W9-BVG-505

FRANK CAPRA

Cry Wilderness

A NOVEL

A VIREO BOOK | RARE BIRD BOOKS
LOS ANGELES, CALIF.

THIS IS A GENUINE VIREO BOOK

A Vireo Book | Rare Bird Books
453 South Spring Street, Suite 302
Los Angeles, CA 90013
rarebirdbooks.com

Set in Dante
Printed in the United States

HARDCOVER ISBN: 9781947856301
PAPERBACK ISBN: 9781644280034

10 9 8 7 6 5 4 3 2 1

Publisher's Cataloging-in-Publication data
Names: Capra, Frank, 1897–1991, author.
Title: Cry Wilderness : A Novel / Frank Capra.
Description: A Genuine Vireo Book | New York, NY: Los Angeles, CA:
Rare Bird Books, 2018.
Identifiers: ISBN 9781947856301
Subjects: LCSH Tourism—Fiction. | Conservation of natural resources—
Fiction. | Environmental protection—Fiction. | Nature conservation—
Fiction. | Sierra Nevada (Calif. and Nev.)--Fiction. | BISAC FICTION /
General | FICTION / Small Town & Rural.
Classification: LCC PS3603 .A68 C79 2018 | DDC 813.6—dc23

Introduction

To the reader—

I N 1971, I WAS a teenage actor who privately held the unlikely dream of one day directing movies myself. The stories I read and heard about Frank Capra's spirit, tenacity, and vision inspired me as much as his array of great and enthralling movies that had already left me in awe of his truly unique talent.

It Happened One Night (1934), *You Can't Take It With You* (1938), *Mr. Smith Goes to Washington* (1939), *It's a Wonderful Life* (1946)— he directed and produced them all, the first two earning him Academy Awards for Best Director and Best Picture. A Caltech graduate in chemical engineering, he had waited tables, worked at a campus laundry facility, and played banjo at nightclubs. Frank Capra was no "goat," as they say in Italian. For Frank, directing movies was a calling and the hard work was simply second nature. In addition to being a rags-to-riches example of the American Dream, Frank Capra was one of a kind and considered by many, and many legends, to be one of the best directors ever.

> *John Ford: "Frank Capra heads the list as the greatest motion picture director in the world."*

> *John Cassavetes: "Maybe there never was an America. Maybe it was only Frank Capra."*

He worked at all levels of the film industry. From a gag man under Mack Sennett to an editor, script writer, producer, and as a brilliant director. Because of the stories he told, people say Frank had a deep insight into people and events and that he loved the "little man." Whether Mr. Smith was going to Washington or Mr. Deeds was going to town, Capra swept us all along on the journey with characters we can all relate to. In any case, there is no denying that Frank Capra brought some of the greatest stories of American life to the screen.

In *The Name Above the Title*, Capra tells the story of his life so masterfully that when I read it, it was the rocket fuel I needed to propel me to new levels of passion and ambition to be a moviemaker and to, by god, dare to quit being quiet about it and declare it to the world!

This expansive autobiography winningly frames the stories of Capra and his family coming to America as poor, illiterate Italian immigrants; how he worked his way up to the top of the business; his service in World War II; the McCarthy era, and beyond. Spanning decades, Frank Capra served his country with distinction both in military and civilian life. Earning many medals while serving the United States during World War II, he also earned the Order of the British Empire from Winston Churchill. Throw in six Academy Awards and many other awards too numerous to mention and Mr. Capra cuts an historic silhouette.

Yet his career success never dulled his compassion for writing stories about the human condition and creating work such as the perennial, decades-long holiday favorite: *It's a Wonderful Life*, an unparalleled pan-generational hit built on values and the characters who stand up for them.

Unfortunately, when Frank was in his mid-sixties, it seemed the film industry had turned its back on him. He couldn't find a studio willing to hire him to make a motion picture he believed in and he began losing his confidence. At some point he went north to his family's second home in the High Sierras, did some soul-searching, and it was then that he began to write stories again. To this date, the extent of his writing output can't be known for sure, but over three decades after his passing, his family found galleys of two unpublished novels in an old storage locker. These two novels titled *Night Voices* and *Cry Wilderness* were both written in 1966 with changes made in 1968, and prove that Capra's drive to tell stories was still alive!

Told against the backdrop of two famous mountain ranges, the geologic masterpieces known as the Sierra Nevada and White Mountains, *Cry Wilderness* is yet another classic Capra story. In this tale, a seemingly minor investigation leads to an epic court case that pits two points of view of human nature against each other. These two perspectives and the definition of civilization and culture itself are brilliantly put in play here by Capra who, without question, gives the reader much to ponder after turning the last page. The story is articulate, thoughtful, profound, and, most importantly, told without pretension.

Cry Wilderness is a classic Capra tale we can all fall in love with and indicates in sharp relief that well past the supposed "peak" of his professional directing career, Frank Capra was creating characters and scenes that were quintessentially his own. Once again Capra has brought pages to life with his undiminished and unparalleled humor involving an abundance of great characters and, in an ironic twist, includes himself!

Yes, at center of it all is Frank Capra, the Hollywood big shot, called to action and moved to take on the establishment. The story could certainly suggest that maybe he never really left Hollywood, that perhaps it was Hollywood that left him, and well before his time. Nevertheless, here it is on the page, evidence that roughly twenty-five years before his death in 1991, the undaunted Frank Capra was creating a new chapter in his career. He was writing a book. A novel. And then some.

Cry Wilderness is genuine, intriguing, and wonderfully Capra-esque. Read it and enjoy! It is my sincere hope that you'll be inspired by Frank Capra the same way I was.

—*Ron Howard*

Every effort has been made to preserve the original text of Cry Wilderness *as penned before Frank Capra's death in 1991. On pages 56, 58, and 101, where the original text was unable to be recovered or faithfully transcribed, the passage has been omitted and marked with the following symbol:*

CHAPTER ONE

I FEEL IN THE mood to tell a tale in print. All my professional life I've tried to tell tales with film. Now I'm seized with this strange yen to tell one with words. Nothing new, this yen. Writing is a virus that strikes almost everybody at some time.

Fortunately the disease, though virulent in some, lasts only a short time, building its own immunity against reoccurrence. The victims recover nicely to pursue their own trades. Any aftereffects? Yes... an increase in their humility count, a bruised ego, awe and admiration for Chekov, Maugham, de Maupassant, and Twain; and adoration and reverence for such gods as Tolstoy, Dante, and Shakespeare.

For such unique men the writing virus is symbiotic. Disease and victim combine to grow and flourish into an artistic marriage, pollinating each other into producing such imaginative fruits as novels, plays, poems, and tales. But for us mortals?

Anyhow, the bug has bitten and driven me to pleasant wanderings in the forest of words. If you, too, feel like wandering, come along and help me unravel this odd tale—a tale full of half-truths, whole-truths, and no-truths at all.

What probably started this nonsense was spending a few months in our wilderness cabin on Silver Lake in the High Sierras; where the air is like wine, the wine is like vodka, the vodka like women...and the women? Well, they've got one more rib. Honest. I counted my wife's. But don't go around trying to prove this by counting *your* wife's unless you know some good Judo holds. Wives object violently to being undressed just to have their ribs counted. They squirm and fight with tooth and nail. But it's okay. Before you get to the fifth rib you get other ideas. The resulting romp is—Mamma Mia! You never knew you had it in you.

Anyway, three months ago I realized a certain Hollywood studio was giving me the salami treatment; you know, cutting off one slice at a time, which you don't miss until you wind up with just the string.

So I said to hell with Hollywood! And anyway, trout season was opening, and I have a wife (Lu) who'll fly right out of a beauty shop in the middle of a hairdo to go fishing. So Lu and I pack up and drive 350 miles to our cabin on Silver Lake. I had a plan, of course. I always have plans. But this one was the best plan I'd thought of in years. I was going "native"! Yes, sir—forget Hollywood, and go native. While I'm still young. In the most primitive mountains in the world.

But which path should I follow in "going native"? There were two well-known hermits that had already gone native in our neck of the woods. One was known as "Bear Bait," a wino; the other they called "Dry Rot," a kind of a wraithlike fellow. Should I go "animal" like Bear Bait, and maybe freeze happily while soused? Or go "aesthetic" like Dry Rot, and desiccate into dust and let the winds blow me round the world? Should I roam, and marvel, and write as a modern John Muir? Or should I create an original way, worthy of an Academy Award winner? A creative way?

All this I tell Lu, in the hope that she would tell me which road to going native I should take. Flatly she listens, and flatly she flattens me with, "Oh, be your age… And will you *please* button that bottom button on your fly!" And off to the kitchen she goes to make coffee.

I'm crushed. Sometimes I wonder if woman is the best thing that's happened to man. After all, she was just an afterthought, something the Almighty took more pains to make attractive after He looked at Adam and said, "What has God wrought?" Anyway, I up and bellow at her through the kitchen door: "All right, laugh. But I'm going native in my *own* way. You'll see. I'm going to build me a hutch on top of the highest peak. And I'll roll snowballs down on the stinking world. And when planes fly over me, I'll write dirty words in the snow with you-know-what. And I'll write left-handed so they won't recognize my handwriting, and…"

Lu comes running in with a light in her eyes. "Look, darling, the fish are rising!" I look. They are *jumping*.

"Oh, boy. Come on!" I yell. "Get your fly rod...put on a mosquito...number twelve..." And we both go flying out to our boat. When brownies rise on Silver Lake, going native can wait.

Where's Silver Lake? It's in Mono County, California, nestled in the Eastern High Sierras. Switzerland can't even hold a yodel to it. It's a jewel of sparkling water set deep in a circle of towering tree-green peaks and capped with snow-white diamonds. When sun and ripple combine their magic, the lake is a sea of shimmering silver. But when in the depths of its stillness it reflects the cobalt of the sky, the passing white clouds stop, Narcissus-like, to primp and admire themselves in this most exquisite of mirrors.

I was introduced to Silver Lake by that great actor, Wallace Beery. Around 1925, Wally and Raymond Hatton (co-stars in several film comedies) each built a cabin on Silver Lake. Wally built his on a very small island, about fifty yards from shore. It became known as Beery's Island. And Wally had two boon fishing pals: Al Roscoe, a good-time Charlie actor, and Frank Capra, a Mack Sennett gagman. Al and I loved to pal around with Wally, mostly because he'd send us into hysterics with his exaggerated animal noises while eating, drinking, or at stud. Then, too, he owned a Travel Air biplane, which he could fly into the craziest places, as he did on our many fishing trips to his Silver Lake cabin. If men needed proof that they are born fools, those trips provided ample evidence.

The nearest landing strip to Wally's cabin was in Bishop, sixty-five miles away and about three thousand feet lower. But Wally had to have a closer runway. So he, Roscoe, and I hand-cleared the sagebrush off a sloping sand dune at the edge of June Lake (four miles away) and called it "Beery Field." The quarter-mile "runway" ran downhill from the top of the sand dune to the icy waters of June Lake. A four-wheel-drive Jeep would have spun its wheels on "Beery Field."

Beery managed to *land* on Beery Field—with the three of us in the plane—with all the comforts of landing a roller-coaster that had jumped its tracks. Coming in low, he'd bounce his wheels off the top of the sand dune, make three or four kangaroo leaps down the runway, then, squashing the Travel Air in a slithering side-skid, he'd finally jackass the gutty plane to a shattering stop in a cloud of sand and dust.

But *taking off* down that sand dune, with *three* people in the plane, at an altitude of 7,600 feet, was sheer suicide. So Wally would take off alone, leaving his chauffeur to drive Roscoe and me to the longer, lower airstrip at Bishop. But the takeoff with Wally alone was *also* impossible with a normal "rolling" start. In the deep sand, the plane couldn't pick up enough speed to keep from plunging into June Lake. So we contrived a goofy way to give the plane a "jump" start. The boggled June Lake natives always managed to gather on nearby hills to see the "fun."

On the top of the sand dune—the beginning of the "runway"— there was an old, lightning-shattered pine stump, to which we hitched the tail of the plane with a looped rope. I crouched at the tail with a hatchet, ready to cut the rope on the signal. When Beery yelled, "Contact!" Roscoe spun the propeller by hand.

Wally warmed up the motor, then shoved the gas throttle to full power. The earsplitting noise bounced back in thundering echoes from the surrounding peaks.

Up went the tail of the Travel Air. Like a leashed hound eager to chase a cat, it leaped, shook, and tugged at the tie-rope. I scrunched against the stump to keep from being blown away by the cyclonic sand blast, a blast that would have flayed my hide off had I not been muffled and hooded with gloves and raincoat. In the roar of the motor and the hurricane of sand, I was deaf, dumb, and blind to any normal signal. But tied to my ankle was a long rope that led off to Roscoe.

When Wally waved out of the cockpit, Roscoe yanked the signal rope. I whacked at the tie-rope. Unleashed, the plane leaped forward in a cloud of dust and noise and rolled like a drunken sailor toward the icy water. Only Roscoe could see what was going on as he ran after the plane yelling, "Keep her tail up, Wally, keep her tail up!" I would be blind for half an hour. The plane teetered and jounced right to the water's edge, then—by some miracle known only to Saint Jude—with one last death-defying lurch, it lifted its wheels and lumbered slow and low over the water like a pelican that had swallowed a horseshoe.

Each takeoff was heart-stopping. Each should have been the last. And each time Wally got airborne, Roscoe would jump up and down, shouting, "He made it! He made it!" To which I—prostrate, blind, too sandblasted to give a blasted damn—weakly answer, "Olé." Then Roscoe would lead me to the lake, wash a quart of sand out of my eyes, ears, and nose—and lift my tail feathers with a slug of bourbon. (And all the blahs were quickly replaced by laughs and the joy of being alive again.)

After our marriage, Lu and I spent many happy weekends in Wally's cabin. And when in the early thirties a snow avalanche engulfed Beery's Island and spread his plush cabin over Silver Lake's ice in pieces no bigger than matchsticks, we rented Raymond Hatton's cabin, or stayed in one of Pop Carson's leaky log huts in what is now Silver Lake Lodge. In 1947—in celebration of making my favorite film (*It's A Wonderful Life*)—we built our own cabin right on the edge of Silver Lake. It will sleep thirteen. And it is, without question, the most heavenly place on earth. Allow me to drool a little.

Around our cabin are the he-men lodgepole and Jeffrey pines, standing Texas-tall and straight as branding irons. Huddled head-to-head in excited groups below them, like teenage girls adoring their heroes, the quaking aspen quiver and giggle. A nod from one of the pines sends them into a dither of leafy applause. While in between them, gnarled, stunted junipers look up at the pines with the same sour expression potbellied men once cast at Valentino.

But through them all the fresh winds blow; on them the clean rains fall and the sunlight glistens, pristine and unfiltered. Breathing here is a joy, not a prelude to coughing. And when it thunders in the peaks...oh, man...like giants bowling strikes. Add to this a half-mile, hard-to-negotiate forest road, which isolates us from the nearest pavement... Ah, Wilderness!

And just one more beauty only Lafcadio Hearn could describe—before I get on with the plot. Sure I've got a plot. I'm not one of those new breeds of directors to whom a plot is something they sell at Forest Lawn...Autumn: summer surrendering to winter in a month-long ceremony of pomp and panoply, with riotous colors flying; refusing to yield the flaming sword until the last autumn leaf has floated past in review.

11

Autumn! You stand in a patch of quaking aspen…in an aura of red, yellow, and gold; the shimmering colors suffusing and warming everything they touch—especially your heart. In the mountains around you, the aspen that line the tumbling creeks are now transfigured into waterfalls frozen in gold!

Selah! Now for the plot… Selah? What does that mean? "So there"? "Take it or lump it"? I looked it up. And I learned that psalms are the poetical lyrics of songs that were sung; and that "Selah!" was a "music up!" musical direction to punctuate a particularly pithy statement in the psalm—a modern cymbal crash or a choral "hallelujah!" Okay, my "Selah!" goes double. For my plot is not only pithy, it's… Oh, I just heard the end of the legend; the folktale of two nameless characters who "went native" up here. I say nameless because even at their fantastic trial at the Bridgeport Courthouse they refused to reveal their names. And I say legend because I've pieced together the story from the romantic vaporings of old-timers, and you know how old codgers can blow up a minor miracle into a Genesis.

Anyway, with me it all started one evening about ten years ago, as I was coming out of the June Lake General Store with some groceries. Right behind me was Deputy Sheriff "Lefty" Wakefield, a big, tough, ox of a man, but as friendly as a Labrador retriever. He was carrying a roll of cheesecloth and some nylon rope, which he threw in the back seat of his sheriff's car.

"Hi, Frank," he greeted me.

"Hi, Lefty. What's with the rope?"

"You very busy tonight?" he asked cryptically.

"No. Not if you've got a better offer."

"I have." Then, lowering his voice, "Can you keep your trap shut?"

"When I'm alone, maybe."

"Okay. Get in."

I hurriedly got into the car, secretly thrilling at the thought of aiding a sheriff with red lights and siren and all. He was just about to close his door when he got out again.

"Oh, I forgot," he whispered, "you'll need a knife, too."

He dashed back into the store. *A knife?* I thought. *Are we going to scalp somebody?*

I was about to take flight when back he came, handing me a long hunter's knife in a leather sheath. Then, as he started the car:

"You can do a better job with that than I can. I've seen you."

With the amber light flashing, we cruised through June Lake's crowded, crooked main street, and out past June Lake's "balanced boulder," which looms fearfully over the road—a ninety-ton, egg-shaped hunk of glacier-deposited granite that balances magically on the small end of its egg, and on a smaller rock, yet. I looked at the knife in my hands and began to worry...and sweat.

"Look, Lefty," I began nervously, "I...I ain't much for...I mean, what's the caper, as we say in crime movies?"

"You promised to keep your big Hollywood mouth shut, remember?"

"I promised nothing," I retorted hopefully. "You don't trust me? Fine. Let me out."

"Just kidding, Frank, just kidding. But on the level. Keep this to yourself, will you?... As a favor?"

"Okay...but where're we going?"

"I got two deer in the back of the car."

"Oh." I brightened. "It's the game warden I shouldn't talk to, huh?"

"Naw...Wes knows all about it. You see, deer knocked off by cars on the highway, we're supposed to take to the county prisoners or the hospital." Then, jabbing a banana-sized finger into my arm, he growled, "But not these two, you hear?... These are for Bear Bait and Dry Rot, and I don't really give a damn *who* you tell about it."

I looked at Lefty with great affection as he gruffly swung the car north on Highway 395. Big bullet head, big hairy hands, big three-hundred-pound body that seemed to fill the whole car—and, for me, a heart big enough to fill Mono County. You see, Lefty was not only a dear friend. He was my hero.

Bear Bait and Dry Rot? They were two disreputable nuts that had been holed up in the woods for years and years. Bear Bait I had seen several times, but Dry Rot only once, years ago. Following an old logging road into Jeffrey Pine Forest in my station wagon, I had stopped to cut up "slashings" (the limbs left by lumbermen) for firewood. I was alone. But as I looked up from sawing wood, I saw

I wasn't alone. In the gloom of the thick pines, a ghost was moving. I froze in fright.

But as I watched, I saw it was a man walking...a tall, very thin man...with long silver hair falling down his shoulders, and a long beard, white, down to his waist. His tattered clothes hung on him like white robes. Then I realized he was covered all over with white volcanic dust, giving him the appearance of a wraith.

He stopped to look at me. Although he was fifty yards away, I thought I saw him smile. With his right hand he made the sign of the cross in my direction...and I thought I heard the words "Pax vobiscum." I say "I thought" because as I stood there in open-mouthed amazement, I wasn't sure of anything.

Then the wraith stepped behind a tree and disappeared. Moments later, I thawed. "What the hell was that?" I asked myself. I rushed out to where I had seen the apparition and looked around. Nothing. I looked for footprints. But the ground was covered with pine needles. I ran back to my station wagon, jumped in, and tore out of that forest as if there were no trees in it.

Back at June Lake, I made for The Tiger Bar for a quick drink. I was still shaking. Red, the bartender, looked at me funny-like as he poured a bourbon.

"Frank...you're pale. What'd ya see, a ghost?"

"Yeah..." And I told him what I saw. Red laughed.

"That was Dry Rot you saw."

"Who?"

"Dry Rot...a harmless nut...been in the woods for years."

"Who is he?"

"Nobody knows."

"Where's he live?"

"Oh, out there someplace. Nobody's ever found his hideout."

"Well..." I stuttered, "Dry Rot?... Is that his name?"

"Naw... Never would tell his real name. Us merchants around here hung Dry Rot on 'em... You ever fish with grubs?"

"Those big white grubs?... Sure."

"Well he digs grubs out of the dry rot of fallen logs...puts 'em in cans we leave him, and hides 'em in a hollow log by the highway.

Then us store guys pick up the grubs and sell 'em to you fishing Joes. That's why we call him Dry Rot."

"Well, for Pete's sake... Hmm...and you leave him money?"

"No. He won't touch money. Never has. No, he just leaves little notes... 'Some socks, please'... He' s always so polite... 'Some shoes'...'some tools'... Lately, Ed Krouse, the hardware guy, told me he's been askin' for heavy gloves and cement."

"Cement?"

"Yeah... Bugs me what in Christ's world he'd do with cement... First few years all he asked for was whiskey. That's how I got hep to the hollow log. Then all of a sudden he's off liquor. Not a drop since. Funny guy."

"Whatta you know... How about food? Doesn't he ever..."

"Never. But you know old Piute Joe from Mono? He was in here years ago putting the bite on me for a drink...said he'd tell some good gossip for a bourbon. So I said, 'Give with the gossip first.' So he told me Dry Rot had been down to Mono Lake pesterin' old Indian biddies about what they ate as kids. Cost Dry Rot a little whiskey, but they opened up... Pinon nuts, they told him, and Mono Lake 'shrimp'— you know, those fly eggs Indians eat like caviar..."

"You mean the fly larvae that wash up on shore..."

"Yeah, fly something... Ain't eatin' none, tell you that... Another drink? Okay...and they told him about the big Jeffrey pine caterpillars you smoke down out of trees...and about wild onions, taboose, berries, squaw rice, and all the rest of the junk the Indians ate...and that's what Dry Rot's eatin' I guess. Funny guy."

"Well, whatta you know. I'd like to talk to him."

"Save your breath... He sees you, he disappears...wants no truck with nobody. Wish I had guts enough to get the hell out of this bar and do what he does."

"Yeah," I mused. "Wonder why he went native?"... And I was still wondering when deputy Lefty slowed up and eased the car off the highway, down a bank and onto no road at all, just an opening in some thick Jeffrey pines. He weaved in and out between the spooky red-barked, diamond-quilted trunks for about a hundred yards, then stopped in a secluded draw. Our headlights eerily illumined a ghostly pine with a low horizontal branch. A hanging tree, of course. Cold fingers brushed my spine.

"What foul deed is afoot here?" I secretly parodied in Shakespearian conceit.

"Okay, Frank," said Lefty. "Let's hang 'em up here." He turned out the car lights and lit a pocket flashlight.

From under a canvas cover on the floor of the back seat we dragged out two deer, a doe, and a young spike buck. We tied two nooses around their necks, threw the ropes over the tree limb, hoisted up the deer until their hind feet were off the ground, and tied the ropes to the tree trunk. Then we unsheathed our knives. But I couldn't figure out why all the secrecy.

"Look, Lefty. I don't mind helping you with the cleaning and skinning. But why act like two guys that just robbed a bank?"

"Because," he snapped angrily as he slit the belly, "the rich, fat, real estate bastards, the big new-money city guys investing 'round here...they're needling county officials to run Bear Bait and Dry Rot the hell out of here. 'Bad for business,' they say... 'Lots of children in the woods now... These two nuts could be dangerous for them... Think of the publicity... Blah, blah, blah! The dirty moneygrubbing, sons of... Neither one of these two loners would hurt a fly."

We started cutting out the entrails, careful-like because of the weak flashlight.

"So," continued Lefty, waxing madder by the minute, "the word sifted down to us officers, the storekeepers and the forestry guys, not official mind you, just hints... Give the two hermits the bum's rush. So all doors are closed to Bear Bait, now...and Dry Rot...his grubs are rotting in the old hollow log. The bastards." He paused, then continued.

"Know what the chief said to me this morning? 'Lefty,' he says, 'pick up those two bums on a vag charge and bring 'em in... We'll roust 'em around a little... Maybe they'll leave the County.'

"'Chief!' I told him. 'That's not fair and you know it. I know the heat's on you from the new big shots, but if Bear Bait and Dry Rot are vags, I'm Al Capone. Not me, Chief, I won't pick 'em up, not even if it means my badge. And if you send somebody else to pick 'em up, send big guys...'cause I'll be there to be picked up with 'em.' And he said, 'Keep your temper, Lefty...or it *will* mean your badge.' So I walked out...and I picked up these deer cars knocked off near Fern Creek... and I'm gonna skin 'em and clean 'em and *take* 'em to those two hermits! Chief or no chief."

Then he turned to me, shaking his bloody knife.

"Frank... Don't ever tell this to nobody...but two years ago, there was this head-on crash at night this side of Deadman's Summit. I got to the accident first. Bodies all over the highway. One of the bodies, young he was, waves me over to him...

"'Officer, officer...there was somebody here...big long beard... all in white like a ghost...kneeled down by those people over there... Then he heard your siren and disappeared.' 'Well,' I said, 'probably was an angel...means you're gonna be all right'... And the young man says, 'Oh, my God,' and starts reciting the Lord's Prayer... Dry Rot, of course... Dangerous? Those bastards."

By this time we were wiping out the insides of the deer with cheesecloth. I had a zillion questions to ask. But before I could frame one, Lefty was off again.

"And Bear Bait...dirty old whiskey-souse Bear Bait. I was passing Silver Lake Lodge when Bill Johnson flags me down. A fisherman from Rush Creek was on the floor inside with a chicken bone in his throat. The phones were out, and could I rush the man to the Bridgeport Hospital? Sure. They carry him out and lay him on my back seat. He's gasping and making awful noises trying to breathe. It's gonna take thirty-five minutes to Bridgeport flat out, and I'm scared the man won't make it.

"I turn on the red light and the siren and lead-foot through the Loop toward three ninety-five. Then I think of Bear Bait. I've always had a hunch about him... Just a hunch, mind you...that he was some kind of doctor... So I take the chance. I turn off the highway and bust through the woods to his shack...about a mile from here. He's in... and soused as usual. I opened the back door of my car and pointed inside. 'Bear Bait, I've got a man here with a chicken bone in his throat. He's dying. What'll I do?' Before I could finish he was in the back seat feeling the man's throat. The man was blue and out.

"'Quick,' he orders, 'your knife.' 'Me?' I ask, scared to death. 'Your knife…hurry.' I took out my pocket knife and opened it. 'Now stab…right between my thumbs.' 'Bear Bait, I'm a cop, not a…' 'Stab, you stupid idiot…quick…right between my thumbs…'

"I stabbed where he told me. Air came in and out of the hole making the blood burble. 'Now,' he tells me, 'hold the wound open till I come back.' I held the cut open with my clumsy thumbs. Color comes back into the man's face, but me, I got no blood left.

"Then Bear Bait came out…with a dirty old pipe stem from a corn cob. He stuck the pipe stem halfway in the cut. Air whistled in and out of it. 'Now get this man to the hospital. Quick!'

"Well, when I got to Bridgeport the man *walked* into the hospital… Bear Bait… Dangerous? The bastards!"

"Lefty… How'd you get the hunch… I mean, about him being some kind of a doctor?"

"Oh, that… Still not sure. First year he'd holed up in his shack, it was. I used to nose around and check on him 'bout once a week… and maybe take him something the wife had cooked to try to make him talk. Two pecan pies this time I had in the back seat. Oh, not because I was Santa Claus, no sir…just a cop makin' sure he was clean…you know…

"Well, as I rolled up, there was his fire outside the shack with a pot on it. I toot my horn to let him know it was me…and out busts a tall guy…looked like a scarecrow, hobbling on one foot and going Billy-be-damned through the trees, with Bear Bait after 'im.

"Well, I jump out of the car, shoot a couple of shots in the air and yell, 'Hold it, Hold it!' But Bear Bait had tackled the guy and waved to me for help. Only his name wasn't Bear Bait then. I called him Mister No Name. And he was Mister No Drink then, too. He took to the flit later.

"'Who is he?' I ask No Name as I got to 'im.

"'Sick man, Mister Lefty. Please don't let him run away,' he tells me. 'I'll get a blanket…'

"I grab the man as he keels over. All rags and bones he was. And whiskey breath? Liked to knock me over. 'Sick, hell… He's drunk, No Name.'

"'No, no,' as No Name spreads a blanket near the fire. 'Bring him here, please.'

"I pick up the scarecrow. He's hot as a firecracker and about as light. 'No Name, he's running a fever. I'll take 'im to the hospital!'

"The fuss that No Name put up. 'No, NO. They ask questions. Just a leg infected, that's all. A thorn... Lay him down here.'

"I lay the man down on the blanket next to the fire. On his shinbone I see an ugly red-and-blue swelling big as my fist. No Name's passing the blade of a bone-handled knife through the flames. I'm worried.

"'No Name...suppose he dies?'

"'He won't die if we hurry. Oh, Mister Left...needle and thread... we need a needle and thread.'

"'I'll look in my kit.' I find threaded needles in my first aid box... but I also find my senses as a cop. Picking up my radio mike, I yell at Bear Bait:

"'Hold it, No Name... Don't touch him! I'll radio for an ambulance...'

"'I'm finished. Bring the thread.'

"'Finished?' I walk back to 'em. Bear Bait had slit open the big lump down to the bone and was squeezing out big gobs of yellow stuff. Between squeezings he washes the wound out with whiskey. The man starts to moan and tries to sit up.

"'Sit on him, Mr. Lefty...and here,' hands me the whiskey pint, 'pour some of this into him.'"

"Ordered you around like a nurse, huh?" I chimed in, still wiping out the inside of the deer with cheesecloth.

"Frank, I was so flabbergasted I obeyed the orders, too... Me! A tough cop who don't mind knocking heads together. But while I dribbled whiskey into the sick guy's mouth, I remembered something.

"'Hey, No Name,' I threw at him, 'you lied to me. You said you didn't drink.'

"'I don't,' he answered, 'he had it on him. Thread, please.'

"I hand him the threaded needle. He puts the needle in the fire first, then straddles the man, sits on his knees to keep the legs still, and over his shoulder I see his hand come up and down as he's sewing the guy up. Fine deputy sheriff, I thought to myself. How do I report this?

"'What's the guy's name?' I ask No Name.

"'Don't know, sir,' he answers, in between stitches.

"'Ever see him before?'

"'No. Just limped in a few moments before you came, and collapsed. When he heard your horn, he up and ran.'

"'Oh...saw me and ran, huh?' I was the cop again, and about time. 'Ten to one he broke jail someplace. I better frisk him.'

"Well, I go through his pockets...and nothing! Not a penny, no wallet, no cards, no nothin'! Only in one pocket I find a few pine nuts and a crazy string of beads. So I'm writing in my book, pine nuts and beads, when Beat Bait gets up and says: 'Thank you, Mister Lefty. He's okay now.'

"I look down at the man's leg. A piece of bark is over the stitches, tied on with strips of his shirt. Bark, plain bark.

"'Take that junk off, No Name, I got bandages and tape in the kit.'

"'No bandages, please,' as he follows me to the car, 'I don't know about bandages... He'll be fine—everything's clean here in the woods...'

"'Okay, I'll bandage him,' as I open the kit. 'I can't take him that way when I've got real bandages.'

"'Take him where, sir?'

"'To the station.'

"'Why, sir?'

"'Because...sir! I'm a policeman. That joker may've stuck up forty banks... Hey!' I'm pointing at nothing. The man's gone. Up and disappeared while I yakked with No Name.

"Well, I run around hollerin' and bellerin' into the woods... shooting warning shots...looking for footprints, which made me madder 'cause footprints're all Greek to me.

"So I run back to the car to report in, yellin' to No Name that if I got my tail in a crack over this I was gonna run him out of the county.

"I call headquarters. The chief himself answers. Cornhouser was his name, 'Pop Cornhouser' we called him, a wonderful guy, he was— almost eighty. I reported how this scarecrow suspect had lammed out on me while getting bandages, described him, and so on...when Pop starts to laugh.

"'Relax, Lefty,' the chief says. 'The Inyo County Sheriff told me last week this egg might be headin' our way. Said he's been hanging round Bishop Creek for over a year...soiling worms and grubs to fishermen. Wouldn't give his name or nothing, so they checked out his fingerprints... No record... Got all his marbles, too. Just a harmless nut who wants to live with squirrels. Well educated too, but he likes the bottle. He's clean, Lefty. Don't bother him unless he starts breaking laws.'

"'Okay, Chief.' I hang up the mike. 'Well, Mr. No Name,' I says, 'got ourselves *another* stray cat for my wife to worry about. Here.' I hand 'im the pecan pies. While he had a pie in each hand I drop in a quick question:

"'No Name...were you a doctor once?'

"'No!' he gave me back fast. Then slower, 'I think I worked in a butcher shop once.'

"'Where?' I shot back.

"'Oh, I forget where...'

"Then I asked him point-blank: 'No Name, I'm your friend. What's eatin' you? Why do you *want* to forget everything?'

"And, Frank, he stands there," Lefty pantomimes it, "a pecan pie in each hand, blinking his eyes fast on account they're startin' to wet up.

"'Mr. Lefty,' he says, 'I wish to God I *could* forget everything... if there is a God.'

"Then he says the nicest thing *anybody* ever said to me:

"'But one thing I won't ever forget...your kindness. You and your wife. Thank you, sir.'

"Well...I gunned that motor and got out quick."

•••

THE DEER WERE CLEANED inside. Now to skin them...a long, tedious job. That gave me time to think of my experiences with No Name—I mean Bear Bait, because that's the only name I knew him by.

I'd heard tales about Bear Bait. Ex-college man, some said... from Yale, Stanford, what have you. Others said he was a black sheep prince... Most said he was just a drunken bum.

But when I first met him, he was fast deteriorating into an animal. His once curly black hair had grayed, knotted, and clotted into a mane of mops. The dirt on his face was old enough to interest geologists. Two boozy, red-lined eyes peering out through matted hair were all that proved he had a face. His clothes, which he never took off, hung heavy with the weight of grime. No one could get that dirty in one lifetime.

And yet...and yet...he fascinated me as he did many others. Underneath the filth you sensed a gentleness...even a nobility. Who is this pathetic wretch...or rather who *was* he? What was it he was trying to forget, alone in this beautiful wilderness—and failing?

Many a time when I was fishing on a lake or a stream, Bear Bait would find me. I was one of his pet patsies. Like the time on Rush Creek when I suddenly became aware of his standing behind me, swaying from side to side. He startled me, because at first glance he looked more like a pint-sized Abominable Snowman than a human being; his little red eyes smiling and blinking, his chapped mouth making sounds that only those of us who knew him could translate into: "Clean your fish, Mister? Clean your fish, huh, huh?"

"Oh, hi, Bear Bait." Calling a man by that debasing name always made me wince. "Sure, go ahead." His body jerked in small fits. I knew the dreaded craving for alcohol would soon rack his tortured nerves.

With a happy grunt, he squatted down to my creel, took out a sharply pointed, bone-handled knife, half the bone of which was gone, and began cleaning fish. I cast out aimlessly but observed him closely. He held the knife like a good calligrapher holds a pen. After opening each fish, he expertly slit the stomach to minutely examine what the fish had fed on.

Suddenly I had a hunch. I spitballed it out as carelessly as I was casting my fly line.

"Bear Bait...was it at Stanford or Yale that you learned to hold a scalpel like that?"

He froze, still peering into the fish, a silent statue. A pause. Then he abruptly dropped everything and, stumbling, hanging onto branches, he scrambled away along the riverbank.

"Bear Bait!" I called, "Wait a minute... Come back!"

To him I was throwing rocks, not words. Then I yelled out the clincher.

"Bear Bait...stop...I've got a whole bottle for you!"

He froze again, his back still to me...with one hand on a limb and one foot in the water. I imagined the agony of his struggle...one last shred of dignity against a whole bottle of whiskey. The shred lost.

He came back smiling and bowing to finish the rest of the fish. There is nothing that can choke you up more than to see the degradation of a human being. Was I helping or hurting him? I wasn't sure.

The fish cleaned, he took my rod, jacket, and creel, and like a puppy dog leading you on to play, he went ahead of me up the bank, holding branches back, giving me a hand up steep places, until we got to my car on the road. There he opened the car door for me, giggling, dancing, and urging me in...a child anxious to get to a picnic.

I had auditioned this pitiful little act before. I knew what it meant. His shaking body screamed for liquor. The craving was on: a thousand little devils gnawing his insides for alcohol...alcohol.

I put him in the back seat and opened all the car windows in order to survive. But it didn't help much since he leaned forward on the front seat and chortled Frankie Fontaine noises into my ear.

The smell of Bear Bait was not one to kid around with. It was gargantuan, classic, and so royally offensive that goats and skunks have turned tail and fled. In fact, the story has it that it was this miasmic aura that earned him his moniker in his early hermetic days. The June Lake Postmaster bumped into him on the street and stopped short, his lungs paralyzed. Turning, he rasped out:

"Jesus, man...you smell like bear bait."

To which the un-fragrant eremite had replied with a flash of unexpected wit:

"Oh, no, Mr. Postmaster...in the words of Samuel Johnson: You smell, sir...I stink."

It was this crack that set the locals off into a rash of conjecture about his past. Anyway, the name stuck. Bear Bait. And some twenty years later he was in the back seat of my car with all four windows open as I drove him back to my cabin for a bottle.

It had been thundering, and now the rains came, as they can only come in the mountains. The peaks turned on their firehoses, while the angry winds tried to blow the water back up to them. I didn't dare put up the windows for fear of being anesthetized. So I got drenched—and so did Bear Bait.

Well, if you think a *dry* Bear Bait was tough to take, you should have tried him *wet*. I breathed out only...never in. I stopped the car some fifty yards from my door and told Bear Bait to wait, while I walked slowly toward the house hoping the rains would wash me clean. I got a bottle of scotch and came back out. There was Bear Bait at the door, bouncing eagerly up and down, his paws in front of him for balance, like a wet sheepdog just learning to stand on his hind feet.

I handed him the bottle. As he took it, he made a sucking gasp of happy surprise. A whole bottle! He bowed and bowed his thanks, then, hugging the liquor to his chest, he disappeared into the wet night, gibbering as happily as a potted Mortimer Snerd.

This childlike, nameless, repulsive, disintegrating human flotsam, having lost man's most priceless possession—his dignity—would now stupefy himself and pass out blissfully and soggily under a dripping tree...and nobody cared—not even he.

I remember silently asking God to bless him and all the other Bear Baits in the world.

•••

"WHAT BLOOD?... OH..."

Think fast, man... Then, from left field, that magic pasture of instant creativity whence spring full-blown ideas, inventions, alibis, and immortal phrases such as MacArthur's "I shall return"...Bastogne's "Nuts I"...Whistler's "You Will"...Churchill's "Blood, sweat, and tears"...the fight manager's "We wuz robbed!" came:

"Oh, I mean aye...'tis the blood of charity. Wist thee not that I am Robin Hood?"

"Go on...I'm wisting."

"There's hunger in the land, me wench. So bearding the Sheriff in his lair, me and Friar Tuck, Lefty to thee, we ventured bold in

Sherwood Forest. Risking all, we caught two stags with our bare hands, dressed them deftly, wrapped them in cheesecloth to foil ye flies, then secretly hung one on a tree for Bear Bait, and t'other oyer a hollow log for Dry Rot. A noble deed I wot...what wot thee, Pigeon?"

"Between wisting and wotting...I'm worried, that's what I am."

"A fig for thy fears, Maid Marion," as, playing the stout of heart, I made a pass at her derriere. She swished so neatly I missed completely. I sat down, faint with my good works.

"Aye, 'tis thirst that marred my aim. So prithee, fetch me a goblet of nectar, 'ere I plant a kiss upon thy ruby lips."

"Prith to thee, Master Robin. You were bringing the nectar from the store... Doth remember?"

"ZOUNDS!! A pox upon me for a clumsy lout!"

I rushed to the door and turned to wow her with my curtain line.

"I left the flagon in the Friar's car. I'll have the varmint's hide!"

•••

SEVERAL DAYS LATER I was drifting along in my boat on Silver Lake, casting a fly toward shore under the willows, when I heard a bell clanging furiously—the little ship's bell on our front porch. Looking up, I saw my wife urgently waving me to come in. Something was up.

"What's on fire?" I asked as I leaped out of the boat.

"Just the phone. The sheriff's calling from Bridgeport."

"Sheriff! What's he want?"

"Just a female hunch...but you did throw a stag party last week."

"Ha, ha...funny," I said as I ran into the house for the phone. "Hello?... Yes, Mr. Sheriff, this is Frank Capra talking..."

As with all sinners, a guilt complex comes over me when speaking to the police. I give it away by being overly polite.

"...You're having a what?... An informal hearing?... Oh... internal discipline. Well, how can I help you, sir?... I see... Not over the phone... Yes, sir... I understand. Two thirty this afternoon... No, no trouble at all... Second floor, Supervisor's Room, Courthouse... Yes, sir, I'll be there..."

My wife had been listening, of course.

"So?" she asked.

"So nothing. They're having a hearing."

"Should I blow the horn and round up your merry band, Robin?"

"Lay off, willya? This may not be funny, you know. What suit shall I wear?"

"Your Lincoln Greens, of course…"

CHAPTER TWO

A s I BACKED OUT of our red-cindered driveway for the forty-mile
trip to Bridgeport, I began to speculate on why the sheriff had
called *me*. Had to concern Lefty, I was sure. His prediction that he
might get his tail in a crack over Bear Bait and Dry Rot had probably
come true. Interesting man, this Lefty. As a deputy sheriff, he enforced
the law in isolated Mono County with Javer-like tenacity. No one
had enough "pull" to sidetrack Lefty—not even for the pettiest of
misdemeanors. And he was fearless. So fearless he once sailed single-
handed into a tough gang of black-jacketed motorcycle hoodlums
bent on terrorizing June Lake. Using only his fists against chains,
clubs, and knives, he knocked so many of the toughs galley-west they
finally took to their roaring cycles and fled, with Lefty harassing the
bullies out of town with his car—like a sheepdog running sheep. Yet
this fearless giant was determined to champion the rights of two
other apparently worthless tramps against all the powers of Mono
County, if necessary.

Yes, I thought—a strange guy, this Lefty—and then, coming out
of a leafy tunnel, I topped the rocky knoll on our back road, whose
granite ledges have all been staked out, claimed, and "worked" by
juniper trees, now as old and gnarled as ancient sourdoughs. And there
it was, spread out before me. Our meadow. Beautiful even in daytime.
But at night—my wife, my children, my grandchildren, all must stop
at the meadow after dark. Why? To catch a performance of the "Ballet
of the Green Eyes" as we call it; a fantasy only Scheherazade could
have described to the Sultan.

With a station wagon bulging with hushed but highly excited moppets, and my headlights high and my spotlight mobile, we'd turn the car toward the meadow and gape out the windows. There they are! A dozen pairs of large luminous green eyes—poised on Nature's stage, waiting for my baton. I count the rhythm—one, two, three—and I tap the horn. The ballet begins…green eyes in slow motion…moving, crisscrossing, leaping, bounding…executing ethereal choreographic patterns with the poetic motions of deer. For they *are* deer!

What beauty there is in the world. And the admission price? Only that the beholder stop, look, and enjoy. I reached the paved road and began circling Silver Lake. Through the tremulous, coquettish, last autumn leaves of the toe-dipping aspen, I catch glimpses of our cabin. Across the smooth waters, the ribbon of its reflection keeps pointing at me as I roll along, tying me to my home. Home! And nostalgic pains. Of all the places I've lived in, from the ghetto shacks to the Bel-Air mansions of affluent film years, this home in the high Sierra is the one I cherish most.

Here our children learned to fish and hike and love the mountains. Here I came for healing when torn apart by the frustrations of filmmaking. Here should come all the beats, the acid-heads; all the sick of heart and mind; all the walking dead, and let Nature renew their ideals, their courage, their manhood. It is impossible to be despondent in the Sierra wilderness. For here there is "Balm in Gilead."

As I circled Silver Lake and passed the Edison powerhouse—whose spinning turbines tamed the wild power of Rush Creek's roaring falls (that plunged over 1,200 feet of glacier-burnished granite cliffs) and domesticated that power into California's obedient lamplighter—and then as I passed by Silver Lake Lodge with its acres of trailer parks, and by campers and trailers jammed "hub-to-hub" along Rush Creek's noisy two-mile frolicking jaunt from Silver to Grant Lake, Lefty's intransigence was becoming more understandable. The primitive wilderness of Mono County had been "discovered."

If the reader is mildly surprised at the unpredictable behavior of some of the characters in this tale, I can only say they were reared in an environment as unpredictable and poly-behaviored as the Los Angeles Dodgers. In 1963 (the year I was answering the sheriff's summons to Bridgeport), Mono was the only county in the state, and perhaps in the nation, that was without a bank, a movie house, a dentist, an incorporated city, a boxcar, or a single foot of railroad track. It was a 50-by-150-mile stretch of wall-to-wall paradoxes—half hot, half cold; half Swiss Alps, half Mojave Desert.

Mono County mines rock that floats (pumice) and grows wood that sinks (iron wood). It has the freshest of waters and the saltiest (Mono Lake); the youngest of volcanos (Mono Craters) and the oldest of rocks. (Near Convict Lake some reddish rocks contain fossils of graptolites—tiny marine animals four hundred million years old!)

Here the closest peak to heaven in the continental United States (Mount Whitney, 14,494 feet) looks down on the lowest hellhole (Death Valley—282 feet below sea level). Here the Arctic cold of the Sierra peaks meets the burning heat of desert valleys, and in between the few miles separating these two environmental extremes, one finds complete sequences of flora and fauna. From arid Owens Valley one does not have to travel thousands of miles to reach the Arctic tundra; one climbs a few miles up the Sierra wall. Many of the plants that grow in the hot valleys also grow in the cool mountains, but with notable differences. Desert plants have become ingenious at coping with hundred-degree weather and years of little rainfall. They developed small leaves, some like thorns, to prevent evaporation. They grew far apart to reduce competition for moisture. Their mountain cousins, however, have much broader leaves to catch the sun's rays, and huddle close together in warm spots since they have plenty of moisture.

In fact, Mono County is a child of paradox. "For here is a land," writes Genny Schumacher in the Sierra Club's handbook *The Mammoth Lakes Sierra*, "born of fire and sculptured by ice…for millions of years fire and ice have played their antagonistic roles, shaping the landscape as we see it today—the one forcing up mountains, building, adding; the other quarrying, carving, grinding down, carrying away…"

Here, nature must have put on its grandest fireworks show— erupting volcanoes, hot rivers of lava, gargantuan earthquakes; here, the violence of nature must have fulminated at its most terrifying fury, as the lava rivers cooled and solidified, only to have other rivers flow over them, layer upon layer as the hot innards of the earth shot up through the cracks in fiery roars and spread bubbling molten magma over areas deep with former spewings, all under a hellish pall of hissing steam and raining ashes.

Then came the Ice Ages (four of them) and the great glaciers, those powerful rivers of ice that scoured the uplifted granite mountains and gouged out the Sierra's valleys and bowls. There are some fifty glaciers still active. John Muir wrote that from the glaciers on the northern flanks of Mr. Ritter flow the beginnings of four of California's major rivers—San Joaquin, Tuolumne, Merced, and Owens—their sources all within a radius of four miles.

And speaking of paradoxes, there are rock glaciers in this area. Yes, rock! In Bishop Creek, one finds solid rivers of loose rock, each moving downhill as a mass, lubricated by ice as they slide over solid granite.

The Mono (Piutes), who had lived around Mono Lake for hundreds, perhaps thousands of years before they saw their first white man, must have been as wacky as their environment. The word "Mono" (short for Monache) was pinned on them by the Yokuts from across the Sierra (Yosemite). It means "fly" people, which aptly describes them for their happy-go-lucky living habits as well as for one of their main sources of food and trade—the Mono Lake fly pupae, a small white worm that surfaces, then turns into a fly. What was wacky about them? Well, those Mono, so lowly they slept mostly in the open, so lethargic they lived on Mono flies, pinon nuts, lizards, and Jeffrey pine caterpillars, and so backward they never discovered how to make pottery, domesticate an animal, or plant a seed—yet, paradoxically, those primitives had discovered and perfected an art form incredibly intricate, unbelievably beautiful, and amazingly utilitarian: basket weaving.

Baskets were not only vital to the very existence of the Mono; they were also their literature, their music, their "soul" art. No two designs were the same; they followed no drawn sketches, but created the patterns as they wove. Baskets were their all; they used them as dishes, for carrying burdens, winnowing seeds, scooping flies, cradling babies, for headgear, and, most importantly, for carrying and storing water (when pitched) and for cooking. As creative basket weavers, the "fly" people were unsurpassed among all other Native Americans. Another paradox is that these "primitives" had invented a picture-writing code that is still unbroken. On the trails between Mono Lake and Owens Valley, they carved the soft "tufa" rocks with petraglyphs—circles, symbols, and arcane designs whose meanings are as yet a mystery. Present-day Piutes disclaim any knowledge of them, and present-day jokesters say the "scratchings" are but the Piute equivalents of "Gilroy was here!"

And if one thinks the first white men to rush into Mono to moil for gold were less kooky than the Mono, this should dispel that illusion. When, in the early 1860s, they established and surveyed the county, the county capitol they selected (Aurora) was not in the county. It wasn't even in the state. It was in Nevada! When the mistake was discovered—and Mono moved its county seat back into California (Bodie, then Bridgeport)—the rights to previously collected tax money ended in a mish-mash that is still as unresolved as the Piutes' petroglyphs.

But the grandest paradox of all—a millennium-old saga that pales the tales of Scheherazade—is still taking place on the lonely, twelve-thousand-foot plateaus on top of the White Mountains. For on these great heights, where only naked crags should exist, live and flourish the oldest living things! Bristlecone Pines. Two thousand years old when Christ walked in Galilee; one thousand years older than the oldest Giant Sequoia!

Scrawny, less than thirty feet high, starving for soil and water, wind-scarred, ice-cracked, gnarled, and twisted beyond all belief, the Bristlecones survive high above the timberline for all other trees—survive alone with Homeric courage against impossible odds. The discoverer of Bristlecones, Dr. Edmund Schulman, found old "Methuselah," 4,600 years old (perhaps 7,000 years old if a San Diego scientist, Dr. Hans E. Suess, is right in contending that Carbon-14 underestimates ages), still defying starvation, bitter gales, and disease. For again paradoxically, and unlike other forms of life, Bristlecones survive not in spite of adversity, but because of it. The oldest trees are found in the poorest soil (dolomite rock) and in areas least protected from icy winter gales. Rugged individuals they are, fiercely challenging all that nature can throw at them and actually prospering on the catastrophic. They remind me of one of the Biblical Patriarchs who grew in stature by defying, railing, and thundering against La Dolce Vita.

But not all is bizarre in Mono County. Most of it is beauty, the pure, wild, pristine beauty of nature's wilderness. The kind of beauty that inspired John Muir to cry out as he stood one morning on a rocky ledge and viewed the magnificence of Vernal and Nevada Falls in Yosemite Valley: "This is the morning of creation, the whole thing is beginning now. The mountains are singing together!"

To better understand the grandeur of it all, the reader should be given a simple thumbnail sketch of how the grand forces created the great Sierra Nevada mountains. Imagine, if you will, a huge, flat, solid block of granite—one mile thick, four hundred miles long, and two hundred fifty miles wide—extending from what is now Central California to Central Nevada in width, and in length, from the Mojave Desert in the South to Mount Lassen in the North. Now cover this granite block with several thousand feet of softer sedimentary rock deposited by oceans that had overlaid the granite several times in the past millions of years. And then imagine that underneath our block of granite, the hot molten magma was roiling and boiling under heavy pressure.

So we have a geologic layer cake: the bottom layer—hot, liquid rocks; the middle layer—a block of solid granite half as big as the state of California; the top layer—softer sediments deposited by oceans. This nicely arranged layer cake would have been content to stay as it was—but it couldn't. The earth's skin was cooling and shrinking, and the enormous pressure of this shrinking was forcing the granite block to occupy less and less of its share of the shrinking skin. To do this, the block (like a dieting fat man's face) had to wrinkle, fold, tilt up, break, or do something. With contracting pressures pushing in from its sides, and hot gaseous pressures pushing up from below, the least pressure was from on top. So the great granite block bent upward into a dome, like the top of a Quonset hut.

But granite, like a piece of hard toast, cannot be bent much without cracking. And that's exactly what happened to the arching granite block. Two large irregular cracks opened up along its full length (north and south). These cracks, or faults, divided the granite dome into roughly three equal segments: West section, Middle section (top of the dome), and East section; each section approximately four hundred miles long and seventy-five wide. Then a curious thing happened. The Middle section (top of dome), being under the greatest bending stress, began cracking here and there within itself. Hot gases, superheated steam, and molten rock from below began escaping up through the local cracks, relieving pressure from underneath the Middle section. And lo! The Middle section began to sink, tearing itself away from the West and East sections along the two original fault lines, while the side sections (East and West), still under compression pressure from the earth's shrinking skin, kept being pushed inward and upward. For over a million years, the Middle section sank in small drops—five feet here, twenty there—each drop creating a tremendous earthquake. And all the while, through its own small cracks, hot lava and pent-up gases roared up and covered the Middle section's top with lava flows thousands of feet thick.

Today, the Middle section—once the top of the granite dome— has sunk some three miles below the tops of the East and West sections, forming a deep canyon between almost vertical walls of granite—the exposed faces of the two faults along which the Middle section sank. That Middle section is now the Owens Valley; the Western section is the Sierra Nevada Range, rising gently from the San Joaquin Valley up to the crest, then dropping almost straight down along the fault where the Middle section broke away and slipped; and the Eastern section is now the Inyo-White Range, which forms the eastern wall of the deep canyon.

One might naturally ask: Why don't the White Mountains look as sheer and jagged as the Sierra range? Because nature's master sculptor, Mr. Weather, got into the act, with his winds, rain, snow, ice, and his headliner, the great glaciers. The reader will recall that the huge granite block that domed up was covered with layers and layers of sedimentary material left by oceans that came and went. These sedimentary rocks, of course, rose with—and still covered— the arching granite.

Now Mr. Weather filled his clouds with Pacific moisture and blew them in from west to east. As the clouds climbed the Sierra wall, they dumped most of their rain and snow on the gently rising western slope, leaving Owens Valley and the White Mountains to the east in the rain shadow or, as author Mary Austin called it: "Land of Little Rain."

Now we can answer the question, why don't the White Mountains look as sheer and jagged as the Sierra range? Rain, snow, and the great glaciers eroded and gouged out most of the original covering sedimentary layer from the Sierra crest and peaks, exposing the great granite layer. The White Mountains, however, with much less rain and snow, and practically no glaciers to contend with, are still covered by the original sedimentary layer. Whatever little erosion took place has only served to round the peaks without as yet exposing the hard granite that lies beneath.

And so, out of the cataclysmic forces of fire and ice, the wild pristine beauty of the Sierra wilderness was born. And many of those who have experienced it can exalt with John Muir: "This is the morning of creation, the whole thing is beginning now. The mountains are singing together!"

Here is the beauty of still undiscovered lakes and creeks, unnamed peaks, and untrodden meadows. Here is the longest mountain wilderness trail in the world—the John Muir Trail—that winds among the monarch peaks of the Sierra Crest from Yosemite to Mount Whitney, passing no settlement, nor crossing a paved road along its two-hundred-mile length. Here hikers—secure from all intrusion, secure from self, free in the universal beauty—may look up into the pink shining faces of the Sierra peaks, all scrubbed clean and bright by their glacial sculptors, and all fringed with the Sierra's pine-green beards—the forests. Here, in nature's bosom, one may wander, look, touch, see, hear, and imagine; with no aim but to wonder: What kind of *Men to Match My Mountains* were the first who saw and sealed this mighty unbreachable wall of jagged granite, four hundred miles long and two miles high? Whose tracks made these delicate patterns on the sand? What caused those concentric, crescent-shaped great mounds of rounded boulders and gravel that guard the entrance to the great canyons? Who nibbled the leaves off this bush? Why does that very high and very long cigar-shaped cloud stand motionless in the sky, while other clouds sail swiftly by on the Pacific winds?

What can match the spine-tingling beauty of gale-driven snow streamers that festoon the mountaintops in the spangled sunlight? "Snow-banners the wild winds hang on peaks," John Muir called them. Or the ineffable beauty of the Alpenglow—that predawn Alpine burst of rosy light that heralds Aurora's entrance with a fanfare of color; and in the evening says "sleep well" to the peaks with a fleeting pastel echo of the sunset colors that have just faded? "…One of the most impressive of all terrestrial manifestations of God," wrote John Muir, Sierra botanist and poet. "At the touch of this divine light, the mountains seemed to kindle to a rapt, religious consciousness, and stood hushed and waiting like devout worshippers. Just before the Alpenglow began to fade, two crimson clouds came streaming across the summit like wings of flame…then came darkness and the stars."

If it is remotely possible—and scientists cannot affirm or deny it—that life and man and beauty (and the eyes to behold it and the souls to hunger for it) are uniquely limited to planet Earth, then how much more rare, more beautiful, and more sacred is a lily, a chipmunk, a fir tree, or a whale?

And if God gave man dominion over all the earth, how great, how special, is man's duty to preserve, cherish, and love the miracle of each blade of grass, of each fish that swims, or bird that flies and creature that runs? For this is our Eden in which all life is One and all is Divine. When man pollutes or destroys its pristine beauty, man is polluting and destroying himself.

Yes, it was pleasant driving through this magnificent country, daydreaming about its primitive wilderness. And somehow Deputy Sheriff Lefty Wakefield kept intruding into my musings. Was I equating Lefty with the country's primitive strength?

Had Mono's primeval beauty—in which there is no evil, no hypocrisy, no envy, greed, or hate; no ghettos, no discrimination, no wealth, no poverty; where there is only grandeur, awe, and wonder as mountains, sky, water, snow, forests, flowers, birds, and animals live in joy and harmony obeying the immutable laws of nature—had this beauty and goodness of nature suffused into Lefty's mighty hulk and lodged in his soul as a rock of faith?

Could be. He, his father, and his grandfather had all been born in Mono County. His grandfather, a gold seeker, must have belonged to what Mark Twain called that "driving, vigorous, restless population... the only population of its kind that the world has ever seen... an assemblage of two hundred thousand young men—not simpering, dainty, kid-glove weaklings, but stalwart, muscular, dauntless young braves...no women, no children, no gray and stooping veterans— none but erect, quick-moving, strong-handed giants—the finest population, the most gallant host that ever trooped down the startled solitudes of an unpeopled land..."

I drove through the narrow gap where, in a short fifty yards, rushing, rollicking, singing Rush Creek, bursting out of its cool tree-lined banks, suddenly put on its brakes in terror. Ahead was a bleak, shocking sight—hot, treeless, deserty, sagebrush-rimmed Grant Lake. And I know what Lefty feels like shouting to Rush Creek each time he drives by here: "Turn back, fool, turn back! The bastards will murder you. Stay outta Grant Lake! Flow back up to Silver...leap back up the falls to Agnew, Gem, and Alger... And get lost in that snow pack! Know what those rich bastards got waitin' for you at the other end of Grant Lake? A tunnel! An eleven-mile black tunnel to deport you to the Owens Valley, where they'll shove you through four hundred miles of slimy ditches and lakes and pipes and tunnels to Los Angeles, where the bastards will store you, douse you with chlorine, and squeeze you through millions of pipes and into millions of dishwashers and stinking toilets, and you'll become another river—a putrid, stinking sewer river carrying civilization's putrid, stinking pollutions out to what will soon be a putrid, stinking ocean. So turn back, you fool creek, turn back!"

And that's about what gross, inarticulate Lefty was trying to get across to Mono officials about Bear Bait and Dry Rot. To him, the clean fresh waters of Rush Creek, and those two peaceful hermits, were both part of the unspoiled, unpolluted wilderness scene.

The groundwork for Lefty's problem had been laid long ago, in the 1860s and '70s, when newly discovered gold-and-silver ledges brought thousands of prospectors back from the depleted California mines, and Mono's mining towns such as Dogtown, Monoville,

Mammoth, Masonic, Aurora, and Bodie sprang up like mushrooms and died almost as fast. Cattle-raising, logging, and farming went up and down with the boom and bust of the mines. But cattle-raising and farming were well on the rise on their own in the early 1900s, when water-thirsty Los Angeles bought up, finagled, or stole practically all the freshwater rights in Inyo and Mono Counties. Ranches dried up. The sagebrush moved back in. The wilderness that was Mono was ready to be abandoned and handed back to the Piutes. But the paradox that was Mono was not to be denied. Few realized that Mono's magnificent unspoiled wilderness was to be a greater bonanza than half a dozen Comstock Lodes.

For, by an unpredictable turn of events, the city that had bought up and stolen Mono's water so that it could grow and prosper now brought prosperity and lasting abundance *back* to the Mono area it had once impoverished. Smog-ridden Southern Californians seeking clean air and quiet solitude found their vacation paradise in the land whose waters they had "appropriated." Fishermen, campers, hunters, skiers, artists, rock hounds, photographers, and lovers of mountain and desert turned Mono County into a year-round vacationland.

Mono boomed again. The new gold rush was on. Millions were being spent for ski lifts, motels, trailer parks, restaurants. Fix the roads. Tear down unsightly shanties. Get rid of crotchety old-timers and dirty old "characters." Spruce up; prepare the way for the great king, the VACATION DOLLAR!

And, of course, getting rid of two unsavory hermits like Bear Bait and Dry Rot was part of the big cleanup. And Lefty burned with indignation. Deep down in his gross, material soul, he loved these two derelicts. He didn't know who they were, why they holed up in the woods, what sins they were expiating, or what ideals they were trying to recapture, but he would fight for them. His weapons were hopelessly inadequate, almost ludicrous: righteous indignation and insubordination.

I didn't quite believe Lefty's assertion that the community was in a tacit conspiracy to run Bear Bait and Dry Rot out of the county. So I had asked some casual questions here and there. Yes, the storekeepers had quit bartering for Dry Rot's grubs. Resort owners admitted they warned all fishermen against letting old drunken Bear Bait clean their fish for whiskey, food, or change. "Starve them and they'll get out" was the general idea.

These thoughts seesawed in my head as I hurried along, hardly noticing the four-mile drabness of Grant Lake, now doubly drab since the autumn-hued aspen clustered around seepages (that only days ago suffused both lake and sky with auric tints, and ennobled the sage-covered hillsides with lightning flashes of frozen gold which revealed the zigzag courses of unseen rivulets) now had had their autumn cloak of gold ripped and weathered into a few faded tatters which, like hardy penitents, hung on to beg with their last quake and quiver for the white mantle of winter to cover their nakedness.

But as I left Grant Lake and topped a crisscross of moraines, I saw a sight that, although I had seen it a thousand times, always emptied my mind of all thought. A sight that makes one rash enough to cry out, "This has to be one of the rarest, most dramatic, and most spectacular sights in all the world!" On the left of the highway is the inspiring beauty of Swiss Alps, on the right the repelling harshness of the trackless Sahara.

Lift up your eyes to the left with me. There, in majestic splendor, with no intervening lesser heights to mar its grandeur, one sees and feels an overwhelming spectacle—a fifteen-mile panorama of the snow-mantled Sierra Crest. Six noble peaks brush the sky; the first five, Mount Wood, Parker Peak, Koip Peak, Mount Lewis, and Mount Gibbs, are all just under 13,000 feet; Mount Dana is just over. Two notable passes are also plainly visible. One is 11,100-foot Parker Pass, notable not only for its inaccessibility, but more so for the 1,000-foot glacial moraine that lies athwart the mouth of Parker Canyon— the only terminal moraine in the area that remains as whole and as perfect as when it was first deposited by a glacier eons ago. All the rest of these great rounded ridges, that look like man-made earth dams across canyon mouths, have been cut through and partly washed away by streams. In Parker Canyon, the creek cut through a lateral (side) moraine, leaving the terminal unchanged.

And the second pass, Mono Pass (10,604 feet), a rocky saddle between Mount Lewis and Mount Gibbs, is, historically speaking, second only to famed but much lower Donner Pass. For untold centuries, the Mono, heavily laden under basketloads of Mono "flies," pinon nuts, and black, glassy obsidian rock (to fashion into arrowheads, knives, and other tools), trudged up their well-worn Mono trail—from Mono Lake up Walker Creek to Walker Lake, then up to two small above-timberline lakes (Sardine Lakes), followed by a short but dangerously steep rocky climb to the Crest and Mono Pass. From the Pass, the trail meanders gently down through the west side forests to beautiful Yosemite Valley, where the Mono bartered their cargos with the Yokuts for deer meat, acorns, and certain black and brown willow bark (for basket-weaving) found only in Yosemite.

It was over that Mono Pass (plainly visible to the naked eye), and the ancient trail down this Walker Canyon—better known as "Bloody Canyon"—that the reverse gold rush took place in the sixties and seventies when Mono's siren cry of "Gold!" was heard in California. In 1863, William H. Brewer, leader of a Whitney survey party, wrote: "...a terrible trail...utterly inaccessible to horses, yet pack trains come down, but the bones of several horses and mules and the stench of another told that all had not passed safely...horses were so cut by sharp rocks that they called it 'Bloody Canyon'..." (Note: from the Sierra Club handbook *The Mammoth Lakes Sierra*).

John Muir wrote of Bloody Canyon: "I have never known a... mule or a horse, to make its way through the canyon, either up or down, without losing...blood, from wounds on legs. Occasionally one is killed outright—falling headlong and rolling over precipices like a boulder..."

Now shift your eyes to the right (east) of US Highway 395— that thin silver strand that here separates antithetical worlds—and you will gape at some of the wildest and most desolate country found anywhere.

Less than ten airline miles from the Arctic beauty of the Sierra Crest, a forbidding, treeless, half-mile-high chain of twenty volcanos (Mono Craters) scars the horizon as it curves to the south, its open craters as ragged and ugly as earth wounds made by emerging bullets shot from below. To the east and north, great waterless wastelands stretch beyond the heat-withering horizon; powdery pumice deserts difficult and often impossible to travel, for boots sink in the volcanic ash and stir up clouds of choking dust.

But the central figure in this inhospitable scene is Mono Lake, twenty miles long and fifteen wide; a dead lake, its alkaline waters saltier than the ocean. There is a local joke:

"Dip your dirty clothes in Mono Lake once, they come out clean. Twice, they disappear." Add the lake's two treeless islands (one black, one white), the alkaline scum that froths its shores, and the ghostly white, weirdly fluted tufa "towers" that stick out of its shallows, and—well, if Jupiter's moons have lakes, they would have to look like Mono Lake.

And Mono Lake must have looked just as dreary eons or at least a century ago, when Mark Twain and his genial hobo pal, Calvin H. Higbie, while seeking (if it entailed no work) the legendary riches of the Lost Cement Mine, stumbled onto the "Dead Sea of California," as Twain called it in his very amusing adventure book, *Roughing It*: "...one of the strangest freaks of nature to be found in any land... so difficult to get at that only men content to endure the roughest life...will consent to such a trip...Mono Lake lies in a lifeless, treeless, hideous desert...[a] solemn, silent, sailless sea...[surrounded by] upheavals of rent and scorched and blistered lava, snowed over... with drifts of pumice stone and ashes, the winding sheet of the dead volcano whose vast crater the lake has seized upon and occupied..."

Despite Mono's repelling prospects, Twain remained to explore it and make notes more humorous than scientific: "Half a dozen little mountain brooks flow into Mono Lake, but not a stream of any kind flows out of it...what it does with its surplus water is a dark and bloody mystery..." A meteorological comment: "There are only two seasons...round about Mono Lake—and these are the breaking up of one winter and the beginning of the next..." A chemical observation: "Its waters are so strong with alkali that...if we threw water on our heads and gave them a rub...the white lather would pile up three inches high...we had a valuable dog. He had raw places...more raw places on him than sound ones. He was the rawest dog I almost ever saw. He jumped overboard one day to get away from flies...bad judgement...it would have been just as comfortable to jump into fire.

The alkali water nipped him in all the raw places simultaneously and he struck out for shore with considerable interest. He yelped and barked and howled...and by the time he reached shore...he had barked the bark all out of his insides, and the alkali water had cleaned the bark all off his outside...[and] he finally struck out over the mountains at a gait which we estimated at about two hundred and fifty miles an hour..."

An ecological observation: "...millions of wild ducks and seagulls swim about the surface, but no living thing exists under the surface, except a white feathery sort of worm, one half an inch long, which looks like a bit of white thread frayed out at the sides..." Then Twain describes hordes of flies, "something like our houseflies," which he says blacken the beaches to eat the worms that wash ashore: "a belt of flies an inch deep and six feet wide...clear around the lake—a belt of flies one hundred miles long..." Throw a rock among them, he writes, and they will swarm up "like a cloud." And they don't mind being held underwater, he noted; in fact, they loved it: "When you let go, they pop up to the surface as dry as a patent-office report." But all things, he philosophized, have their use "and proper place in nature's economy ducks eat the flies—flies eat the worms—Indians eat all three—wildcats eat the Indians—white folks eat the wildcats and thus all things are lovely..."

And Twain observed another instance of nature's wisdom. He was told that thousands of seagulls flew over from the Pacific to lay their eggs on Mono's smaller, black island. And since the islands were "utterly innocent of anything that would burn; and seagull's eggs being entirely useless unless they be cooked, Nature had provided an unfailing spring of boiling water on the largest island [where] in four minutes you can boil them as hard as any statement I have made during the past fifteen years." And he was told that within ten feet of the boiling spring there was a spring of pure cold water, sweet and wholesome. "So, in that island you get your board and washing free of charge—and if Nature had gone further and furnished a nice American hotel clerk who was crusty and disobliging...I would not wish for a more desirable boarding house."

So Twain and Higbie had to explore that big island—whether to boil seagull eggs or look for a crusty hotel clerk, old Samuel Clemens didn't say. One hot blistering morning, he and Higbie rowed a boat to the island; that is, Higbie rowed, because Twain (anticipating his Tom Sawyer's labor-saving knavery with the fence-painting gag) swore that it made him deathly sick "to ride backward when I work." But, he added with pious-tongue-in-impious-cheek, "I steered."

On the island they found jets of steam, scorched and blasted rocks, and "a small pine of most graceful shape and faultless symmetry" that was kept brilliant green by steam that "drifted ceaselessly through its branches…" But no fresh cool water: "We hunted everywhere for the spring…climbing ash-hills patiently, and then sliding down the other side in a sitting posture, plowing up volumes of gray dust…nothing but solitude, ashes, and a heartbreaking silence. Finally we noticed that the wind had risen and we forgot our thirst in a solicitude of greater importance…we had not taken pains about securing the boat. We hurried back to the landing place, mere words cannot describe our dismay—the boat was gone!… We were prisoners on a desolate island…with neither food nor water. But presently we sighted the boat. It was drifting along, about fifty yards from shore, tossing in a foamy sea…it approached a jutting cape, Higbie ran ahead and posted himself on the utmost verge and prepared for the assault. If we failed there was no hope… When [the boat] got within thirty yards of Higbie I was so excited that I fancied I could hear my own heart beat… When, it seemed to go by, only one little yard out of reach, it seemed my heart stood still… But when [Higbie] gave a great spring the next instant, and landed fairly in the stern, I discharged a war-whoop that awoke the solitudes!"

Why all this personal affinity with Mono Lake and Mark Twain? Because two weeks earlier a local lawyer friend, Steve "Boat-court" Gorski, had presented me with his copy of Twain's *Roughing It*, and I hadn't stopped laughing since. I'm certain I'll never drive by Mono Lake again without laughing. One last Twain titter:

"In speaking of the peculiarities of Mono Lake, I ought to have mentioned that at intervals all around its shores stand picturesque turret-like masses and clusters of a whitish, coarse-grained rock that resembles inferior mortar dried hard," and that if one breaks off fragments of them, "he will find perfectly shaped and thoroughly petrified gull's eggs deeply imbedded in the mass. How did they get there? I simply state the fact—for it is a fact—and leave the geological reader to crack the nut at his leisure..."

Well, I just had to crack that nut. The petrified gull's eggs bit earned me some queer looks. But the gargoylish white rocks—that I had always imagined Mono's little water demons had sculptured to guard Mono's shores against desert demons, like Quasimodo's gargoyles guard Notre Dame's spires—turned out to be a fascinating natural phenomenon. They are freshwater coral! Limestone buildups of the limey secretions of certain tiny plants (algae) that multiply around freshwater springs; a cousin of the ocean coral, a similar deposit secreted by tiny sea animals.

I left Mono Lake and its dead sea mysteries, and began climbing the grade to Conway Summit (8,138 feet). But I couldn't help stopping near the top of the grade—at "View Point"—for one last look at the desolate area where Twain had had so much fun. For Mark Twain is a disease. When his laughing bug bites, it enslaves. Yep. Way down below me in the withering heat waves, Negit, the small black island, was still the hot "incubator" for the eggs of thirty thousand seagulls. And the larger, whiter island, Paoha, was still wreathed (suggestive of its name) in the wraithlike vapors ascending from its hot springs— Paoha is the Indian word meaning "small spirits with wavy hair." That's the island that nearly claimed Twain's life, but which within a few years was to save the lives of hundreds of Chinese. It seems that the wild mining town of Bodie, said to have had the best water, the worst climate, and a killing a day, also had the biggest Chinatown in California, next to Sacramento. And it also seems that the bad men of "Shooter's Town"—who boasted they had themselves a man a day for breakfast—all got drunk together and went on an "anti-chink" shooting hellbender just for the hell of it. Learning of their plans, the engineers building the Bodie and Benton Railroad, hurriedly gathered all their coolie workers together, and rafted them out to Paoha and kept them there, until Bodie's bad men had run out of enthusiasm and liquor.

It must be that islands have always fascinated men. Show a man an unclaimed island anywhere and he will come up with an uncontrollable yen to claim it and build his castle on it. Paoha was no exception. Over the century, many white men have planted their flag on Paoha and dreamed of building castles, only to have their dreams shattered by Paoha's harshness.

But strangely enough, the "spirit island with the wavy hair" has been hospitable to the animals left behind by would-be castle-builders. Today there are some three hundred wild goats and a large population of Belgian hares roaming the bleak island.

Did I say they were building the Bodie and Benton Railroad, after saying that there was not one foot of railroad track in Mono County? That's right. The thirty-one-mile railroad, that was built to carry lumber and wood fuel from Mono Mills (in the Jeffrey Pine Forest) to Bodie, died and was dug up when Bodie died and was abandoned.

Jeffrey Pine Forest! By George! I've forgotten to mention the most astounding of Mono County's paradoxes: That distant expanse of cool green that lies hidden behind the Mono Craters' scorched row of volcanos—the northern flank of the largest stand of stately Jeffrey pines in the world! As anomalous alongside Mono Lake as a two-hundred-square-mile forest of green pines would be if it were smack in the middle of the Sahara Desert.

But how can a cool forest of great pines possibly exist in the arid "Rain Shadow" of the Sierra wall? Is there a chink in the great wall through which Pacific storms can spill over? Yes. There are gaps (passes) in the Sierra Crest—like the gaps of missing teeth. But most of these gaps are protected from the brunt of winter storms by other high peaks (other teeth) west of the gaps. There is one notable exception: the Mammoth gap. Here the windblown storm clouds can race straight up the Middle Fork of the San Joaquin River unhindered by any peaks, and slide smoothly over the relatively low rounded saddles of Mammoth Pass and Minaret Summit, to drop their rain and snow over a highly favored two-hundred-square-mile area of the Rain Shadow. Result: the world's mightiest stand of Jeffrey pines in the middle of desert country.

And the Jeffrey pines reminded me that both Bear Bait and Dry Rot were holed up in their shady fastness. My God, yes. Forget Mark Twain. Get going. There's a sheriff waiting at Bridgeport to ask questions about Lefty. But what could I say in defense of Lefty? I was certain he had disobeyed orders. What defense is there against insubordination?

I stepped on the gas up the grade. Would charity be an excuse for insubordination? Why, yes…of course…charity. Without charity we are tinkling cymbals. If charity is greater than hope and faith, it must be greater than minor disobedience. Big charity organizations were always "blackjacking the rich" for the poor. When you donated to charity weren't you "stealing" from yourself, or your children, to help the poor? That's it. I would make my pitch for Lefty in the name of charity. Would the sheriff swallow it? I had my doubts as I topped Conway Summit and began to descend into Bridgeport bowl.

CHAPTER THREE

Bridgeport, the county seat, population: 460, lies in the middle of a cattle-dotted, lush green meadow surrounded by Sierra peaks. In summer, descending into the bowl from Conway Summit, the distant town always reminded me of a white wedding cake on a green table, around which the mountains sit as wedding guests.

But in winter, the master pastry cook goes berserk. He pours thick icing all over the cake, the table, and the mountain guests, making the bowl one of the coldest spots in the country.

As you arrive at the courthouse itself, all white and trimmed with red, you have to admit it is one of the prettiest buildings in California, even though built in 1880 at a cost of only $31,000. Fashioned of native wood, quaintly carved, its two stories, red roof, and graceful cupola, together with its tall narrow windows, all blend into a harmony most pleasing to the eye.

Outside, a delicate iron fence surrounds the grassy courtyard, while a row of handsome silver maples separates the rush of twentieth-century traffic from the nineteenth-century leisure of lawn and gardens.

Pushing open the tall main door, I entered a high, dark-paneled hallway. The floor creaked with age, as did the stairway I started to climb. I couldn't help wondering about all the stark human dramas that had been played on the creaky boards of this old frontier theater of Justice.

At the top of the stairs a skinny, far-out young man buttonholed me. I thought he was one of the four Beatles.

"Excuse me, Mr. Capra, Jake Ziffren, Mono Herald..."

"Hi, Jake. What's cooking?"

"Not much. What brings you to the county poorhouse?"

"I dunno. Sheriff asked me up to a hearing... Supervisor's Room, he said."

"Oh-ho-o..." His long ears pricked up like a setter's pointing at a pheasant. "That's where they're meeting."

"Who?"

"The Civil Service Commission, the Sheriff, the DA, and I dunno who else."

"What's the meeting about?"

"Search me. My boss said to me: 'I think that hearing's gonna smell from herring. Go up there and nose around.' But nobody'll talk. The whole building's clammed up."

"Okay. Wait here till I come out."

"Oh, boy...will I?... First door on your left there."

I knocked. A uniformed deputy sheriff opened the door a crack.

"Frank Capra, sir. The sheriff..."

"Oh, come in, Mister Capra."

He squeezed me through the door, then locked it behind me.

I found myself in a high-ceilinged, paneled room, dimly lit by the pale light of a cloudy day and the still paler glow of overhead neon tubes.

Against the narrow windows, on a raised dais, flanked by federal and state flags, and looked down upon by pictures of George Washington, the father of our country, and Lyndon Johnson, father of the Great Society, sat an owlish man at a large raised desk that commanded the room.

Facing this raised desk, on the floor level, was a long crescent-shaped table, with leather chairs on its outer perimeter. Only one man occupied this long table, a large slouched man in uniform—the stout friar, Lefty Wakefield.

On the left, between the crescent table and the raised desk, three middle-aged men sat around a smaller desk. The Civil Service Commission, I assumed. Opposite them, on the other side of the room, stood a tall handsome man in shirtsleeves. Alongside him, at a small working table, sat a beefy, bald-headed man in a braided uniform. The sheriff—a comedown from the Sheriff of Nottingham, I thought… Next to him, a bouncy, blonde secretary pulled at her short skirt. Behind the sheriff stood another young uniformed deputy.

My escort deputy introduced me, first to the small man with large glasses at the main desk.

"Mister Capra, this is County Supervisor Guy Hanford."

"Mister Capra," welcomed the supervisor, as he rose, all smiles, and offered his hand. "Well, well…always a privilege to meet a movie celebrity," to the whole room, "especially when he's in *my* district."

"Well, thanks…I…" This "celebrity" stuff always leaves me with a handful of worms.

"Now over here, Mister Capra," said my deputy, leading me to the table with the three men, "these gentlemen are the Civil Service Commission: Boyce Dickinson, cattleman and owner of the BD Guest Ranch. You may remember him as a rodeo champion…"

"Oh, yes," I said, wincing at his handshake, "I think I saw you at a rodeo at the Pan Pacific in LA."

"That was my brother," he answered flatly as he crossed a long blue-denimed leg. I tried to stammer out an apology but the deputy took my arm.

"And this is Nino Jacobetti, owns Italian restaurants in Mono County."

A round, pink-cheeked extrovert waved and greeted me in Neapolitan.

"*Goompa…chi si deech?*"

"*Tutto bene, grazie,*" I waved back. Whereupon he slapped the rodeo rider on the back and gloated: "Boyce, didn't I tell ya he could make with the Italiano, huh?"

"Big deal," shrugged tight-lipped Boyce, his thumbs in his Levi pockets.

"…And this third commissioner was born in Bridgeport… Kyle Sommes."

"Better known around here as Mister Real Estate, Frank," interrupted the extrovert Nino, "owns half the county and is trying to steal the other half. Right, everybody?"

The small titter was drowned out by Nino's own hearty laugh.

"Nice to know you, Mr. Sommes," I said as I extended my hand.

In it he dropped a languid, cold fish, then withdrew it quickly, before it could warm up.

"Howdy," he wheezed nasally through his hawk-like nose.

As a "celebrity," I was a bust and knew it. I looked for a chair.

"Where do I sit?" I asked my guide.

"Just a moment, sir," he said, and he led me clear across the room to the bald, potty sheriff. I couldn't help noticing his wild, twitching bushy eyebrows that curled upward at the ends.

"Mister Capra, this is County Sheriff Tom McMahon…"

"Yes, yes…hello, hello!" the sheriff rasped out irritably. "What is this, a social tea? Can't we get the hell on with this crummy hearing? Guy!… Come on… I gotta county to police…"

I could have kissed his bald head.

Supervisor Guy Hanford coughed, nodded, and rapped his knuckles on the table. But the tall man in shirtsleeves was not to be left out. He introduced himself.

"Frank Capra, I'm Tony Caldwell, District Attorney…" We shook hands. "My wife wouldn't let me in the house if I didn't tell you how much she loves your movies."

"Oh, thanks, Mister Caldwell, and thank Missus Caldwell for me."

"I will, but don't include me in your thanks. I never go to movies." A statement that never failed to rile me.

In the theatrical world you learn quickly to recognize the old zingaroo. He certainly was handsome, this bushy-haired performer with his flashing cuff links and polka-dot bow tie. And he knew the actor's attention-getting trick of being the only coatless man in the room. I quickly put him on the list as a TMLO: troublemaker look out. Complex characters they are, these good lookers who resent show people yet ape them. Complex and dangerous, their hostility bordering on the psychotic. They are the ones who buy drinks for stars in public then pick fights with them.

"I don't blame you for not seeing movies," I said, letting him know I had felt the zing. "You see better performances every day in a courtroom."

"Tony! For God's sake," interrupted the sheriff with eyebrows lowered fiercely. Then raising them high, he pleaded, "How long you gonna keep me on my can here?"

Supervisor Hanford rapped again for order. He invited me to sit down at the end of the long crescent table. As I sat I glanced over at Lefty. There he slouched, huge and lumpy, eyes fixed on a blank pad of paper, chin on a fist that distorted his massive face.

"Hi, Lefty," I threw at him. He didn't look up or answer—just raised the little finger of his fist in acknowledgement.

"Guy!" the sheriff boomed out to Supervisor Guy Hanford.

"Okay, okay, Tom," answered Mister Hanford as he turned to me, all milk and honey. "Mister Capra, we appreciate your coming here of your own free will to give us the benefit of…of your valuable thoughts…and we thank you. Do you know why we asked you here?"

"No, sir, not exactly."

I suddenly remembered the jokes the June Lake working stiffs made up about Supervisor Hanford at their early morning breakfast hangout; that he wore a weather vane for a hat, and his theme song was "Every Little Breeze…"

"Well, sir…I'll be brief," said Weather Vane. "This is a confidential hearing before the Civil Service Commission there, involving a county employee. Nobody's under oath…no official minutes are kept… all informal. The commission can resolve these little interfamily spats, so to speak, easier and quicker if we keep the discussions within… within our four walls. Do you understand, sir?"

"Perfectly."

"Now…we'd like you to become a member of our family here… and join us in a gentleman's agreement not to discuss this hearing with any…uh…outsiders…especially the press. Have we your word on that, Mister Capra?"

"No, sir."

Seats squirmed and feet shuffled.

"I'm sorry, Mister Supervisor, I can't go along with you about the press for two reasons. First of all, I think the press *should* be sitting right here in this room…to act as a sort of a watchdog…make sure the hearing is kosher…"

Nino, the Italian restaurant owner, jumped to his feet. "Just a goddam minute, Frank. Are you saying our commission here needs a watchdog?"

"Well," I answered, "maybe my eyesight's getting poor, but I can't see any halos on your heads, so I take it you're human beings like the rest of us. And as human beings we all need watchdogs."

"Now, let's keep things friendly," cooed the supervisor. "You said you had two reasons, Mister Capra…"

"Yes, I did…and the second one's personal. I'm in show business. We can't afford to deliberately mislead or offend the press. So if I'm asked, I've got to level with them."

"Tom…there you are," snorted the DA to the sheriff, "I told you it was a mistake letting Lefty con you into calling this Hollywood character. He's in the movies! He'll do anything for publicity…"

"Almost anything, Mister Caldwell," I shot back, "especially when I walk into a meeting of public servants conniving to avoid publicity."

They all spoke up at once:

"What d'ya mean, conniving?"

"Who told you that?…"

"I resent that remark…"

Supervisor Hanford rapped his knuckles red. When quiet was restored he motioned the DA, the sheriff, and three commissioners over to his desk, where they huddled in animated whispers.

To say I wasn't enjoying this Perry Mason stuff would be a lie. I began to wish there were some cameras around, when my eye caught Lefty. There he was, looking straight at me over the gargantuan fist still at his chin. When our eyes met he gave me the biggest, fattest wink I ever saw. I gave him back the Mack Sennett wink, in which you screw up the whole side of your face.

I looked back at the huddle, where under the watchful eye of our first and thirty-fourth presidents, Mono County officialdom was figuring out the next play to call, after being stopped for no gain. The DA was doing the quarterbacking, while the supervisor's weather vane swung from player to player.

Watching from the sidelines were the young deputy and the DA's bouncy secretary. Catching my eye, she tugged and tugged at her very short skirt, either to cover or to call attention to a pair of shapely knees. Tug as she would, the skirt ended up higher. But she threw me a quick smile, then went back to skirt-pulling. Aha! I had an ally.

The young pokerfaced deputy was looking straight ahead with arms folded. But a hand hidden under his folded arms, opened up, made a discreet "okay" sign with its fingers, then closed again. Ha, Ha! Another ally.

Only one more person left—the deputy at the door, my introducer. I looked at him. No soap. With some feathers on his head they could have stood him up in front of a cigar store. Not bad, though, I thought. The help was two to one for our side. Later it was to be about fifty-fifty among the hundreds that stormed the courthouse.

The huddle was over. The DA announced the verdict.

"Mr. Capra, your uncooperative attitude is a great disappointment to the commission. But...since your zeal for publicity overshadows your responsibility as a citizen, the chair ruled you are to be excused from this private hearing. You may leave, sir."

"Fine." I nodded as I gathered my hat and stood up. "But I should warn you. There's a time bomb planted in the hallway...a reporter. He tried to pump me when I came in...and is waiting to nail me when I come out. He already feels pushed around and suspicious. So when I tell him I was thrown out on my ear for refusing to enter into an agreement to lie to the press...well, you know reporters. It's an article of faith with them, that where there's secrecy, there must be chicanery. Goodbye, gentlemen."

I was stopped in my tracks by a loud: "Wait a minute!" One of the commissioners, Boyce Dickinson, rodeo champ and dude ranch owner, was up on his feet.

"These remarks about Mr. Capra's lack of cooperation are uncalled for. We asked him here and he came, didn't he? I know what he means about the press. The year I was champ on the circuit, if I didn't talk to reporters, they'da crucified me.

"And another thing. Why all this crap about...sorry, Miss Laura, I mean why the locked doors? The sheriff fired Lefty Wakefield for disobedience, right? Lefty said it was unfair and appealed to this commission for a hearing, right? Now it's up to us three here to decide if Lefty's right or wrong, right? So why all the secrecy? I'd like to hear what Mister Capra has to say about Lefty's firing, if that's what he's here for. And I don't give a horse's pizzazz who he talks to."

The supervisor felt the changing wind and called another huddle. This one was different. All the players were quarterbacking. The old sheriff particularly was all fret and sweat. It trickled down his furrowed neck. His armpits were black circles of wetness, with thin, concentric lines of white salt surrounding the edges in sweat rings, some thicker than others. I wondered: Could they be indicators of stress and strain, maybe like tree rings reveal the years and their rainfall? I thought of a comedy scene in which a wife counts her husband's sweat rings to see if... The huddle broke up.

"The hearing will now resume," announced the chair. "Mister Capra, you may be seated. Tony?" he said, giving the floor to the DA.

Handsome Tony, the DA, waited for all to be seated, then strode theatrically toward a rear corner and up to a hanging curtain, which I hadn't noticed. Grabbing a curtain rope, he paused dramatically, riveting everyone's attention, then jerked the curtain open and walked away.

My eyes bugged out. Our two deer, still trussed and wrapped in cheesecloth, dangled from a bar like two corpora delicti.

Back at his desk, the DA shuffled papers, savoring the surprise of his staging. He'd certainly bowled me over. Wha' happened? I looked at Lefty. He was still the same amorphous lump. I wondered if he was still breathing.

"Mr. Capra," the DA addressed me, as he paced up and down clicking a pencil against his beautiful teeth, "have you ever seen these objects before?"

"Yes, sir!" I smiled vaguely, "they look like the two deer Lefty and I cleaned, skinned, and delivered to Bear Bait and Dry Rot. How'd they get here?"

"Thank you, Mister Capra," he said, ignoring my question. "Now, sir, will you kindly go to the carcasses and read to the commission the two notes that are pinned on them?"

"I know what the notes say. One reads: 'To Bear Bait. A gift from Lefty,' and the other: 'To Dry Rot. A gift from Lefty.'"

"In Lefty's handwriting?"

"I saw him write them."

"Any other writing on the notes?"

"Yes. While Lefty wasn't looking, on an impulse, I added 'and F. C.' to each note, after the words, 'from Lefty.'"

"I'm glad to see you're meticulous about your details."

"I'm a film director, Mister Caldwell. Careful about details— but never meticulous." The quick look he threw was translatable— he would have to up me in class as an opponent.

"You say you added 'and F. C.' to each note on an impulse," he said, now choosing his words. "Could you clarify the impulse for us?"

"Well, I don't know…an impulse…probably the same impulse," I said jokingly, "that prompted you to pause dramatically before you pulled the curtain on the deer. Show business, I guess."

"I see…show business. Can you forget make-believe for a moment and more correctly describe the impulse that impelled you to help Lefty dress and deliver the deer to those two gentlemen with such appetizing names?"

"I can describe that exactly…a charitable impulse."

"You knew those deer were hit by cars?"

"Yes, Lefty told me." I was determined to admit everything, then rely on the charity pitch.

"Did you know that deputies are under official orders to deliver highway deer to the county prisoners?"

"Yes, Lefty told me that, too."

"Then, sir…" he said, leaning forward to emphasize his point, "would it not be fair to say…that you knowingly and willingly…aided and abetted a peace officer in the dereliction of his sworn duty?"

The audacity of the question took the wind out of my sails. So this was the play the DA called in the huddle: incriminate him and he won't be so anxious to talk to reporters. Smart play. I better go into a huddle with myself.

"Oh, beautiful, beautiful," I mocked, while stalling for time, "worthy of a Darrow…innocent little legal words strung out into barbed wire… Oh, yes…I like that statement…"

"It happens to be a question. Did you understand it?"

"Does a nail understand the hammer? Did Caesar understand the dagger?"

"But does Frank Capra understand my question?"

"Understand it? I can repeat it word for word: 'Then, sir… would it not be fair to say…that you knowingly and willfully…aided and abetted a peace officer in the dereliction of his sworn duty?'"

"Mister Capra," interrupted Weather Vane, "if you don't think the question is fair, you don't…"

"Oh, it's fair, Mister Supervisor…loaded dice couldn't be fairer… or a covered bear trap…"

"Well, IS HE GONNA ANSWER IT OR NOT?" shouted the impatient sheriff, building up another sweat ring.

"Yes, sir, Mister Sheriff…I'll give you an answer…with honest dice. Yes, it's fair to say that Lefty there has a heart as big as his body. It's fair to say that while the 'Vacation Dollar' people were trying to evict the peaceful hermits who had lived in these mountains for nearly a quarter of a century, Lefty was seeing to it they didn't starve this winter. And it's more than fair to say that I helped Lefty…helped him in the same spirit Robin Hood aided and abetted Friar Tuck… in diverting a deer or two from the Sheriff of Nottingham's well-fed minions, to feed the hungry poor…"

"WAIT A MINUTE!" shouted the DA, taking the floor from me. "You can't escape legal responsibilities with romantics. Do you realize what would have happened, even to your Robin Hood and Friar Tuck, if the sheriff had caught them red-handed?"

Neophyte that I was in this legal stuff, his outburst led me to think I had hit pay dirt. So I followed the same vein.

"Oh, sure…anybody knows that. With the help of Robin's merry outlaws, they'd managed to escape."

The sheriff blew a fuse…and another quart of sweat. "Tony… for Chrissakes! Do I have to listen to these crummy fairy tales? I'm the sheriff of Mono County…elected by the people. I fired a deputy for disobedience. Now it's him or me. Get the hell to it!"

"Tom! Keep your shirt on!" the DA angrily fired back at the sheriff. "Lefty's basing his whole appeal on what Hollywood, here, has to say about his dismissal. So let me nail him as a publicity-seeking accessory, or that movie guy can—"

A quiet settled over the whole room after the surprisingly angry exchange between the DA and the sweaty sheriff. Everyone shuffled around collecting their thoughts for the next move. I was enjoying myself immensely, of course. I began to imagine plots, chicanery, graft; and that these big boys had to knock me off to save faces—or was it necks? Was there more to this hearing than just firing Lefty? I mean—were there some bodies around? Wouldn't that be a doozy of a plot twist…

During this quiet moment, the confused supervisor folded and unfolded his white little hands, while his weather vane swung wildly seeking a favorable breeze. It came from an unexpected source—Kyle Sommes, the commissioner whom the Italian kidded about owning half the county and trying to steal the other half. Sommes cleared his throat and rose shyly to his feet.

"Guy?" he asked dryly. "Could an innocent bystander have a word?"

"Innocent bystander, he says," breathed the relieved supervisor. "Only the head man of the commission… Can *he* have a word?… Oh, you're a riot, Kyle… Yes, sir…*you* may have a word."

"Well, my first word is, will somebody pull that curtain on those spooky stiffs hanging there? They're bugging the hell

good here. I admire you. Funny thing…forgive me fellas, this is off the subject for a moment…I say funny thing, Frank, because I voted against you…I mean, a few of us old-timers have organized a land investment syndicate, and my partners wanted me to ask you to join us…and I said, 'NO!'…and as Fiorello LaGuardia said: 'I don't make many mistakes. But when I do, it's a beauty.' So Frank, my apologies, and if you'd care to share in the prosperity of the fastest rising land values in the state, I'm personally inviting you to join us… and your grandchildren will be very happy you did."

"Why, thanks, Kyle. Very generous of you."

Was he holding out a golden carrot, this wheeler-dealer with the Midas touch? But why? Couldn't really be a bribe…too big for the occasion. Besides, what was I being bribed *about*? These thoughts chased each other through my head as Sommes resumed talking.

"Now…as to the small matter before us…and I say small because we're blowing up an anthill into Mount Whitney. Incompatibility… that's all it is. Incompatibility between subordinates and superiors. I, myself, have fired many a good man I couldn't get along with, and they walk across the street and get better jobs. Happens all the time.

"Now with the permission of my two compadres here, I'd like to present a solution that will be good for everybody. We separate…and I emphasize *separate*; we separate Lefty Wakefield from the sheriff's office… Reason? Incompatibility. Safe. No stigma to anybody. Millions of husbands and wives have been separated by incompatibility…"

I looked around the room. Each face stared open-mouthed in admiration of the Solomon-like words. All but Lefty. He had yet to move an eyebrow.

"But here's the best part," continued "Solomon" Sommes, "with no loss of pension time or fringe benefits, we place friend Lefty with another county agency…Highway, Tax Office, Building permits… whatever he likes…and…and a slight increase in salary. Now who's the loser? Nobody. Who's the winner? Everybody. Fair enough, Frank?"

His question caught me in the middle of mulling over his solution.

"Huh?… Well, maybe, Kyle. That's up to your commission…and certainly up to Lefty, himself…"

"Quite right, Frank." He turned to Lefty, "Lefty, my boy? Could you ask for anything fairer than that?"

Unnoticed, the central figure of the hassle had sat there, a hulking, frozen statue. Now he was squarely in the spotlight. One word from him and all the shouting would be over. The room was so quiet you could've heard a subpoena drop.

Slowly, Lefty pulled his clenched hand out of his massive red face, leaving a bloodless fist-print as big as a mule track. Without looking up, he gave his quiet answer.

"Gentlemen, I didn't ask for this hearing to get my job back… or any other job. All right, I disobeyed an order and got fired. Fine. The sheriff was right. All I ask is that my wife and kids and friends and everybody else know the *reason* I disobeyed the order. I couldn't *make* myself arrest two peaceful nobodies, charge them with vagrancy, and run 'em out of the county. That's all I want everybody to know."

There was actual consternation at the unadorned simplicity of this ox-like man. Kyle Sommes recovered first.

"My boy…I admire your loyalty to those two unfortunates. Admirable. But there's a hundred million acres of woods right out of Mono County they can move into. We've got a cleanup program going on… Millions of visitors from all over the world will be coming here…"

"Those two unfortunates," quietly countered rocklike Lefty, "They were here long before the ski lifts and the shiny Las Vegas motels…living alone, no more trouble'n a couple of chipmunks. They ain't got money, they ain't even got names, but damn it all, they got rights…and I'm gonna fight for 'em if I have to go to the governor, the president, or to who the hell ever you gotta go to…" And, putting his fist back in his face, he solidified into a statue again.

ruling as more than fair. Representing the people of Mono County, I move this hearing be adjourned and closed…"

"Mr. Chairman," I yelled, "you adjourn this meeting now, and I'll tell the press the whole hearing was phony…"

The DA turned on me with venom in his eyes.

"What do you mean, phony? Do you know the import of what you're saying?"

"Yes, I know what I'm saying. The issue here is Lefty's concern for human rights…not his disobedience of the sheriff's order. What Lefty disobeyed was the pressure that was put on the sheriff to give that order…"

The sheriff came at me like a wounded grizzly.

"Goddam your soul, that's slander! I'll sue you for every dime you got in the world, you loudmouth Hollywood show-off…"

"Sue and be damned!" I yelled at him, nose-to-nose like Leo the Lip to an umpire, "and I'll sue you all right back for conspiracy…yes, conspiracy…to slander my character to save your own necks. The DA made that statement right in this room…"

"Order!… Gentlemen… Order!" cried Weather Vane. Order, hell. I was wound up. Everybody was yapping something, but I yapped louder.

"Who's got the notes? I want the notes… I want a copy of what everybody said…!" I cried out.

"No notes, no notes…" the anguished supervisor wailed.

"You all heard him," barked the sheriff at everybody, spraying sweat with every wild move, "he slandered me… I want you all as witnesses…"

"Tom, Tom," the supervisor pleaded, "we gave our word not to repeat…" but the DA had yanked the sheriff off to a corner.

I rushed up to the supervisor and shook a finger right under his frightened nose.

"Mr. Chairman…as a taxpaying citizen who pays your salary, I demand you recess this meeting until you get a court reporter in here to take notes, so I can repeat everything I've said here officially… so the sheriff can really have something to sue me about!"

With that for closure, I made for the door. Wild with excitement I was, yes. But not really sure what the devil I'd been saying or doing. The deputy barred my way at the door.

"Open that door, Buster…or I'll add unlawful detainment to my other charges." The deputy looked to the supervisor for orders. "Yes! Yes!" shouted Weather Vane over the hubbub. "Recess granted! One hour, everybody! One hour—"

The door opened—just a crack big enough for me to squeeze through into the hall. It nearly cost me a foot, but I kept the door ajar just long enough for those inside to hear me shout: "Reporter! Jake! Jake, over here!" The door banged shut. But I had played my ace… or had I?

CHAPTER FOUR

J AKE, THE EAGER-BEAVER REPORTER, rushed up to me panting for news. But he wasn't alone. Right behind him was "Hoppy" Hopkins, his boss. Hoppy Hopkins...an ex-publisher of one suburban LA paper, who retired to Bishop to get rid of the ink in his veins...and ended up publishing five weekly tabloids serving Inyo-Mono Counties.

"Hoppy," I greeted him warmly. "What are you doing here?"

"Hi, Frank... Well," indicating his reporter, "my fifth Beatle here called in with a song and dance about you being in the hearing, so I came up to cover the Hollywood social angle. Got any juicy items?"

"Yeah," butted in Jake, "what went on? I heard a lotta yelling..."

"And how... I'm still a little deaf. I need some coffee, Hoppy..."

"Across the street."

"Come on... I've got plenty of social news..."

The three of us clattered hurriedly down the creaky stairs to the front door. As I opened the massive door, I collided heavily with a slovenly dressed fisherman, hip boots turned down, battered hat stuck full of colored flies.

"Excuse me, sir," I apologized and tried to go by him.

"Wait a minute, Frank... Steve Gorski," he said merrily, as he turned to greet the other two. "Jake... Hoppy... Someone's in bad company here, but I don't know who..."

Steve Gorski...eccentric, rich, witty, and an avid fisherman. Between fishing dates he was the "name" lawyer of the Eastern Sierras; the legal messiah for cattlemen, motels, ski lifts, resorts—and anyone else with money. "Boatcourt Steve," they call him affectionately and unaffectionately, because instead of trying lawsuits in the courts, he takes his opposition out fly-fishing in a boat. By the time they get back, they've usually arrived at a settlement. It's because "fish make the smartest juries," he tells everybody, "and a pint of bourbon doesn't hurt none, either."

"Steve Gorski!" I greeted him, pumping his hand, "am I glad to see you. I need a lawyer, quick… Oh, not you, Boatcourt, you're an institution. I mean a…you know, just a lawyer…"

"Caught you with more than ten fish, huh?" he kidded, lighting his beat-up pipe. "Put him on the front page, Hoppy…"

"No, no, serious… They're tying a can to a wonderful deputy sheriff…for being a human being. Know a struggling beginner that'll take a case for a bag of peanuts and a…a carload of principles?"

"Tried the Salvation Army?" he quipped.

"Okay, I'll laugh later, Steve…so long. Come on fellas…"

We were halfway down the walk when Gorski called after us. "Hey, where're you going, you guys?"

"For some coffee. Join us?"

"Make it brandy and I'll tell you a fish story…"

Hoppy, the publisher, grabbed my arm as Steve Gorski joined us.

"Frank…sure you want to talk in front of old Boatcourt here? He's the mouthpiece for all the big money boys…could end up your opposition, you know."

"Good…then I'll take him fly-fishing in my boat…"

Over coffee and brandy, at an isolated back table in the coffee shop, I told lawyer Steve Gorski, publisher Hoppy Hopkins, and reporter Jake Ziffren everything that happened, word for word, from the skinning of the deer to the sheriff bellowing he'd sue me. When it was all over, Boatcourt looked squarely at me with a sly grin.

"Frankie, my boy…now level with me. What's been your interest in this two-bit squabble?"

"Two-bit squabble?" I cried, climbing on my soapbox. "Steve… can't you see? Human rights are involved…the rights of little people… Bear Bait and Dry Rot are symbols…"

"Whoa, whoa, whoa… Save that bleeding heart stuff for Hollywood. Come on, now… What? Stirring up a movie out of this? Want to be another Truman Capote?"

"You may have an idea..."

"You know this, don't you, dreamer boy... The sheriff's got you over a barrel. You did slander him. Right, Hoppy?"

"I'd say so," said Hoppy as he leaned back and swayed on the hind legs of his chair. "You can't go round accusing public officials just on flimsy rumors, Frank."

"But nobody in that room can talk... They made an agreement..."

"Oh, boy," sighed Steve in disgust. "How'd you live so long without being run over? A court order will make 'em talk fast in a libel suit, stupid, and under oath! You need a lawyer more than Lefty does."

"Wow!" popped in eager-beaver Jake. "Can I quote you directly in my story, Mister Gorski?"

"No!" snapped his boss Hoppy.

"But, Boss...aren't we covering this?"

"SHUT UP!"

That made us all shut up and begin thinking. Steve sipped brandy with one hand and twiddled flies on his hat with the other. Hoppy tipped back and forth on his chair, pulling his lower lip into grotesque shapes. Outwardly, I drummed out a rhythm with my fingertips on the table, but inwardly, the word "libel" was beginning to drum up a panic.

"Fellas," said Boatcourt, breaking the silence, "I got to tell you a story about Dry Rot...you'll die. All of you know how nobody's ever found his hideout. So the subject came up at a Lion's Club luncheon, when up jumps that little fat banker... What's his name, Hoppy? Gruber, that's the guy, with those thick glasses, like beer bottle bottoms. Well, Gruber had had a gin or two, and he up and says: 'I'll lay eight to five my two hound dogs can find Dry Rot's diggings. Any takers?' Well, there were lots of takers, so fifteen smart businessmen pile into their cars, follow Gruber to his kennels where he picks up his pooches, and up we go to Deadman's Summit, to the hollow log where Dry Rot trades grubs for things.

"Well, little fat Gruber unloads two powerful hounds that could pull a truck, and they're rarin' to go. But he holds them back, a leash in each hand, looking like Ben Hur driving a chariot, only he's got no chariot and no waistline like Ben Hur, either. His little potbelly does all right holding up his pants when he's sitting in the bank, but not when he's hanging on to a seventy-pound hound with each hand. But he's game, this Gruber.

"'Stand back, everybody,' he tells us, sneaking a hoist at his pants, 'give Greenie and Brownie a fair chance... There's money on this... Stand back... Don't confuse the smells.'

"Well, us scoffing Lions stand back, while Greenie and Brownie sniff and slobber and make asthmatic noises all over the hollow log and Dry Rot's grubs, with Gruber ordering them, 'Smell, Greenie... Smell, Brownie'...when Greenie suddenly lifts a leg against the hollow log and destroys every other smell within the radius of a mile...

"The Lions snickered and laughed...and when the other pooch, Brownie, lifts his leg on the same spot, the Lions howled...they knew they had a pigeon now... 'Gruber, twenty more they don't find Dry Rot.' The odds go down... 'Two to one, Gruber...' 'Three to one...' But Gruber's game. 'Name your poison, fools. I'll cover anything... Remember your bets...'

"With that he aims the tugging hounds into the woods and yells, 'FETCH!'

"Well, they fetched with such a jerk they nearly yanked Gruber off his feet...and off they go, with Gruber leaping and stumbling, hanging on for dear life to the leashes and his pants. And off we trot after him, whoopin' and hollerin'...fifteen smart businessmen, full of lunch and liquor.

"We hadn't gone a hundred feet before Gruber stumbles on a root, and off fly his glasses. Now he's blind...but he's got a bigger problem...his pants. But he's game, old Gruber. He just keeps shouting, 'Fetch! Fetch!'...and the hounds answer him with yowls that would wake the dead.

"Round and round we race through the pines, with brave Lions collapsing right and left what with the altitude and the hooch—and there they sprawl on the ground, laughing and panting like beached dolphins...until there's only about six of us stalwarts left to urge old Gruber on with horn noises, and 'Yoicks! Yoicks!'...'On Donder!'... 'On Blitzen!'... 'On Greenie!'...'On Brownie!'

"The poor hounds hadn't the slightest notion of what anybody wanted them to do, so they ran in all directions at once, and it had to happen. One runs this way, the other runs that way, leaving poor Gruber spread-eagled between them, his arms pulled out of his sockets. Well, that made him a little thinner…and down came his pants…down to his ankles…and he yells for help…

"So we rush to the rescue. We hang on to the dogs while we try to pull his pants up, but he says: 'Pull 'em off, pull 'em off!' So we pull his pants off and try to get him to call the whole silly thing off. But not old Gruber. 'Quit? ME? We've just started…' So he puts his arms around the panting pooches and talks to 'em. 'Greenie, Brownie…sweethearts… Don't let me down…I got money on you… Find Dry Rot…' And the hounds slobber all over his face while he kisses them back.

"Then he lines them up again, yells 'FETCH!' and the hounds race right toward a big pine tree, with blind Gruber on the leashes. One dog takes the left side of the tree, the other the right side, leaving poor Gruber with no place to go except right at the tree… which he smashes into with such a whomp, it starts raining pine cones around us.

"Gruber is knocked cold. He slides down the tree like a rag doll. Well, there's no more laughing. We turn poor Gruber over. He's out, and his face is a mess, and his manhood a bigger mess. So while we're slapping him around trying to bring him to…we hear a voice behind us: 'Gentlemen…can I help you?'"

Cutting off his tale right there, Steve Gorski stood up from the table, yawned, and said: "Well, Frank, thanks for the drink…"

"Wait a minute," said Hoppy, "who was the voice? Dry Rot?"

"Yep," answered Steve, "there he was, not twenty feet away from us…Dry Rot…skinnier and whiter than ever. And not only that…the two hounds were stretched out at his feet…panting with their tongues out a mile…" He drained the last drops from his glass. "And when old Gruber came to at the Bishop Hospital, and we told him what had happened, he sat up and yelled: 'Aha! I win all the bets. Told you my hounds would track him down! Pay up, you dopes, all of you!'

"Well, on account he had a hospital bill, we all paid off…then went to the nearest saloon to laugh it up…"

Then Steve yawned again and waved to us: "Hoppy…Jake…I got fish to clean. See you, Frank…"

He started out but I grabbed his arm. "Hey…Steve. You said I needed a lawyer, remember?"

"Like the flowers need the rain, boy…"

"Well…shall I get some big guy from Beverly Hills?"

"A foreigner? Up here in the woods? Don't be silly…"

"Well, who, then?" I asked, beginning to feel like Linus without his blanket… "Not you? Would you want to, Steve…?"

He was lighting his pipe, but he paused to look at me.

"Frank… I wouldn't touch your case for the deed to the Taj Mahal. A show-off Hollywood director insults and slanders an upright small-town sheriff, with no evidence? It's loaded against you. A million dollars couldn't buy you one cent of sympathy."

He relit his pipe; then, very casual-like, he added: "But Lefty… Lefty's different. If he were to ask for me as a public defender…" He hung back a moment or two, pulling at his ear, then casually sat down again and talked to Hoppy face-to-face.

"Hoppy…are you game? I mean…as game as old Gruber? Because that's what it's going to take."

"Steve, I've told you. You can afford to lose your rich clients, but my papers can't afford to lose their advertising. Simple as that."

"Hoppy, it's the break we've been waiting for. A gift from heaven. If I become public defender for Lefty, Wonder Boy will have to talk for my rich clients. See what that means? It puts the rich and the DA's crowd together. A rich mob against two little people. Get it?"

"Call Lefty and Frank, here, little people?"

"No, no! To hell with them. I mean Bear Bait and Dry Rot. They're the gimmick. Through them we make unmerciful tyrants out of the DA and the sheriff's henchmen, and a hero out of Lefty. That'll clear him, and," pointing to me, "it might even get this guy off the hook."

Somehow these gentlemen were taking my ball and running away with it. Besides, I wasn't quite sure what they were talking about. "Look, fellas," I said, trying to make my presence felt again, "All Lefty wants is to—to—"

The words expired in my mouth. So absorbed were they in their own thoughts, I just wasn't there. I turned to Jake the reporter—the fifth Beatle—and poked his arm. "Jake… What's with all the heavy thinking?"

"Who, me? Oh. The election, of course."

"What election?" I asked.

But Boatcourt had suddenly become aware of the young reporter's presence. "Hey, Hoppy! Your boy here...I mean..."

"Gotta trust him now, Steve," said Hoppy. "He knows too much. Jake? What's your reaction to this clambake?"

"Boss, I'm drooling! Biggest thing that—"

"Then drool over your typewriter," urged Steve. "Pour it on. Feature the secrecy. Where there's secrecy there's got to be chicanery."

"Steve!" I butted in proudly. "I made that same speech today—"

"Who hasn't?" he said without even looking at me. "Hoppy... you know as well as I do what they're incubating in that little old courthouse across the street. A premature little monster!"

Surprisingly, the words "little monster" came out of Boatcourt with unexpected heat. He pushed his misshapen, fly-spangled skimmer forward over his smoldering eyes and clamped his jaws so hard the veins swelled in his neck. Odd bloke, this Steve "Boatcourt" Gorski. He had the wit and certain mannerisms of a Will Rogers, but all similarity ended there. His body had the shape of a lumpy carrot—wide bottom, narrow shoulders, and an almost pointed head. The great George Randolph Hearst had somewhat the same shape. But Boatcourt's face puzzled you most. It was not suntanned like a fisherman's, but pallid; as if it might have been grown in a cellar like a mushroom. But his skin did have a slight color—the age-old yellowish color of ancient parchment. In fact, his face looked like a Dead Sea scroll with eyes.

And his social life was also unusual enough to nourish rumors. Rich (nobody knew how rich), unmarried, he lived alone in a magnificent chalet high above June Lake. Yet he entertained lavishly—as if he wanted to share it all with everybody. And everybody thought that was a fine idea and helped him out.

"Be a lot of fun plowing up this county a bit, Hoppy," said Boatcourt, resuming his pitch to the publisher. "You yourself said in one of your editorials that there was a hardpan forming just below the surface that needed breaking up and airing."

"I wrote that line, Mr. Gorski," interjected Jake the Beatle.

"Good line, son."

After putting papers to bed for forty years, Hoppy Hopkins had become too hard-boiled and cynical to be stampeded into emotional causes. He listened to Boatcourt, but wasn't buying. "Steve!" he said, blowing out some air. "I'll lay it on the line. Everything's fine with me right now. My family, my papers—all fine. And I'm too old to enjoy being seduced by you, and too damned tired to want to reform the world. So unless you've got a better idea than knocking off Wonder Boy…"

"I have, Hoppy. Every man, and I mean every man, should experience the holy catharsis of being on the side of the angels at least once in his lifetime before he dies. I mean, lash the moneychangers! I mean a go-for-broke, gung-ho fight for some lost cause for the downtrodden, if you will!"

Well, after that I was ready to sign up, carry the torch, wave the flag—anything!

"The downtrodden don't buy ads," shot back Hoppy, throwing a bucket of ice water on my enthusiasm.

"Aw, come off, Hoppy!" said Boatcourt heatedly. "After forty years yet. Nobody buys ads. Ads are sold! By circulation. Sure you'll get cancellations. So you publicize them by printing: 'The ad in this space was cancelled by so-and-so because of lack of human compassion.' You'll murder them—Oh, what, the hell… Anyway, Hoppy. I wouldn't dare take it on without your help."

There was an awkward pause. Hoppy broke it up by kicking his chair back and pacing up a minor storm. Stopping suddenly, he poked an angry finger under Boatcourt's nose and said:

"Look, Mister Big Rich Lawyer, I played up the bastard as big as Lindbergh in my papers. Remember that. So let's pull the chain on this downtrodden stuff and talk turkey. You're running against your own protégé because the eagle you thought you were nursing turned into a cobra. Right? And you know I hate the son of a bitch as much as you do. But I can't see how in Christ's world you, or me, or anybody else can blow up a penny-ante case of two dirty old bums into a lost cause that'll keep Mister America out of Sacramento. It's too crazy! Too screwy to even talk about."

Another pause. Something new had been added. Politics was rearing its ugly head. Who needed politics? I tried to formulate a sentence that would tell them that all Lefty wanted was to let Mono County know why he disobeyed his orders. Boatcourt got in ahead of me.

"Hoppy," he drawled, pushing back his fly-studded hat. "Wasn't it you who told me the yarn about how Hitler's uncle said he could have saved thirty million lives if only he had shot down the little monster before…"

"I know, I know," interrupted the annoyed Hoppy. "If he'd have stepped on young Adolf the first time he got out of line, and all that. But Tony Caldwell's no paranoiac house painter. He's a brilliant political genius. Smart. Tough. Popular. He's bound to plow a helluva row in Sacramento, and maybe a deeper one in Congress. Stop Tony with Bear Bait and Dry Rot? You're out of your mind. That guy can make political hay out of—"

Hoppy was interrupted by a deputy sheriff approaching our table. It was the door deputy at the hearing.

"Excuse me, gentlemen," he said. "But we are ready to resume the hearing. With a court stenographer present, as per your request, Mr. Capra."

"Oh, yes…thank you…I'll…I'll be right there."

"Yes, sir." And the deputy left. In the excitement of meeting Boatcourt and Hoppy, I'd forgotten all about the hearing and my grandstand demand for a court reporter. "Now what, Steve?" I asked plaintively.

"Frank, go back and make a sincere apology to the sheriff for the record. Maybe they'll forget your silly remarks."

"What about Lefty? You mentioned something about being his public defender?"

"Tell Lefty to accept the commission's ruling and go to work for the highway."

"But, Steve… You know he won't accept it. He's going for broke—like you said…"

"I'm sure Saint Peter will take note of it."

"Then you won't defend him?"

"Huh? Oh, yeah. Well, I thought it was a good idea. But I'm glad Hoppy, here, wised me up to how screwy the whole thing is. Forget it, Frank."

"Forget it? But Steve... Bear Bait and Dry Rot...you said..."

"Can't you Hollywood guys take a hint?" he said, losing patience. "Who gives a damn about two worthless derelicts...unless you can make it pay off?"

My confusion turned to anger. I'd been had. I felt a great sense of betrayal; a great shame of men in general...and I wanted to hurt somebody. Anybody.

"Great feet of clay, I salute you!" I said and bowed mockingly to Steve. "But I tell you what, you big respectable people. I'm not apologizing to anybody. And if Lefty refuses to wave the white flag, I'm sticking with him—even if it lands me in the clink. And Jake! If you want to write up this little meeting, you've got my permission to quote me verbatim. You'll find somebody to print it."

I flung my chair aside and started to leave. I was stopped suddenly, by a leg that shot out from below the table, barring my way—Steve Gorski's leg. I angrily turned on him but he was innocently lighting his pipe. Then I noticed that Hoppy was pacing the floor again—this time yanking and releasing great handfuls of his mop of iron-gray hair and mumbling to himself. "How?...How?... Jesus!... It would be a helluva service to America to stop big 'I AM' right here in Bridgeport. But how?... How?... We go to press tomorrow," he said, still talking to himself. "But I could delay it a day...a special issue...screamers on the front page...inside, whole-page petitions...asking for a public hearing before the whole Board of Supervisors... My correspondents in each little town will 'get signatures... It's crazy...a fifty-to-one shot...that handsome DA plays ugly...and they're organized in that courthouse... Take a shot at one and they all fight back like kamikazes." He stopped ruminating. "Okay, Boatcourt. If you aren't just beating your gums, be at my office at eight o'clock tonight. I'll have some copy. You, too, Frank. I'll need some quotes. Come on, Jake. You can forget about sleeping..."

"Geronimo!" shouted Jake the Beatle as he gathered notes and knocked over chairs trying to keep up with his long-striding boss heading out the door.

I didn't sit—I collapsed in a chair. And there was Boatcourt puffing his pipe and grinning like—it was his own expression, the Felix Domestica that ate the Serinus Canarius.

"Frank, we're in. That's a great fighting fool just went out of here—when he gets hooked on a principle." Then the professional took over, the gleam of battle in his eyes. "Now you! Capra, go back to that hearing, quick! Get hold of Lefty privately. Say you want a private conference. Tell Lefty to neither accept nor reject the commission's ruling, but to say that he would like to consult an attorney. And having no funds, he asks them for a public defender. That's all. Nothing else. Just that, and not another word! Tell Lefty I'll do the rest. I'm on call this week, understand? Now go!" Then he added a compliment of sorts, "Feet of clay...you stinker! Right out of one of your terrible movies, I'll bet."

About ten that night, I called my wife from Hoppy's press office in Bishop. She hadn't heard from me all day.

"Darling! Where are you?"

"In Bishop, honey. Don't worry."

"Don't worry? Are you in jail?"

"Naw. Little private poker game, sweetie. We may play all night... so go to bed, honey. I love you."

"But, Frank. You haven't told me anything—" I hung up. I was quite sure she banged the phone and said, "All men are idiots!" And the point is, I think we love being idiots.

CHAPTER FIVE

D AWN. WEDNESDAY MORNING, NOVEMBER 3, 1960. A light snow was failing as Hoppy and I flung the last bagful of individually wrapped *Mono Herald*s into a mail truck—the weekly delivery to be stuffed into subscribers' PO Boxes. "Get going!" shouted Hoppy hoarsely. We hadn't slept. My arms hung like lead, my tail sagged like a sandbag, my legs were concrete that wouldn't harden. But ink-stained Hoppy was a roaring, driving Simon Legree. "Bring up those Volkswagens. Come on! Come on!" he shouted to some sleepy high school boys. Hoppy had hired three Volkswagen panel trucks and boy drivers to deliver stacks and stacks of extra tied-up bundles of *Herald*s to restaurants, stores, bars, hotels, motels, trailer parks, and pack stations for delivery into the high country. Not five regional editions this time. Everybody got the same paper. And not the usual 7,500 copies. No, sir, Wild Man Hoppy had shoved 21,572 copies through his old rickety flatbed press before it bucked, rattled, gasped, and came to a grinding halt from exhaustion. And no amount of extra foot-kicking by Hoppy could make it roll out another copy.

A half hour later, three tail-heavy Volkswagen trucks labored up Sherwin Grade in low gear packed solid with tied-up bundles of *Mono Herald*s. I lay like a dog on top of the bundles in the leading truck. Hoppy had thrown me in. "Now get the hell home and get some sleep." But now sleep was impossible. What had I gotten myself into? The top paper of each pile I laid on, exposed to handling and rubbing, was so smeared with barely dried ink it was hardly legible.

But no amount of smudging could stifle the scream of the foot-high headline. You could hear it in the dark:

SHAME! MONO!

Now, before you can fully appreciate the power of a newspaper headline in Mono County, California, you must remember that the county has no local radio and very few telephones. The county newspaper is still the only mass medium of communication. The only other communication link worth mentioning is US Highway 395, which ties together nine-tenths of the locals as it snakes along at the foot of the great, two-mile-high Sierra Wall. This is the word-of-mouth road; the joke line; the gossip freeway, down which rumors, amplified from mile to mile, speed faster than the traffic.

But these 150 miles of two-way chitchat, delectable though they may be, are still subject to the aberrations of word-of-mouth transmission. You can believe it, build on it, cut it in half, or call it hogwash as you pass it on.

But the printed word in Mono County—Ah! That carries power and authority. Yes, siree. You read it in the paper and it's *there*, hot off the press, firsthand, no in-betweens. Just you and the paper and the clout of the printed word.

For we must remember that one can fly from San Francisco to New York in half the time San Franciscans can reach the Eastern Sierras. Boundaries may be shrinking all over the world, but the Inyo-Mono area is a holdout. And small wonder. It is incredibly isolated and insulated by boundaries that don't shrink: On the west by the sheer granite Sierra Wall; on the east both by desolate mountain ranges and waterless valleys (Death Valley); on the south by one of the world's great graveyards of bleached bones and withered hopes (Mojave Desert); and on the north by a harsh jumble of volcanic outpourings and dead inland seas (Carson Sink).

And we must also remember that California, on the other (western) side of the Sierra Wall, had been a thriving, populous, "civilized" area for almost two hundred years before white men came to Mono. The great western migration routes of the Gold Rush and covered wagon years lay far to the north, where the Sierra Passes were lower. When the "reverse" Gold Rush did hit Mono, it came east from California, as a belated backwash of the 49er tide. So out-of-the-beaten path are these three thousand square miles of mountain and desert that even today, Mono's population of Native Americans and whites is still less than ten thousand. And yet, in recent years, almost two million yearly vacationers come to camp, fish, hunt, hike, or ski in its primitive wilderness.

As mentioned before, there is no local radio in the county. The reception of outside radio is almost nil in the daytime, while at night so many stations "come in" it is almost impossible to separate them. And as for TV, one or two small districts have managed to arrange for weak signals to be relayed down from community aerials on high peaks. But that is all there is of modern electronic communications. The air lanes and airwaves still belong to the hawks and the eagles.

But the press? That's a different story. Here the country newspaper still plays the same important role it enjoyed in all rural areas fifty years ago.

"Hoppy" Hopkins is the publisher and editor of five such county weeklies, three for Inyo County and two for Mono. All are continuous extensions of the rip-roaring "mining town" papers that once spread the heady news of rich strikes from the now ghost towns of Aurora, Bodie, Mammoth, and Lundy.

These weeklies are truly provincial. If it has no Mono slant, no statewide, national, or world news is printed. But all local items (scenic, political, sports, social; births, deaths, marriages, lodge meetings) are covered fully and in detail—fifteen village correspondents contributing weekly columns about the comings, goings, and doings in their particular community under signed bylines. Editorials are rare, but names and photos are used, lavishly. To Hoppy's weeklies, Mono County is a world all its own; a proud, provincial, primitive world. Nothing that happens on the "outside" is worth printing, but everything on the inside is. And for Hoppy Hopkins, that "local" formula, and the power of the printed word, had gained him prestige and a mighty good life.

Now he was laying it all on the line in his go-for-broke crusade for the rights of two worthless derelicts against the pressures of the new vacationland.

Unusual? No, not really unusual for the independent, fearless breed of frontier journalists. When America was a brawling, gangling, juvenile delinquent seeking fame, fortune, and meaning in the West, it was the journalists and their makeshift presses who guided, needled, wheedled, blasted, humored, inspired, and served as the "conscience" of America.

Many of the adventurers who "won the West" acquired fame and fortune with guts, trigger, pick, and plow. But meaning was implanted by the frontier newspaper. Hoppy Hopkins might have been an editor out of his time, but not of his historic mold.

•••

THE FIRST OF THE Volkswagens, loaded with me and the all-powerful printed "words," pulled up to Rock Creek Inn and slid to a stop on the thin snow. Waiting for the papers, Lloyd, the stone-faced innkeeper, was standing on the porch smoking his morning pipe. One of the two high school boys on the truck, earning twenty bucks for this single special delivery, hopped out and ran to the back of the truck. He was red-haired, irrepressible, and wildly imaginative.

"Lloyd!" he cried out to the innkeeper. "Oil up your old musket… we're bringing the message to Garcia… Here it is!" he said laughingly, as he hefted the bundle of papers at the innkeeper's feet. "Careful how you handle that, Lloyd. It's liable to explode!"

"Come on, Gabby…we're late," yelled the other high school boy who was driving; a dour, mule-eared, pimply youth who wouldn't go around the corner to see Lady Godiva wrestle a tiger. He threw the truck in gear, making his gabby friend run to get in.

"You know what, Muley?" said the irrepressible one as he banged his door shut, "we oughtta hang red flags all over this heap…"

"I'll bite," muttered the dour one.

"We're carrying explosives!" the redhead exclaimed, holding up the screaming front page.

"You're nuts!"

"Look at that, man. Two words…two bombs, man… 'SHAME! MONO' Heads will fall! Mono Craters will erupt again! The Indians are coming!… Think I'll be a newspaperman."

"That figures. Yesterday you were an astronaut."

"So what? I'll start the first paper on the moon."

"Aw, grow up, earache," Muley growled. "Know what your load of bombs will be by tomorrow night?"

"They'll be shots heard round the world!"

"They'll be cut up toilet paper."

At each stop all the way up to Topaz, the irrepressible redhead threw out bundles of papers and shouted American slogans: "Extra! Extra! The Redcoats are coming!" "Paul Revere rides again! Extra!" "One if by land, two if by sea!" "Man the ramparts, men!" "Four-score and seven years ago!" "Give me Liberty or drink the ink!" "Tippecanoe and Tyler, too! Extra!" "Massa's in the cold, cold ground!..."

Well, I couldn't miss all this fun. Instead of going home, I stayed on the truck and watched and listened. In the post offices, in stores and restaurants and on the streets, I saw the natives avidly read and reread the eye-bugging edition. And as in most sparsely populated areas, a local burning issue raises blood pressures quicker'n a declaration of war. At Convict Lake Inn, where workers gather for early breakfast, the papers created quite a hullaballoo. A waitress later told me that eggs, bacon, and hash browns were left uneaten as men, cooks, and waitresses devoured the juicy headlines.

"Hey, Hank!" yelled out a construction worker wearing a red safety helmet. "Read it out loud, I left my glasses."

"With or without gestures?" quipped Hank, who ran the pack station and, as with all horse wranglers, wore a week's growth of scraggly beard.

"Try it with English," cracked a loud mouth from the counter.

"I save the English for my pool balls, you pigeon," retorted the bearded wrangler. "Okay, Sy, listen to this for a kick in the pants..." He read out loud for the helmeted one as the hubbub quieted down:

"The headline reads: 'SHAME! MONO!' which you can read from a mile away without glasses. "COUNTY OFFICIALS TAKE ORDERS FROM ARROGANT LAND DEVELOPERS TO DRIVE OLD CHARACTERS OUT OF MONO.' Then: 'OLD-TIMERS DON'T FIT NEW VACATIONLAND IMAGE, SAYS THE NEW MONEY. BEAR BAIT AND DRY ROT FIRST ON EXILE LIST.

WHO'S NEXT? YOU?'... How do you like them apples, you dirty old-timers?" asked the bearded wrangler of the whole room.

From my wife, my friends, and the exciting gossip that flew up and down the "rumor lane" (Highway 395), I got other breathtaking "eyewitness accounts":

The checking counter at the June Lake General Store was surrounded with customers and clerks listening to butcher Franz Schwartzenburg reading the paper.

"Listen...just like Dusseldorf before the war: 'BEAR BAIT AND DRY ROT, TWO LOVABLE HERMITS, PEACEFUL RESIDENTS IN OUR WOODS FOR OVER 25 YEARS, HAVE BEEN ORDERED ARRESTED AS "VAGS"... TO BE TAKEN TO THE COUNTY LINE AND TOLD TO "GIT!" THEIR CRIME? THEY WOULDN'T LOOK GOOD IN BIKINIS.'"

"What's bikinis?" asked the puzzled German butcher.

"Oh, little things," volunteered a shapely guest in skintight slacks, "little black... Oh, shut up and read..."

"Excuse me," apologized Franz the meat man, then resumed reading from the paper: "'INCORRUPTIBLE DEPUTY SHERIFF WAKEFIELD WAS STRIPPED OF HIS BADGE AND FIRED FOR REFUSING TO ROUST THE TWO HERMITS OUT OF THE COUNTY. WHO'S NEXT? YOU?'"

•••

THE QUAINT WHITE COURTHOUSE at the county seat of Bridgeport was a bedlam of excitement. All work stopped as county employees ran into each other's offices waving copies of the "sheet." Tax Assessor Tobias Greenwald was livid as he read excerpts to his office help:

"Can you tie that for yellow journalism?" he muttered as he turned a page. "And here's a whole page of interviews by that slimy little beatnik, 'the enquiring reporter':

"'CASE CLOSED,' SAID SHERIFF TOM MCMAHON WHEN REACHED BY PHONE, 'I FIRED LEFTY FOR INSUBORDINATION, PERIOD. CASE CLOSED, CASE CLOSED...'"

•••

Two DEPUTY SHERIFFS WERE parked in a sheriff's car on the Pole Line road to Hawthorne. One was reading to the other. "'OH, NO, MR. SHERIFF,' RETORTS NOTED ATTORNEY, STEVE 'BOATCOURT' GORSKI, WHEN QUESTIONED ABOUT SHERIFF'S REMARKS. 'THIS CASE HAS JUST BEEN OPENED. I'VE BEEN ASKED BY LEFTY TO BE HIS PUBLIC DEFENDER…'"

"Wow!" remarked the other deputy. "Old Boatcourt ain't about to take on a case unless it's big. This could start a civil war…"

"You can say that again," answered the reader as he continued with Gorski's interview;

"'…AND AS LEFTY'S ATTORNEY, I'M ASKING FOR A PUBLIC HEARING BEFORE THE ENTIRE BOARD OF SUPERVISORS. IF THE BOARD REFUSES SUCH A HEARING, OPEN TO PUBLIC AND PRESS, THEN I'LL FLY TO SACRAMENTO TO PETITION THE STATE'S ATTORNEY GENERAL TO ORDER A SPECIAL HEARING BEFORE DEPUTIES FROM HIS OFFICE.'

"'WHAT HAPPENED TO BEAR BAIT AND DRY ROT CAN HAPPEN TO ANY SHEEPHERDER, CATTLEMAN, PROSPECTOR, OR FARMER WHO ISN'T DRESSED IN HART, SCHAFFNER, AND MARX'S LATEST FASHIONS.'"

The radio in their car crackled: "Number one to all cars…all cars… Report at once to Bridgeport station. Repeating…"

"Look's like the civil war's starting…" said the driver deputy as he turned on the ignition key.

•••

THE EMPLOYEES OF THE Great Sierra Motel (forty rooms) hurriedly assembled in the "help's quarters," hanging on to the chambermaid's every word. Fanny Welch, a refugee from amateur theatricals, was not just reading—she was auditioning. But the almond-shaped, rhinestone glasses she normally wore were not on her nose; they twirled in her hand as she held the *Mono Herald* within an inch of her naked eyes and projected her voice: "'IT'S THE SAME OLD BALONEY,' answered old-timer Gabe Palastra, when queried by your reporter. 'MONEY, MONEY, MONEY'S GOT ALL THE RIGHTS. NEVER USSENS!'"

"Oh, my stars…here's an interview with Indian Joe," exclaimed Fanny, putting on her glasses to bring the others into focus. "That would be your uncle, would it not, Mary John?"—this last directed to a squat Indian dishwasher.

"What he say?" grunted Mary John.

"Him say plenty," emoted Fanny, taking off her glasses and bringing the paper up to her nose again: "'WHAT THE HELL, IT'S US INDIANS NEXT,' answered old Piute Joe when asked for comment, 'TELL WHITE POLICE WE ALL GOT RIFLES NOT, NOT ARROWS!'"

Mary John untied her apron and dropped it on the floor.

"Now me go home," she grumbled as she started for the door.

"Wait a minute, Mary John. You Indians holding a pow-wow?" asks the fry cook.

"We talk," cryptically answered the Indian dishwasher, shuffling out.

•••

FROM THE SIERRA PEAKS to the White Mountains, from Topaz to Sherwin Grade, the "Bomb" reverberated and the echoes swelled. Monoites stopped everything to read and discuss. Of particular interest were the printed interviews with people they knew personally, such as:

Resort owner Gabrielson of Mammoth: "YOU CAN'T STOP PROGRESS. I CONGRATULATE THE SHERIFF AND THE DISTRICT ATTORNEY. AND YOU CAN PRINT THAT IN HEADLINES."

Lupo Gallegos: "WHAT ABOUT ME? I'M SHEEPHERDER. BEAR BAIT AND DRY ROT IS LOOK BETTER'N ME."

Pack station "Hoss" Toomey: "YOU MEAN US MULE SKINNERS GOTTA SHAVE AND SLICK DOWN OUR HAIR TO STAY IN THE COUNTY? HORSE----!"

Realtor Hathaway of Twin Lakes: "THOSE BUMS ARE A BLIGHT TO VACATIONLAND. WHO NEEDS LICE WHEN WE GOT BEAR BAIT AND DRY ROT?"

Tackle storeowner Ned Hicks: "WHAT D'YA MEAN, THEY'RE RUNNING PEOPLE OUT OF THE COUNTY? WHAT THE HELL IS THIS, SIBERIA?"

Bridgeport drugstore clerk: "ON LODGE NIGHTS, I'VE SEEN THE SHERIFF AS DRUNK AS BEAR BAIT."

Bartender Crouse: "IT'S ALL POLITICS. I WOULDN'T GIVE YOU A DIME FOR THE WHOLE CRUMMY LOT."

Mrs. Lucille Lornegan/President of the Women's Club: "DISTRICT ATTORNEY TONY CALDWELL STANDS ACE HIGH WITH US. HE UNDERSTANDS WOMEN'S RIGHTS."

President June Lake C. of C.: "WORST PUBLIC RELATIONS STUNT TO HIT MONO COUNTY. CANCEL MY ADVERTISING."

East Walker housewife: "OH, THEY'RE ALL THIEVES UP IN BRIDGEPORT. JUST RAISED OUR TAXES A HUNDRED PERCENT."

Cabin owner Peter Horgan: "AS A DISTRICT ATTORNEY, TONY CALDWELL SHOULD BE IN THE MOVIES."

Barber Sam Morelli: "WHAT THE HELL'S ALL THE FUSS ABOUT TWO BUMS?"

Garageman Tyson: "BUMS? WHAT ABOUT THE 'SKI' BUMS COME UP IN WINTER? STEAL EVERYTHING THAT AIN'T TIED DOWN, THEY DO."

Store clerk Tilly Feuchtwanger: "WELL, DID YOU EVER SMELL BEAR BAIT? TOOK THE CURL OUTTA MY HAIR."

Tungsten prospector Jerri Jacobi: "BEAR BAIT'S SHACK A PIG PEN? HELL'S AFIRE, YOU SHOULD SEE MINE."

And so went the printed comments pro and con—as pro and con as the readers who read them. Emotions flared, discussion warmed into argument, which boiled into name-calling, which steamed into shoving, which finally escalated into fisticuffs—especially if you didn't happen to like each other anyway.

It was gloomy enough for some headlights to be on when the irrepressible redheaded lad and his friend Muley and I stopped for coffee and donuts at Kellogg's in Leevining—after twelve hours of delivering the Bomb. Muley immediately lay his pimply face on the counter and went to sleep. I was so bushed I sat on the stool like a glassy-eyed zombie—dreaming of peace and quiet. But the redhead let out a war-whoop, "Ya-hoo-o! The revolution!" and pointed out the window.

Across the highway, outside Harry Blaver's Leevining General Store, on the shoulder of 395, I saw a Standard Oil station attendant and a Union Oil man trading haymakers. Out rushed redhead shouting, "Fight! Fight!" Whereupon friends from Standard and Union down the street dropped gas hoses and windshield rags and came a-runnin' to the fray.

Well, that pitted five Standard uniforms against only three Union jumpers, which didn't seem fair to a couple of virtuous clerks in the store, so they rushed out in their aprons and joined the fracas to even things up.

The fighting wasn't fancy, but it was eager and had a purpose—to cold-cock the guy nearest you, be he friend or foe. And what with the thin coating of snow on the pavement, the swinging missing, sliding battle royal edges out into the middle of Highway 395, stopping traffic both ways. In fact, so suddenly did the first cars stop, cars behind them skidded wildly and crashed into them, causing traffic behind them to do some fancy figure skating on locked wheels until they smacked abruptly and noisily against other cars or against the curbs. But the honking of horns, and banging of fenders, bothered the battlers not at all. On the contrary, they added to their zeal; for now they had an audience. One might say they were fighting in a ring of sorts—a ring of broken headlights.

On the covered porch of the Leevining General Store, there was a long bench that was usually occupied by half a dozen overweight Indian buckaroos, sitting on their ever-widening behinds impassively watching the pale-faces scurrying around like ants whose anthill had just been kicked over. This being "paper morning," there were ten "little" Indians sitting on the bench watching the street fight.

Now maybe it was the rallying cry of the redheaded irrepressible high school lad when he threw off the large bundle of papers at their feet: "Oh, noble Red Men! Can't you hear the drums? Put on your war paint!" Maybe the Indians thought the street fight was the opening skirmish of the Piutes' "Der Tag"; that their time to drive out the pale-faces had come at last. Maybe it was because TV had raised rioting to a popular sport. Or maybe it was just the plain old male urge to join any donnybrook and pop somebody in the kisser.

Whatever it was, their leader yelled out the Piute equivalent of "Geronimo!"...and all ten Indians put their heads down and charged into the brawl, swinging like berserk windmills. And Adam was their common father.

But Adam had to have some Irish in him, for from out of stores and garages other stalwarts came running to lend a helping knuckle to the Donnybrook. Even some well-dressed Fancy Dan travelers popped out of their busted cars, shedding coats and pumping fancy straight lefts at the nearest noses. But these city boys went down fast from the first local hairy fists that massaged their chins.

Wayne Fellows, a first-year California Highway Patrolman, was kissing his wife goodbye when he heard the yelling and the screeching of brakes on 395, three blocks away. He hopped in his patrol car, turned on red lights and siren, and burned rubber threading the narrow streets to the Highway.

There he was confronted with two of the worst bugaboos a peace officer has to face: a king-sized traffic jam and a citywide riot. Leaving his flashing light and wailing siren turned on, he radioed for "all cars" and ran toward the brawling men, who now numbered over fifty.

Some were down and bloody from blows. Others were down and panting from swings. But in their middle stood first-year Wayne Fellows, shouting "Hold it! Hold it!"—and shooting his revolver into the snowy atmosphere. He might as well have tried to stop a fighting pack of Dobermans with a peashooter. In fact, only the strict discipline of his training kept him from throwing away his gun and starting to swing himself.

But the wailing siren and the shots did have one un-hoped-for effect. All the rest of Leevining's men, and half the women, came racing toward the riot scene; while from out of the grammar school and high school grounds, whooping youngbloods brought new vigor to the bloody tumult. Like leaping fire starting smaller fires, perimeter fights broke out among the newcomers.

Delano Roosevelt, the half-Indian fire chief, was digging a pipe trench with his tractor when he heard the siren and the shots. He kept his head. In less than a minute he was at the firehouse blowing the big bullhorn. Three minutes later, he had a manned fire truck at each end of the riot scene.

When Delano gave the signal, the rioters were caught in a "cross fire" of ice-cold water. There was nothing much in the way of human passion that a well-directed high-pressure blast of ice water couldn't cool off. Especially if it knocked you down and sluiced you around, reducing you to the ridiculous state of being washed into the gutter as so much garbage. The mob broke and ran, shrieking with laughter.

Delano Roosevelt had won the day for sanity—with water. As he stood on his fire truck, coolly directing streams at foot-dragging groups, he looked down and saw newspapers floating by in the gutter water. He looked down in wonderment as headline after headline floated by—SHAME! MONO!

CHAPTER SIX

Wᴇ ʜᴀᴅ ɪɴᴠɪᴛᴇᴅ ᴏᴜʀ Silver Lake neighbors—Herb Kelly, a retired, successful San Diego corporation lawyer, and his wife, Helen; and Lyle Wright, a retired, Huntington Library expert on American literature, and his wife, Marge—to breakfast to discuss the "SHAME! MONO!" bombshell. Lyle Wright was reading aloud the Hopkins editorial:

"THIS IS YOUR EDITOR AND PUBLISHER, HARRY 'HOPPY' HOPKINS, WRITING WHAT MAY BE HIS LAST EDITORIAL. BUCKING A COMBINATION OF THE 'ESTABLISHMENT' AND 'BIG MONEY' IS GENERALLY CONSIDERED SUICIDE FOR PUBLISHERS.

"BUT AS ATTORNEY STEVE GORSKI PUT IT TO ME: 'EVERY MAN SHOULD EXPERIENCE THE HOLY CATHARSIS OF CONSCIOUSLY BEING ON THE SIDE OF THE ANGELS AT LEAST ONCE IN HIS LIFETIME, BEFORE HE DIES A GO-FOR-BROKE, GUNG HO FIGHT FOR LOST CAUSES: FOR THE RIGHTS OF THE DOWNTRODDEN.' WELL, THIS IS MY ONCE IN A LIFETIME.

"FIGHTING FOR LOST CAUSES, DEAR READERS, HAS PRODUCED SPECTACULAR CHANGES IN HISTORY, AND IT MAY PROMOTE CHANGES IN MONO COUNTY. ANYWAY, REGARDLESS OF CONSEQUENCES, THIS NEWSPAPER IS SHOUTING 'SHAME!' TO MONO OFFICIALDOM.

"SHADES OF THE GESTAPO AND CONCENTRATION CAMPS! SHADES OF CARTING OFF PEOPLE TO SIBERIA!

WHAT ARROGANCE! WHAT INSANITY! WHAT AN INSULT TO THE INTELLIGENCE OF MONO VOTERS… TO THINK THEY WOULD CLOSE THEIR EYES TO THE SHERIFF'S ARBITRARILY DECREEING WHO SHOULD OR SHOULDN'T LIVE IN MONO COUNTY?

"THE ACTIONS OF THE SHERIFF (TO PLEASE LAND DEVELOPERS), IN ORDERING THE ARREST AND DEPORTATION OF TWO PEACEFUL HERMITS, MONO RESIDENTS FOR OVER A QUARTER OF A CENTURY, SMELL TO HIGH HEAVEN!

"ACCORDING TO THE LIGHTS OF OUR ELECTED OFFICIALS, THE GREAT JOHN MUIR, THE FIRST 'HERMIT OF THE SIERRAS,' WOULD QUALIFY FOR BANISHMENT.

"THE ACTIONS OF THE DISTRICT ATTORNEY, AND OF THE CIVIL SERVICE COMMISSION, IN REFUSING LEFTY WAKEFIELD AN OPEN HEARING BEFORE PUBLIC AND PRESS, SO THAT ALL MIGHT HEAR AND KNOW LEFTY'S REASONS FOR DISOBEYING A GESTAPO ORDER TO ARREST TWO MEN ON TRUMPED-UP VAGRANCY CHARGES…THIS TOO, SMELLS TO HIGH HEAVEN.

"THIS NEWSPAPER BELIEVES ONLY AN OPEN PUBLIC HEARING BEFORE THE ENTIRE BOARD OF SUPERVISORS WILL DRIVE AWAY THE STENCH.

"BASIC HUMAN RIGHTS ARE INVOLVED. AMERICAN LAW IS BASED ON COMPASSION AS WELL AS JUSTICE. HUMAN DIGNITY IS SACRED…EVEN TO THE LAW.

"IF YOU AGREE, SIGN THE PETITION ON PAGE 3 OF THIS EDITION, WHICH REQUESTS THE SUPERVISORS TO CALL AN OPEN HEARING.

"REMEMBER, CITIZENS, YOU ARE THE ULTIMATE POWER IN OUR DEMOCRACY.

"SIGN THE PETITION."

"Oh, this is marvelous!" enthused ex-attorney Herb Kelly, "another Dred Scott decision…a Dreyfus ease…another Stokes trial! Another example of man-made laws colliding with God-given human rights. Oh, legal minds have bashed their heads against this rock for centuries. The problem is: Where does Justice end and compassion begin? How far can the Christian ethic of 'Love thy neighbor, even if he's your enemy' spill over into the framing of laws?'

"Should you still love your neighbor if you catch him stealing, or raping your wife? Or should you turn him in to the law? Marvelous, marvelous...the Bear Bait-Dry Rot case... Does a person forfeit his human rights when he disowns the society that gives him those rights? What a field day for legal philosophers... What a headache for the Supreme..."

He was interrupted by the entrance of friend and neighbor, tall John Hewitt, as he stomped in waving a different newspaper.

"Hi, neighbors," greeted pleasant John. Then, turning to me, "Well, Frank, I see you made the out-of-state papers, too."

"Me? What's that you've got there?"

"Minden, Nevada paper. A big, red, Mono County fire truck, blowing its siren like Billy-be-damned, is dropping bundles of 'em off all up and down three ninety-five...Whole-page ad in it by county officials..."

"Let me see that..." I grabbed his paper and read the ad out loud: "'SHAME! SMEARERS!'... That's the headline," I told the others. "'SINCE ALL THE MONO COUNTY PRESS IS A MONOPOLISTIC DICTATORSHIP, CONTROLLED BY ONE PERSON (A LYING MUDSLINGER), WE, YOUR ELECTED COUNTY OFFICIALS, HAVE SUFFERED THE HUMILIATION OF BUYING SPACE (AT OUR OWN EXPENSE) IN A NEVADA NEWSPAPER, IN ORDER TO EXPOSE THREE VENAL MEN AND CHARGE THEM WITH CHARACTER ASSASSINATION.

"'NEVER HAVE SO FEW STOOPED SO LOW TO DESTROY SO MANY. AND FOR WHAT? FOR POLITICAL ADVANTAGE!

"'YES, FRIENDS...IT'S A POLITICAL PLOT!...A PLOT TO ELECT A HANDPICKED HACK FOR STATE ASSEMBLYMAN, OVER YOUR DEVOTED SERVANT, DISTRICT ATTORNEY TONY CALDWELL.

"'THAT'S THE TRUTH AND THE WHOLE TRUTH.

"'THREE MEN, THREE UNSCRUPULOUS VENAL MEN, ARE DISRUPTING YOUR WHOLE COUNTY WITH VICIOUS LIES. THEY ARE:

"'NUMBER ONE: "BOATCOURT" STEVE GORSKI, FOREIGN-BORN, "CHARACTER" ATTORNEY: RICH (AND HOW HE GOT RICH IS STILL A MYSTERY), UNMARRIED, ECCENTRIC, BOHEMIAN, ATHEIST, POWER-CRAZED STEVE GORSKI. HE IS THE BACKER AND 'ANGEL' OF HIS HANDPICKED CANDIDATE FOR THE STATE ASSEMBLY—HIMSELF!

"'HIS AMBITION? TO BE A 'TAMMANY HALL' BOSS OF MONO COUNTY.

"'NUMBER TWO: 'HOPPY' HOPKINS, PUBLISHER AND EDITOR OF ALL MONO COUNTY PAPERS: APTLY NAMED "HOPPY," FOR ONLY A MAN FULL OF POPPY JUICE COULD TREAT ALL ELECTED COUNTY OFFICIALS AS AUTOMATIC "CROOKS."

"'THE MAN HATES...HATES ALL THAT HE CAN'T CONTROL. HE WOULD "ACCUSE" GOLDILOCKS IF IT WOULD PUT NEW LIFE IN HIS MORIBUND CIRCULATION.

"'NUMBER THREE: A MOVIE DIRECTOR FROM HOLLYWOOD, THAT CESSPOOL OF VICE. HE IS FOREIGN-BORN, A CATHOLIC, A 'LIBERAL'—PROBABLY IS FINANCING THE SMEAR CAMPAIGN IN ORDER TO SUBVERT A LIBEL SUIT FOR SLANDERING YOUR INCORRUPTIBLE SHERIFF, TOM MCMAHON.

"'THERE YOU ARE. WE APOLOGIZE FOR HAVING TO GO TO ANOTHER STATE TO BRING THE TRUTH INTO YOUR OWN COUNTY.

"'IF YOU BELIEVE IN YOUR DULY ELECTED COUNTY GOVERNMENT, AND NOT IN FOREIGN-BORN, POWER-MAD, KOOKY OUTSIDERS, THEN:

"'SAVE YOUR COUNTY FROM THEIR DOMINATION BY SIGNING THE PETITION AT THE BOTTOM OF THIS PAGE. TELL THE BOARD OF SUPERVISORS NOT TO BE PANICKED INTO CALLING AN OPEN HEARING OVER A TRIVIAL AFFAIR INVOLVING TWO SORDID MISFITS. EVERY DAY YOUR LAW OFFICERS HANDLE DOZENS OF SIMILAR CASES INVOLVING THE SAFETY AND PROTECTION OF YOUR HOMES AND CHILDREN. AND THEY WILL CONTINUE TO DO SO.

"THE THREE VENAL MEN WANT AN OPEN HEARING, ONLY AS A FORUM TO TRY TO SUBVERT YOUR COUNTY GOVERNMENT.

"SIGN THE PETITION!

"SAVE YOUR COUNTY'S GOOD NAME!

"SIGN FOR JOBS, PROGRESS, AND PROSPERITY!

"SIGN THE PETITION, AMERICANS!

"'Signed:

COMMISSIONER KYLE SOMMES,

SHERIFF TOM McMAHON, and

DISTRICT ATTORNEY TONY CALDWELL.'"

I was shocked. I couldn't think of anything to say. The ferocity of the half-truths, the viciousness of the innuendos...

There they were, printed in black and white, certified with the official county seal and attested to by the highest governing officers. No wonder politicians say the prime requisite in politics is a thick skin.

I looked around at our neighbors—friends of twenty years standing. They, too, were mulling the charges in the unexpected counterattack. Surely they would raise a storm of protest in my defense. They were silent. Was bigotry a dormant disease in all of us, even our friends, waiting to be stirred into virulence by the dirty finger of innuendo? A dirty suspicious finger of my own began stirring up a counter-nastiness. Persecuted skins become supersensitive to the faintest gleam of discrimination.

"Well!" I finally said lamely to nobody in particular.

"Frank, whoever wrote that rebuttal knows his infighting," said ex-attorney Herb Kelly with admiration. "That's a beautiful counterpunch, cunningly devised to confuse the issue."

"I'd say it's a beautifully timed counterpunch, anyway," mused John Hewitt. "You betcha...SHAME! SMEARERS!... A solid right cross over your straight left of SHAME! MONO! They play rough up here in the hills."

"Speaking of prize fights," threw in my already fed-up wife, "having to go out of the state and buy space to tell their side of the case, that pretty much makes them the underdog, too."

"Lu, you're absolutely right," said Mrs. Herb Kelly. "That's one thing I can understand. I think it's terrible that county officials are forced to go to another state to defend themselves against charges."

"My dear, that's just a brilliant piece of strategy to enlist voter sympathy," countered her ex-attorney husband. "All that's being asked of them is to hold a public hearing..."

"I don't care, Herb," she snapped back. "It's just not fair."

"Darling, all is fair in love and war, and a legal fight is mental warfare. Yes, and as in war, the best defense in law is to attack. Attack your opponent's motives. Destroy his credibility; his character. And if his case is clean and logically clear, be a squid and squirt the ink of doubt all over it. Very seldom is a case all black and white, so you attack with grays. Make the sinner seem more sinned against than sinning." He turned to me.

"Frank, that's what those shrewd boys in Bridgeport are doing to your lost cause crusade. You and your friends are fighting for an idea...all right...an ideal—human rights—difficult to spell out perhaps, but nevertheless, very dear to you. But in the process you are threatening political lives...and survival is very dear to them, too."

Herb Kelly's words sounded like the lyrics of a funeral march. My God. My neighbors were taking this whole affair as a game, a contest in which the opposition held most of the legal and moral cards. Not a word about their bigotry. I glanced at my wife. She averted her eyes. She knew what the others didn't know—that I could be as boring and annoying as some blacks, Hindus, and South Americans who take a perverse pleasure in making life difficult for their friends by deliberately misconstruing a careless jocular word, a look, or a silence as a racist statement in disguise.

Lyle Wright, the retired librarian, had sat there all this time, detached, elbows on the table, a coffee cup in both hands—and, I thought, as haughty as a Mayflower descendant. "Lyle?" I asked with an overly honeyed voice. "Haven't you got a witty remark up your white, Protestant sleeve to add to the obit of a lost cause?"

"Why, yes, Frank. I just looked into my white Protestant sleeve and saw an elbow that wants to bend a little."

"Lu, hand me the brandy. That's the best idea you've had in years, Lyle." And everybody laughed, relaxed, and agreed wholeheartedly, thereby proving alcohol's redeeming virtue: a relaxing catalyst.

"In my coffee, Frank," said Lyle, holding out his cup, "that's the way we drank it at the library. Looked better."

"That's the way we drank it branding cows in Texas," added John Hewitt. "Brandied better."

The corny pun got howls of pain.

"Ouch!"

"Did you have to reach way back to Texas for that?"

"Always got a laugh out of the cows," retorted John with a straight face.

And so it went as the brandy warmed away the blues. The chitchat got sillier and sillier. For the moment, at least, everybody forgot about Bear Bait and Dry Rot and Lefty and the rest. Everybody but me, that is. Despite the brandy and banter, I was seething inside. "Foreign-born, Catholic, a movie man," officialdom warned in their statement.

Of all the sins of man, bigotry has to be the cruelest. There's no way to fight it—so you hate it. Then you hate yourself, for hating. Yes, I was kidding around and smiling at our friends, but smiling only with the mouth, not the eyes.

"A toast!" I announced suddenly. "It's the only way to celebrate a wake. The Irish do it, the Jews, the Italians do it, the birds and the bees and the bigots do it..."

"Excuse me, Frank," interrupted Herb Kelly, "But did you say we're drinking to a wake? What Caesar are we burying now?"

"Haven't you heard? Old Causus Lostus, who's been buried and reburied a million times, and we're burying him again, on this lone prairie..."

"I won't drink to that, Frank," said Lyle. "I came to praise, not to bury anybody."

"Lyle," I answered, "didn't you hear Herb Kelly here, Mr. Law himself, make like Marc Anthony? Telling us you can't fight City Hall?"

"Wait a minute, my boy," said Herb, waggling a handful of fingers at me, "I didn't say you can't. I said they'd be tough and dirty; that's all."

"Well, Herb!" broke in Lu tartly, "I hope they have fun." Her tone silenced our friends. They knew my wife as a no-nonsense gal who was made of sturdy stuff—the roots of four generations of hardy Western pioneers nourished her character. "Frank is a sucker for human rights stuff," she went on. "I warned him he was silly to get mixed up with small-town politicians squabbling over who should lead the parade come next Fourth of July. But no. A couple of nice tramps were involved. So what does he get?" She held out the Nevada paper. "A lot of insulting name-calling. So if my husband is thinking of giving Mono back to the "fly people," and going back to that cesspool of vice called Hollywood, where being a foreign-born, or a Catholic, or even a Hottentot doesn't automatically qualify you as a leper, I wouldn't blame him on darn bit."

Lyle was first to comment. "Lu, if Frank left now, it certainly would be a big surprise to me." He was puzzled when he turned to me—as if he had discovered a scar on my face he hadn't noticed before. "Frank! I would never have put you down in my book as a summer soldier."

"Summer soldier?"

"Yes…and I agree with Lyle," interjected Herb Kelly, as he rose and began pacing the floor, waving his arms around like an orating penguin. "You're not a sunshine patriot… You can't be thinking of turning tail and running just because somebody yells 'BOO!' at you… and from way off in Nevada. Right causes never become lost causes until you quit fighting. My God, I wish I were twenty years younger… Frank, you believe in ideals…fine. But when the chips are down, it's not ideals that are on trial… No, sir…it's the men who champion them that are on trial. You're on trial…"

"Oh, fiddlesticks!" interrupted the librarian's wife, Marge, surprising everybody since she hadn't said a word all morning. "Frank's not on trial. He's not running for office. Why should he have to take all these dirty insults?"

"Marge," Lyle replied to his wife with unexpected heat, "Marge, Frank started the insults by insulting the sheriff at the hearing; he told us so. And then he talked that lawyer Gorski, and Hopkins with his newspapers, to join him in a crusade for the human rights of Lefty and the two hermits. You know what Truman said about it—if you can't stand the heat... Well, Frank not only went in the kitchen...he lit the fire. And Frank...your paisano Dante has a special place in hell for those who wouldn't stand in a crisis. You're out of your mind to even think of running out."

"My husband never ran away from anything in his life, Lyle," spoke up my wife evenly. "It's me he's worried about. I thought all this human rights business was just an excuse for a political dogfight, and I didn't want him to be the patsy caught in the middle. If human rights are really involved...well, that's up to Frank."

"Thanks, darling. Yes, dear...there are human rights involved. And there is a vicious political dogfight, too. But that's not what makes me so sick I want to climb in a hole... No. It's seeing public officials, respected men...stoop so low...polluting everything with the dead cats of bigotry... Aw, to hell with it. I'm getting serious. And when I get serious, my yellow slip shows. You know," I went on, "even when I was a kid, before every football game I'd vomit. But after getting knocked down a few times. I'd start laughing and play like hell." I picked up the SHAME! SMEARERS! paper. "The Bridgeport boys are screaming 'foul' as they clip you from behind, so I guess I'd better laugh and get back in the game. And before you say no, Lu, how about another shot of that liquid courage all around?"

Lu filled up the cups with triple sec—and since our guests seemed loath to take the floor away from me, I went on talking.

"Funny thing, if I can make like a big philosopher for a second—I ought to know by now, that...it isn't the world that beats you in the scuffle—you beat yourself. And only when you see the comedy of life can you really understand it. For instance—our different reactions to this screed from Nevada when John Hewitt brought it in here:

"Legal-beagle Herb Kelly, there, praised it as a fine example of tricky in-fighting. Texas John, here, saw it as a beautifully timed counterpunch... While thin-skinned me, wearing my inferiorities on my sleeve, I smelled the putrid odor of dying racism. So instead of laughing at the comedy in it, I burned...and beat myself. I let it hit my stomach instead of my funny bone.

"This is funny, my friends. All this screaming and yowling and appeals to Americanism is just noise…the noise of frightened little men…putting on their high hats of office and beating dish pans in the dark—to scare away the ghosts who point fingers and shout: 'You've had it too good, Fatso…now get out!'"

"You're absolutely right!" cried Herb Kelly, as he jumped to his feet again and flapped his arms like a cheerleading penguin. "We all missed the point. City Hall is shaking. That's why they're whistling hate tunes and rattling skeletons. Who was it said, 'The classic defense of fear is noise?' I've seen it in courtrooms…the lawyer with the weakest ease always yells the loudest. Hell's a-poppin'…I ain't been this excited since I won my first case…a chicken stealer he was… Helen, come on, we've got doorbells to punch. Bring your paper, I'll go get my baseball bat…"

"Where're you going, Herb?" I asked.

"To get signatures on the petition. Think I want to miss all the fun? Come on, Helen…"

"Wait for me, baby," enthused Librarian Wright as he leaped to his feet. "Come on, Marge, off the lead…Bring your petition and a long hatpin. Frank, this'll be the biggest excitement in Mono County since Jimmy Whoosis burnt down Bodie." Then yelling to the receding Kelly, "Herb…you bash heads on Silver; Marge and I'll stick fannies on Gull Lake. To the ramparts, men!"

Then Long John un-jackknifed his six-five frame from the table and drawled, "Well, might as well go crazy with the rest of the world. Frank, looks like you stepped in your own bear trap." Then, to the others leaving the house, "I'll take the power plant, Lyle…then maybe a horse to the high lakes."

Undone by the nutty events of the morning, my wife and I just sat, not daring to look at each other. When I finally turned to her with a silly, "Well, Lu?" we both exploded in loud laughs—even though some tears were trickling down both her cheeks.

CHAPTER SEVEN

Homo Americanus is a political animal. Ever since the classic revolutionary phrases of Tom Paine, John Adams, and Tom Jefferson transfused Liberty and Freedom into our bloodstream, we have been "We, the People!" Three little words: "We, the People"—but they turned history inside out.

Many slogans and battle cries have sparked causes, wars, and revolutions: "Deutschland Uber Alles!," "Workers of the World Unite!," "Remember the Maine!," "Geronimo!," "On Wisconsin!"

However, these "Calls to Arms!" are, to put it crudely, cries of "sic 'em" to incite man against man, gang against gang, people against people!

But "We, the People" is a clarion call for people against ideas; against tyranny, injustice, greed, corruption. Not a few, not some, but all the people—of all colors, class, or clime—exhorting each other to unite against the evils of the times. That is the grand concept capsuled into three little words—words of extraordinary power and meaning; words that spell HOPE!

But for us who live in the home of the brave, the three words not only spell hope, but politics—that grand old game between the "ins" and the "outs." What spearing fish is to Eskimos, politics is to Americans—a way of life. Our national pastime, enjoyed with gusto by every male and female between ten and a hundred, is not baseball or wine festivals; it is elections.

We introduce the game early in grade schools, teaching children how to nominate and elect school and classroom leaders. In high school, the virus spreads from the scholastic confines to infect the extracurricular activities of sports, clubs, and social shindigs. In colleges and universities, the fever rises into all-out election campaigns, with bands, rallies, speeches, posters (some funny, some cruel). This is the boot camp for the "pro" league.

Those of us who leave college for the work-a-day world carry the election bug with us. We join the "amateur league" and elect officers for service clubs, women's clubs, kennel clubs; for unions, industry, professions; sports, churches, jails and prisons; even the Cosa Nostra elects sub-rosa leaders with super-rosa credentials. No one can escape being elected to something. We have become a nation of all Chiefs and no Indians. But that's We, the People—amateurs or not, we love it.

But it's the battle of the "pros" that sends us into a frenzy every other November, when presidents (every four years); congressmen; state, county, and city officials—and the village dog catchers—all come back to We, the People for election or reelection; and to have their heads deflated by the rude reminder that they work for us; that our secret little "X's" will mean thumbs-up or thumbs-down for half of them.

And so we sit smugly glued to our TV sets, as (in between sexy gals brainwashing us into thinking we'd all be more potent in bed if we drink this, smoke that, or gargle both) all the candidates come into our living rooms, wearing makeup, oozing charm and integrity as they "point with pride" at themselves and "view with alarm" at their worthy opponents, who are always nameless. And we love it. But true to the contrariness of human nature, after we elect them—we dare them.

And—we needle them, too. We, the People have contrived a gimmick to get the lead out of political behinds. We call it a petition. They call it a pitchfork. Anyway, petitions keep our political claws sharpened between elections. They are collections of signatures (sponsored by the sane or the nutty) calling for "special action" from foot-dragging public officials.

We blithely sign petitions to "save the cats" or "kill the cats"; for or against taxes, freeways, Bingo, long hair, tight pants, beatniks, smoggy air, fluorinated water, topless waitresses—and—

As happened in primitive Mono County—during a November week of misty, icy weather—petitions for and against the Board of Supervisors' calling of a public hearing concerning Deputy Lefty Wakefield's refusal to arrest and deport two "weirdies"—Bear Bait and Dry Rot.

Hundreds of charged-up Monoites—on wheels, on nags, on foot—banged on doors for housewives, sloshed the streams for fishermen, beat the sagebrush for Indians, and puffed up mountains for hunters to corral their signatures.

The "pro Beavers" (those for Lefty) were mostly waitresses, carpenters, farmers, and sheepherders—the working stiffs. The "con Brigade" were realtors, resort owners, businessmen, and club women—the hiring staffs. Roughly the two groups represented those with little who wanted a little more, and those with much who wanted much more.

All the petitions had to be delivered personally to the chambers of Superior Court Judge Hollingsworth, in the county courthouse, for counting and checking by county recorders against eligibility and duplication. The deadline was midnight, Saturday.

•••

THE FOUR-FACED CLOCK IN the cupola tolled twice—two hours past the midnight deadline. Across Highway 395, in the doorway of the Sportsman's Lodge, I paced and smoked. It was cold. Through the now almost leafless row of silver maples, the lit-up courthouse seemed strangely unreal in the swirling mist of fog and snow flurries. Ghostly moon halos encircled each lighted courthouse window. The spectral glow of an occasional passing car's headlights conjured up yellowish phantoms that raced madly to escape pursuing red demons that followed the taillights.

The setting was MacBethian. The silence eerie. The actors awaited their cues. The government forces were bivouacked in Tony Caldwell's DA office—waiting, pacing, smoking. My fellow conspirators, "Boatcourt" Steve Gorski, Hoppy Hopkins, and ex-deputy Lefty Wakefield, were huddled in a small back room of the Sportsman's Lodge—waiting, pacing, smoking. Outside the hall door of Judge

Hillary Hollingsworth's chambers, waited two opposing emissaries: fidgeting Jake "Beatle" Ziffren, and the DA's composed, dress-pulling, bouncy secretary. For the record, the dress-pulling was not entirely wasted on Jake. He admitted later that, in between nail-biting, he was about to ask for her phone number—when the door opened!

Judge Hollingsworth, seventy-five, short (he wore high heels and sat on a phone book at the bench), stood in the doorway yawning. Behind him, disheveled clerks were putting on their coats and collecting election bets. With maddening deliberation the judge handed each emissary identical written verdicts of the petition count. One emissary screamed and raced up the rickety stairs. Moments later a victory roar exploded in the district attorney's office. I heard the shout from across the highway, heard it rattle the old courthouse's tall narrow windows.

A half hour later, in the main room of the Sportsman's Lodge, it was New Year's Eve. The bureaucrats were howling tonight— howling, backslapping, and singing. The most popular song, joined in by all, and repeated every two minutes, was the old faithful:

"For he's a jolly good fellow,

He's a jolly good fellow—

WHO? TONY CALDWELL!"

...and then a burst of cheering and applause.

One fractured wit made up and sang the theme song:

"Oh, we tell you one and all,

You can't beat City Hall!"

CHEERS! Soon everyone sang it, each to his own tune. And soon the men began acting out the ancient party ritual: sing a song and kiss a secretary and—if you're stoned enough—try for her scalp—that is, her garter. Since there were five Johns for every Jane, happiness was being a secretary.

In the closed-off back room of the coffee shop, there was another meeting—but no cheers, and no singing. Not even talk as Boatcourt, Hoppy, Lefty, and I sat around a small table looking far, far away into our coffee cups. Since Jake had brought the verdict to us, no one had said a word; the dressing room of the losers—ringing with the victory cheers of the winners.

Steve Gorski, dressed in an expensive gray suit and black fedora (which on him still looked like his fishing duds), twirled and untwirled a gray forelock. Hoppy pinched his lower lip, pulling it this way and that; Lefty was his usual hulking "statue of a lump." He still wore his deputy's uniform (since what with six kids he couldn't afford a "civvy" suit), but without pistol, star, or handcuffs he appeared oddly emasculated—like seeing a toothless lion yawn.

One after the other we had read the verdict: 3,956 against a public hearing for Lefty—3,501 for! What a shock! We had all felt so certain... Crusaders for the downtrodden! And they turn us down! The first Crusaders had a holy cause and were certain, too—until they met the Saracens, I thought to myself. An ungodly cheer went up in the party room. The gloom in our room was shattered by a blast of noise as the door opened. And speaking of Saracens, there stood District Attorney Tony Caldwell, his elegant black topcoat and gray hat glistening with fine drops of mist. Behind him stood his cheering section, just finishing up:

"...For he's a jolly good fellow—

WHO? TONY CALDWELL!..."

The cheeky SOB, I thought to myself, he just couldn't wait to look in and crow. He closed the door to shut out the noise.

"Sorry if I'm interrupting," he said with a tired voice. "May I come in?"

Only Steve Gorski recovered enough to answer.

"Sure, sure. Pull up a chair."

We watched him closely as he dragged over a chair and slumped into it without removing coat or hat. If he'd come to crow, he wasn't flapping his wings about it. Somehow he seemed ten years older as he sat there tapping his fingers without looking at anyone.

"How'd you tear yourself away from the victory party?" asked Boatcourt.

"Victory party? Oh, yes..."

"I have to congratulate you, Tony," said Boatcourt. "Those club women went all out for you."

"Yeah..." answered the DA vaguely. He seemed to be trying to ease into a conversation of some sort and finding it difficult. "Never underestimate the power of a woman, they say..."

"Or of bigotry," snapped back Hoppy Hopkins.

The remark stung Tony out of his vagueness.

"I'm not proud of it," he retorted quickly, leaving unsaid the obvious inference that he hadn't been left any other choice. Then he leaned over the table toward Hoppy and began talking, as evenly and impersonally as a man dictating a letter. "Hoppy...I really came over here to see you...to tell you that I've convinced the Board of Supervisors to hold a public hearing, regardless of the petition count. In fact, in spite of it."

He paused to light up an elegant little cigar with an even more elegant gold gas lighter, then continued:

"Many of the Board, and particularly the sheriff, are quite sure I'm out of my mind...and maybe I am. But anyhow, they agreed to it. Now, what I'd like to know from you is this: Will you publish this announcement in your next week's edition of your papers, or will I have to take out another ad in the Minden, Nevada, paper to let the people of Mono know about it?"

Outwardly, not one of us batted an eye. But inside our heads the little computer wheels spun furiously. Was there a joker in this sudden reversal? A booby trap? Why didn't the supervisors give Lefty a public hearing when he first asked for it? Or was this a sawdust trail conversion? The wheels spun, but the computers were as confused as the questions.

"I'm a newspaper man, Tony," answered Hoppy, offhandedly. "What are the facts?"

"Tonight, at two thirty a.m., after the signatures were counted, the full Board met to consider...on its merits only...Deputy Sheriff Lefty Wakefield's appeal for a public hearing on the reasons he disobeyed a direct order from his superior, Sheriff McMahon. The supervisors voted unanimously to grant the request, even though the petition count was clearly against a public hearing.

"The time of the hearing is set for ten a.m. Thursday next. It will be held in the Supervisor's Office at the county courthouse in Bridgeport. Adjacent offices will be opened and seats provided. If there is an overflow, standing room in the halls will be available within the limits of safety.

"The hearing will be open to the public and the press. Court reporters will keep a verbatim record of the proceedings. This record will be available to the press. Interested parties may be represented by counsel, and if any subpoenas are necessary, the Board will issue them on request.

"The hearing will be informal. The Chairman of the Board, Mr. Guy Hanford, will honor questions and answers from anyone in the room, including the public. A formal witness chair will be provided for anyone wishing to testify under oath. No one will be required to answer any question he doesn't wish to answer. The hearing will be purely informational, for the enlightenment of the Board and the public. The Board will not be required to make a formal judgment, or take any formal action unless it wishes to do so. I think that takes care of it. Any questions?"

There were many questions we would have liked to ask, but didn't. So I asked a perfunctory one just to keep the conversation alive.

"Any photographers allowed?"

He looked straight at me for the first time. There was no love in his eyes. I just rubbed this man the wrong way, and that was it.

"You mean movie cameras, I take it?" he asked after taking a deep breath to calm his irritation.

"Skip it," I answered, annoyed with myself.

"Hoppy…we didn't discuss photographers. But if you want two of your men there, I'll arrange it for them. Any other questions?"

"Tony…" spoke up Boatcourt after a pause, "why?"

Tony twirled the little cigar in his fingers, then managed a fleeting wry smile as he looked up at Boatcourt. These two men seemed to understand each other.

"Good question, Steve," he answered slowly as he groped for words. "Well, for one reason…Lefty, here…probably the only honest man at this table. What he did, he did from the heart…and his appeal for understanding has been snowed under by…other matters. Lefty deserves a break." Then, as he rose to leave, "Hoppy… All the details, please…and I hope without editorial comment. There'll be none from my side. See you at the hearing."

"Tony!" called out Boatcourt, stopping him at the door. "Lefty's no more honest today than he was yesterday. What's the other reason?"

Handsome Tony seemed to slump at the question. Then he straightened up and faced Boatcourt, smiling pleasantly:

"Well, Steve, you'll know sooner or later. It's me that's different today than I was yesterday. Doc Slingsby told me this morning I have an inoperable cancer."

•••

"Next bungalow on the right, Frank," said Boatcourt to me as I was driving him up a piney road in the hills back of the post office at Mammoth Lakes.

"Elegant house," I remarked as I pulled up to the curb in front of a very attractive rambling bungalow, all shingles and rockwork. Even in the soft glow from the lighted windows I noticed the well-kept lawn, the rosebushes, and the tall surrounding pines.

"He's strictly first class all the way," said Steve while getting out of the car. "You should see his wife."

Boatcourt had called and asked me to drive him over to Tony Caldwell's house. The shocking news Tony told us the night before at the coffeehouse had taken the fight out of us.

As we sat limply, Boatcourt expressed the feelings of all when he mumbled, "I can't stomach the idea of crossing swords with a condemned man." I had no solution. Neither did Hoppy. And when Lefty burst out with a loud "Damn!"—the only word that crossed his lips all night—we all got up and went home.

"Better if you stay in the car and wait for me, don't you think, Frank?" said Boatcourt through the open car window. "You're fingernails on a blackboard to him, you know."

"I know. Okay, I'll wait."

Good man, that Steve Gorski, I thought to myself, as I watched him trudge up the neat brick walk. Strange man, but a good man. And smart. And gracious. Yes, that was it. He must have done something pleasing to God sometime, for Steve Gorski had been blessed with more than his share of the Almighty's grace, with all its attending humilities and amenities. Yes, sir. Circumstances seemed to relax around old Boatcourt. Old? How old was he? Hard to say—thirty-five? Forty-five? Sixty-five? It was his eyes that one first noticed about him; bright eyes that mischievously danced out of a baby face that was paradoxically furrowed and seamed with premature wrinkles; crinkly wrinkles that curved upward from the corners of his mouth into man's most appealing accomplishment—a warm, friendly smile; a smile that said disarmingly, "Relax, friend. I'm a much bigger fool than you are."

Puck, that's who he was. A wrinkled, overage, benevolent Puck. What envious little devils had started those juicy, sub-rosa tittle-tattles about all those bizarre parties he threw for college students in his mysterious mountain mansion? And why did wives snicker when they unfunnily whispered that "that man Gorski is an old smoothie" and husbands guffaw when they leeringly added, "You mean a 'queer' old smoothie"? Could Boatcourt possibly be a homosexual?

On the porch, Steve Gorski pushed the doorbell button. Three-toned chimes reverberated from inside the house—much like

A Mercedes 300 turned off the road in front of my parked car, slowing to a stop in the graveled driveway.

"Tony! Look who's here," she cried out. "My pet man…"

Interesting voice, too: made of laugh stuff; low; occasionally breaking into rippling highs—like Jean Arthur's.

Steve pulled Grace toward him. Lowering his voice, he whispered something seriously. She looked up at him, puzzled by his words.

As Tony walked across the lawn toward the door, his head turned to keep me fixed in a challenging stare as he wondered who was sitting in the parked car. He was interrupted by the lovely arms of his wife slipping around his neck.

"Hi, darling." Then, with the faintest trace of anxiety in her laughing voice, "Mister Gorski just asked me how you were feeling… Is there something I should…"

"Feeling?… Oh… He means about the hearing…Steve?" he shouted to Boatcourt kiddingly. "I'll show you how I feel about it. Watch and drop dead."

With that he embraced his wife fiercely, kissed her, and held her so tight her toes were off the lawn as he swung her back and forth. Then, as the kiss took effect on both, he gently lowered her down on her feet and, standing there molded in each other's arms, they passionately glued their lips together, unmindful of the world around them. It was a love affair all right, I admitted to myself.

"Oh, Tony…" she chided, as she broke away flushed and flustered, her dishevelment making her cool beauty even more desirable. "Out here in the open? In front of…"

"In front of God and everybody. Now you run in and straighten up that pretty little face, while Steve and I straighten out a few points about the hearing. Go, beautiful."

"I guess I'd better. Excuse me, Mister Gorski. Don't forget to come in for a drink."

She ran into the house, leaving Tony and Steve to walk silently toward my car. When out of earshot of the house, Tony turned to let Steve have it, his voice as cold and sharp as an ice pick.

"Steve…I resent anyone coming to my house without letting me know. And what's all this malarkey about how I feel?"

"Stupid of me to come without calling. I'm sorry."

"Fine. You're sorry. Now will you please explain why you worried my wife with solicitations about my health?"

"Tony, I feel terrible about that. I had no idea she didn't know."

"She didn't know what?"

"Well, about…" Steve said, groping for words, "about…uh… what you told us last night at the coffeehouse."

"I haven't the vaguest idea what the hell you're talking about. I didn't discuss my health with you or anybody else last night or any other night. What're you trying to pull? Another one of your slimy tricks? Are you trying to spread more dirty rumors?"

"Tony, my boy…" Steve answered, on the verge of a blowup, "you have the most wonderful capacity for making things tough for everybody…"

"I have every intention of making things tough for everybody. Especially you, Steve…and that movie guy in the car…and that joker with the papers. I don't know what you came here for, but whatever it was…forget it. And I'm warning you, Steve…come prepared. 'Cause I'm going to use that hearing to break you…and break Hoppy…and break anybody else that's out to stop me. And that's the real reason I made the Board call the hearing. Good night!"

He turned on his heel, marched into his house, and banged the door so hard it started little hanging bells tinkling on the porch.

"Come on, Steve," I said, opening the car door from the inside.

Seething and muttering, Steve scrunched in, jerking the car door shut with a bigger bang. Again the bells tinkled. Then, gathering his accumulating exasperation all in one ball, he exploded it all in one blast:

"That arrogant...egotistical...son of a bitch!"

For the next ten minutes, neither of us spoke a word as I drove slowly down the twisting road through Mammoth. You can't talk when your think gears have just been loused up with a handful of sand. Personally I was as baffled as a scientist who suddenly observed some cosmic phenomenon that made a liar out of Einstein; or one who ran into a group of numbers that kept adding up to different sums.

How do you make logic out of contradictions? Or put in parallel the divergent? Was Handsome Tony's irrational behavior the paradox in logic that mathematicians call "the antinomy of the liar?"—in which some sentences are false only if the sentences are true? The statement: "Tony Caldwell has cancer is false," is false only if it's true. Or is it the other way round? To hell with mathematics. Think of him in film terms. Was Handsome Tony a tragic hero or a no-goodnik? A noble eagle or a tricky cowbird laying phony eggs in your nest? I gave up. The mind boggles, rejects, then lights up "tilt" at the irrational.

Gorski spoke first, his words about as baffled as his thoughts. "And the wunderkind has covered his trail, too. First thing this morning I called up Dr. Slingsby about Tony. His answer was short and sour. 'Listen, Mr. Gorski. I'll give you the same answer I gave that snoopy newspaper publisher. My Hippocratic oath not to discuss my patients with anyone is sacred, sacrosanct, and inviolable. And that goes for my staff and technical assistants or they're fired. Good day.'"

"Steve," I said, "just have to hear myself talk. Tell me, is Fancy-pants a Rudolf Hess or a Macchiavelli?"

"He's worse. He's a Galahad riding a white charger, hell-bent on carrying the Holy Grail of Law and Order to Sacramento, to the Senate, then to the White House."

"Hmmm. Maybe it's just static, Steve, but my hunch antenna is trying to tell me you admire Gorgeous—that maybe there's a slight case of friendship. Or maybe something deeper—right?"

"Frank," he answered, taking out his pipe, "I'm rich and successful. I can afford aberrations."

"You take your opposition out fishing to win cases. Ever..."

"I don't try to win cases. I settle them."

"Yeah, I know. Ever take Tony out fishing?"

"Laughs bore him," he answered, lighting his pipe. "Tony doesn't believe in settling. With him it's legal or illegal, black or white. If you're right you win, if you're wrong you lose. And, oddly enough, he has yet to lose."

"In my business you've got to lose before you can win."

"Fascinating career, this boy," he went on. "An orphan at seven—he watched two burglars hack up his father and mother—he was taken in by an aunt and step-uncle who raised hogs and sold smoked hams and bacon in a tiny store in Bishop. Young Tony worked his way through Bishop High School by collecting pig garbage for his uncle and doing odd jobs for Hoppy's Chalfant Press. He made Eagle Scout and earned such outstanding marks he got a scholarship to Berkeley. I made the commencement speech at his high school graduation. I spoke on 'The Values of Compromise.' Young Tony followed with a valedictorian speech on 'The Evils of Compromise.' When I gave him his diploma I said 'Good speech, son,' and he answered, with an assurance that some might call arrogance, 'As you can see, I disagree with you...sir!'

"Well, before he graduated from Cal, he made student body president, and head of the debate team, set a record for touchdowns as a running back, married the most beautiful girl on the campus, and got a scholarship to Harvard Law School. And would you believe it? He was tapped as a Rhodes Scholar and went to Oxford. Hoppy's Mono papers ballyhooed Tony's triumphs with the huzzahs reserved for astronauts. He was Mono's man in orbit.

"Well, when he returned to Mono I quickly sensed we had a young supernova among us, a man-in-a-million, Frank. He had it all—good looks, courtliness, a super-intelligence, the super-charisma I know your stars have, and that indefinable leadership endowment that men like Moses, Alexander the Great, Aristotle, Saint Paul, Thomas Aquinas, and Napoleon must have had, and that such women as Joan of Arc, Florence Nightingale, and Saint Therese certainly had. And I fell in love with this boy, Frank, and I began to dream the "impossible dream," as the song says. I envisioned this small-town Lochinvar, first in the governor's seat in Sacramento, and then, so help me, I saw him in the White House, another Jack Kennedy but with the drive of a General Patton, if you please. I saw him calming our fears and healing our wounds with the robust vigor of his youth, and bringing fresh hope to a war-sick world that a new, bright, healthy, happy day of peace would soon be coming."

Boatcourt paused to relight his pipe and, I surmised, to re-savor that "impossible dream." How little we know of people that daily fill our lives. The hero of Boatcourt's "impossible dream" had only impressed me as an insufferable, egotistic bore. And what did Gorski mean when he said, "I fell in love with this boy?" Was I sticking my nose into the tawdry tantrums of some sleazy "old man, young man" relationship? I turned north on Highway 395 and began speeding up that pine-scented twenty-mile drive through the Jeffrey Pine Forest. I wanted to get home fast and talk everything over with my commonsense wife.

"What I didn't know then, of course," resumed Boatcourt, as if he had as much need of talk as I had of silence, "was that young Lochinvar had had the same dream—only with him it wasn't just a dream. It was a coldly calculated obsession...his Eastern Star, his Golden Fleece. Well, he was young, Frank, and I had become so fond of him that I brought him into my law office as a junior partner, hoping I could season and humanize the young meteor before he rocketed himself out of the pull of human gravity. By the end of the second month he had grown much too big for my office. Clients offered him big jobs, big pay. So I nudged him, prematurely I knew, toward his goal of politics. 'There is no limit to how high or how fast you can rise in public service, Tony,' I said, 'if you can keep from tripping over your own mistakes. And I'd like the honor of managing your first political campaign.'

"He looked me straight in the eye and said, 'Mister Gorski, I have no plans for tripping, and I don't make mistakes. As for your becoming my James Farley, what's the catch? Your politics and mine are as far apart as the poles. Why should you manage my political career?'

"'Because, Tony,' I answered, 'I love this country and I love its people. And you've got it all to serve them well. I offer you my experience, Tony, and my backing. Free. No strings. Political or otherwise. I just want to become famous. People will point to me later and say, 'There's the bloke that coached the great Tony Caldwell in his first dive into the dirty pool of politics.' So he allowed me to run him for county tax assessor—won going away. Then I ran him for district attorney—a landslide victory."

"Help me, Steve, I'm on a merry-go-round. If you worship Tony Caldwell as God's answer to American politics, why are you running against him for the state assembly job?"

"I don't know about God, but Tony would have been my answer to politics if I could have… You asked me if I had ever taken Tony out fishing. Yes, once. The day he moved into his new job as district attorney, I stepped into his office and said, 'Tony, to celebrate your first day in office, I think I'll do something different and go fishing. Want to come along?'

"Again he looked me straight in the eye and said, 'Steve!'—it had always been 'Mister Gorski' before—'I'd make a bad patient. There's nothing your psychiatric boat can do for me.'

"I laughed and said, 'You wanna bet?'

"He thought a little, then rose from his chair. 'Okay, let's go. I might have a bit of advice for you, too.'

"Within two hours we were fly-casting in the rippling waters of that small but, as you well know, beautifully hidden, rarely fished Parker Lake. I keep a small rowboat stashed away in the willows at the lower end. Well, wouldn't you know? Tony could cast a dry fly some sixty feet and make it land six inches from a log as gently as a fluff of down. Could even lay that fly right on the log, then flip it off into the water. Beautiful. With the disciplined ease of a champ. Like he did everything else. Well, when he began pulling in brookies faster than I, he put down his rod and asked, 'Well, Boatcourt—I haven't got all day. When does the treatment begin?'

"I laughed. But not too easily. It's difficult to relax around wonder boy. 'Laddie,' I said, 'the treatment—as you call it—began with your first fly cast, which you do superbly well. It consists of drifting around in a boat, letting the sun and the beauties of nature soak into you, casting a fly now and then, swigging a little bourbon when you feel like it, and maybe swapping a fish lie or two.'

"It's a very old treatment. Some two thousand years before Christ, an Assyrian philosopher chiseled the prescription on a stone tablet: 'The gods do not subtract from the allotted span of men's lives the hours spent in fishing.' As good advice today as it was four thousand years ago, don't you think? Every day spent in fishing adds one more to your life. And of course you remember Isaac Walton's saying that 'Angling is somewhat like poetry.' An art that was a 'calmer of unquiet thoughts, a moderator of passions…and that it begat habits of peace and patience in those that practiced it.' And President Herbert Hoover paid a wry tribute to fishing: 'It reduces the ego even of presidents… for all men are equal before fishes.'"

Boatcourt interrupted his soliloquy—he was really talking to himself more than to me—to knock the ashes from his pipe. We had just passed Crestview Lodge and had begun the short but steep climb up Deadman's Grade (so called because an old-time mail carrier and his mule disappeared here in a blizzard while carrying the mail from Mammoth to Mono). "Well, Steve," I said, irked at the suspense. "Was Wonder Boy impressed?" He heard my voice but not my words. Like a man reliving an evil day, he resumed his monologue.

"I offered Wonder Boy my pint of bourbon. Disregarding it, he reeled in his line, selected one of his classy little cigars from a classy monogrammed case, lit it with a classy gold lighter, and blew out its smoke with the classy superiority only Oxonians seem to master. Then shaking his head in disbelief, he said, 'Mister Steve Gorski, you are a bloody disappointment. Of course, I've known all along that you had your heart set on becoming my political guru—my own spiritual Iago, so to speak. Well, even though years ago I had discovered and made a pact with my perfect guru, my own intellect, I thought it might prove amusing to see how old famed Boatcourt contrived his pitch. Mind you, I fully expected to be cloyed sick with sugary platitudes, and to be harangued on my need to practice that holy trinity of virtues known as pity, compassion, and humility—if I wished to rise in public affairs.' This he said while carefully inserting his three-piece rod into its velvet sheath. 'But really, Boatcourt, I looked forward to you laying it on with intellectual finesse, with style, but not with a trowel. So if you don't mind rowing me ashore—'

"'No, Tony. Not till you hear me out. Yes, I admit it. You've been on my mind, and perhaps even in my heart, ever since I handed you your diploma in Bishop ten years ago. And yes. It's been my fondest hope, my constant dream, to become your political adviser. Because, Wonder Boy, whether by finesse or by trowel, it comes straight from the heart: You need me! Need me to tell you that it's happened before. To warn you that without the mellowing graces of moral principles, men gifted with your superior capacities have become monsters! And it can happen to you!'

"Well, Frank, I touched a nerve. He shouted, 'Monster? Moral principles?' so loud they echoed back from the rocky banks. His contorted face jarred strangely with his elegance, as he opened up on me like a scourging Jeremiah. 'Why you hypocritical old fart, *you're* the monster. You're the one that hoped the warm sunshine and the scenery would soften me up for your mealy mouthed chestnuts. You're the impious one that doesn't know that in all the beauties and wonders of nature there is not one jot, one tittle, or even one flick of your precious pity, compassion, or humility. Look around you, why don't you, with the eyes of reason. Nature is evolution according to natural law; where the strong devour the weak, and the weak devour the weaker. A doe, a "Bambi," the very symbol of peace and shy innocence, will, if it's hungry enough, ingest the fetus of its own unborn fawn! Babbling brooks will, in flood-time, devastate everything in their path. Soft, beautiful, snowflakes, symbols of Christmas, which your John Muir so nauseously called "heaven's snow flowers," well, those "flowers" will compact into a glacier that will cut the heart out of the toughest granite that gets in its way.

"'Look around you,' he went on, 'Strong trees shade out weaker trees, which shade out bushes, which shade out grasses. And will one strong tree ever say to another, "See that little old weak sapling fighting for sun—shall we give him some room and let him live?" Never. They kill it. That's the great beauty of Nature: the realistic beauty of the justice and logic of its "survival of the fittest" law. And no compromises! No "The Values of Compromise" speeches at Bishop High School. And no hypocrisy in Nature's Law.

"'It gives you great pleasure to hook a fish by deceit, doesn't it? And it's fun to play it on a light line until its heart gives out. Oh, yes. It adds days to your life said some Assyrian jerk. But what the hell does it do to the fish? How many months or years does it subtract from its life? Pleasure for you, but murder for the fish. So where's your pity, compassion, and humility? In your hypocritical dreams, you fake. You live in the jungle world of dog-eat-dog like the rest of us, but you're too scared to admit it. I had a hunch you'd resurrect those Isaac Walton bromides on me, so I came prepared with one of his better ones—on the noble art of torture. Listen—'

"He pulled out a small notebook, from which he read me a quotation from *The Compleat Angler* on how to prepare a live frog for fish bait: "'Thus use your frog... Put your hook, I mean the arming wire, through (the frog's) mouth, and out at his gills; and then with a fine needle and silk sew the upper part of his leg, with only one stitch, to the arming wire of your hook; or tie the frog's leg, above the upper joint, to the arming wire; and in so doing, use him as though you loved him." End of quote. Yes, sir. Pity, compassion, humility. There it is. Ask the frog.'

"Frank, I was speechless," said Boatcourt, as we approached June Lake Junction, "and so sick in the stomach I grabbed the oars and rowed for shore. But he's a killer, Frank. He wouldn't let me up. 'It's hypocrites like you,' he hammered, 'that are really the prime cause of all our national and international troubles. Yes, hypocrites, appeasers, frightened by the rabble into play-acting and glorifying pity and charity instead of nailing them for what they really are—make-believe virtues, counter-evolution myths invented by weaklings to cut the strong down to their size. "Why do the wicked flourish?" has been the despairing lament of weaklings since they first equated strong with wicked.

"'It's the riff-raff rabble that's wicked. They stoned the Prophets...murdered the Apostles...crucified the Christ. They assassinate the Gandhis and the Lincolns and the Kennedys. They multiply our crime statistics. When George Orwell wrote: "All animals are equal, but some animals are more equal than others," you intellectual snobs howled with laughter. You didn't realize he was impaling your bleeding hearts with a perfect squelch: "God did not create a Law of the Strong for Nature, and an opposite Law of the Weak for Men." It is a sin, a reversal of God's and Nature's Law when the weak cower from the strong; when the parasites spit on the hands that feed them. And by all that's holy, Boatcourt, I intend to reverse that trend, and put Nature's Law back on the right track. I intend to emancipate our citizens from the chains of pity, compassion, and humility. And people will listen to me, Boatcourt! And I will be President of the United States before I'm forty-five! So—rich man, lawyer, art collector, do-gooder, fairy godmother, or what the hell ever you are—thanks for past favors, and goodbye! AND STAY THE HELL OUT OF MY WAY!'"

"My God, Steve! That guy's got to be some kind of nut!" I blurted out.

"Unfortunately not, Frank. Nuts can be handled. But at unpredictable times, God sends a hell-raiser to test our human failings. And if you don't believe in God, blame it on a random cosmic ray that knocked certain genes around at conception, and a man-child is born with a messianic mission to lead the chosen out of bondage; the kind of a Messiah the Jews prayed for when the rejected Prince of Peace walked the shores of Galilee—a King on a white horse, they wanted, a warrior King that would lead them in driving the Romans into the sea. Most 'redeemers,' of course, end up as frustrated fanatics, born with the zeal but not the tools of a messiah—like John Wilkes Booth who shot Lincoln.

"But give a 'redeemer' the messianic mission and the inflammatory tools to kindle passions, and millions will follow him in confusing, shaking, and ravaging the world with hate and war—

as they did in Germany not too long ago. And as they may do again, in any country, including ours, if the right 'redeemer' comes along."

We left the June Lake Loop highway and turned up a steep forest road that twisted and turned among the towering trunks of Jeffrey pines—dark red Corinthian columns supporting their dark green vaulted domes. Through the leafy maze ahead, warm, twinkling rays welcomed us to the always-open doors of Boatcourt's popular chalet, especially the beams from the always-lighted two lower stories which housed collections of fine paintings and great books. A museum? No. Those two floors were crammed with musical instruments and record players, billiard tables, ping-pong tables, bridge tables, and tables groaning with snacks, sandwiches, coffee, milk, and soft drinks. Boatcourt laughingly called it "a recreation center for blockheads and eggheads, run by a mush-head." Here the high school boys of the area and dozens of college kids working in resorts during summer vacations came to play, listen, read, or yak it up in bull sessions. And all free, including the books. Any boy interested in any book could take it home and keep it. Old Boatcourt's smile would light up a room every time a youngster left with a volume of Plato, an art book on El Greco, or even a rare copy of Boethius's *Consolation of Philosophy*.

My wife once told me that at a Women's Club luncheon, one needling mother goaded Boatcourt with this prod: "Mister Gorski, some mothers say your influence on our boys is good, and some say it's evil. Which would you say it is?"

"Oh, evil indeed, Madam," Gorski retorted amiably. "You see, I'm a pyromaniac. I like to rub young minds and great minds together. And sometimes they spark, and start fires."

The chalet was built on a steep hillside. We heard voices and music below us as I parked on the third-floor level—the entrance to Boatcourt's exquisite private quarters. Boatcourt was loath to leave my car. Slowly, awkwardly, like a man dredging up words from an inner well of agonizing memories, he began talking again. "I guess I loved that man more than... Anyway, that's why I filed as a candidate to run against him for the state assembly. I didn't want the job. But I had to beat him, Frank. Before his halo got too tight. Understand?

Before he actually believed he was God's answer to our country's crisis. You see, if I could stop him once, just once here at home—prove him fallible, human, teach him humility—then he would have had it all to go places. And now he's going to die. Pity. If I weren't an atheist I'd have to say it was Providence once again sparing our nation from men who have it all."

"Wait a minute!" I said, having had a bellyful of Mr. Great. "You mean that cancer bit? Baloney! I don't believe a word of it. No man with his colossal ego would blurt out 'cancer'—cold turkey—like he did to us. Not even in a 'B' movie."

"You don't believe him?"

"Hell, no!" I said. "He's faking. And I'll give you two reasons why: First—there's too much sympathy for Lefty and his pals, Bear Bait and Dry Rot. They could become public martyrs. Second—he's polluting the issue. The small petition majority he won by could tarnish Wonder Boy's shining armor, perhaps put him behind the eight ball in the race for assemblyman. Therefore: Out-martyr the martyrs. Make a grandstand play for greater sympathy by (a) magnanimously insisting on a public hearing, regardless of winning the petition battle; and (b) paralyzing the opposition's will to win with that corny cancer bit. Result: at the hearing those who know will say, 'How brave!' And when it's all over, when the tumor miraculously becomes benign, or nonexistent, everyone will shout, 'Thank God!' and vote him into the Assembly by a headline majority. Make sense to you, Boatcourt?"

"May not make sense, Frank," he grinned, "but it could make the dangdest soap opera of the season."

"Soap opera?"

"Sorry, Frank. Your hunch would make sense with anybody else but Tony. Wonder Boy is unpredictable because we look for normal, human deviations. When we find none, we can't believe it. But when you know the hardline moral path he follows, so straight, so fixed, he is completely predictable.

"We didn't believe Hitler, or Karl Marx—even though they gave us detailed road maps to the land of the 'Herrenfolk' in *Mein Kampf* and *Das Kapital*. Tony has given us his roadmap to the absolute Rule of Law in his 'The Evils of Compromise' valedictorian speech.

"He, too, has a messianic mission: To enforce justice ruthlessly—without the cloying impediments of compassion and mercy. According to Tony there is neither charity, pity, nor mercy in the Ten Commandments. Therefore: obey the 'Thou shalt nots' or suffer certain punishment.

"If we follow his roadmap, Tony's actions of the last few days, baffling and quixotic as they appear to us, fall into a predictable pattern. You must remember that everything this young man has done so far, is 'right.' His unshakeable convictions—that the Rule of Law will eliminate wars, poverty, ignorance, and color lines—are difficult to fault. Couple these burning compulsions with good looks and charm, and you've got a powerful natural leader. And he knows it."

"Does his lexicon of virtues include lying? He deliberately lied to us—either at the coffeehouse or at his home tonight."

"That wasn't really lying to him," said Boatcourt. "That was making sure no mercy or compassion got in the way of Law. Let us take his actions, one by one, and see if they deviate from his roadmap. He won the battle of petitions; but to him that was a vote of confidence, not a judgement of law on Lefty's appeal. Then too, petitions to him are frenzied, emotional outbursts, based more on energy than on statutes. The 'City Hall' people celebrated their petition victory, but not Tony. I'm sure he had decided the hearing must be held even before the votes were counted.

"The county supervisors were jubilant with the petition results, of course. Now they could sweep the insignificant, but mighty sticky, affair of Lefty and the two bums under the rug. But no. Tony forced the reluctant board into an open hearing. I say reluctant because, being human, board members know sympathy can be more potent in a public hearing than legalities. So Tony won that point for justice, by barreling right down the middle of his planned road: judge Lefty's case, not with frantic petition signing, but by law, in a public court.

"Then Wonder Boy runs smack into an unmarked roadblock. A doctor tells him he has incurable cancer. At the coffeehouse he gives us the shocking news. Why? For sympathy? For a postponement, or perhaps a cancellation of the hearing? No. He was making it crystal clear to us that, come life or death, he wanted no part of humanistic detours around the lethal roadblock. No sir. He was crashing through it head-on. And Tony won himself another battle for justice. Over death.

"All right. At his home tonight, he denied his cancer. Angrily accused me of slimy tricks; warned us against spreading ugly untrue rumors; told us point-blank that he had promoted the open hearing in order to break us! Break us with his Rule of Law; and put us on guard to be prepared to fight for our lives. Why? To make us think he was faking; to make us so fighting mad we could slug him, health or no health. And he succeeded with me. I was within inches of punching him in the nose. Me. Mister Calm himself. So he won that point, too. No compassion from his opponents. And now he can fight what may be his last battle on his own terms—a no-holds-barred scrap within the ring of Law. And with no piddling compromises to compassion, charity, or what have you.

"Oh, yes, prank. He's got cancer. Probably of the brain. Otherwise his actions wouldn't so perfectly fit his roadmap. And maybe it's a blessing. In ten years he'd probably have been governor, after that—maybe higher. And God help us, he would have been a terror; an unassailable terror who did everything right—in the name of God and the Law."

"Steve," I said, more convinced than ever that I was right, "you'd give the devil himself an even shake. No, Steve. That fancy punk is a faking ham actor; trying to steal the spotlight from Lefty and those two nobodies; trying to make himself the issue, hoping to sabotage our human rights pitch. As a motion picture Joe I say he's bollixing up the plot. You're right. What might be another Stokes trial, another Dreyfus case, he's trying to water down to a no-cal soap opera, in which the big suspense is, 'Has Handsome Tony really got a fatal malady, or is he fibbing?' Big deal. The real blessing to all would be if we slapped that faking bastard down so hard in that hearing that— well, we'd cook his goose forever as a public official. Right?"

But Boatcourt was so lost in his own hurt he hadn't heard a word I said.

"You know, Frank, that's why I love this guy, or who knows— maybe I really hate him." A reflecting gleam betrayed a wetness in his eyes. "Anyway, I always wanted a son. And this boy got to me... But I could never get to him. Yes, sir...this Tony has done something very few others have done to me; put me in a position of no compromise. It's either win or lose; break or get broken. 'Sorry I can't agree with you, sir,' he said when I handed him his diploma. And DAMN! It's come to a showdown against that eighteen-year-old boy with his diploma. Funny. Funny. And now... Whether he lives six months or six centuries, my conscience says I've got to smash him, destroy him! The boy I dreamed of becoming. Come on, Frank. Let me out of this blasted car. I've got homework to do..."

CHAPTER EIGHT

W HAT HAPPENED IN THE next few days I will have to piece together from hearsay—eyewitness accounts from such diverse sources as deputy sheriffs, telephone operators, Marine Corps colonels, forest rangers, and talks with many personal friends. I believed what I heard, but, of course, the reader may not. For the reader's credibility gap may have already been widened to the point where a recounting of what I myself saw and heard could be construed as more apocryphal than apostolic.

At any rate, this account appeared in Jake Ziffren's *Mono Herald* column:

> They said he wasn't the oldest or the most toothless coot in Bridgeport but, for sure, he was the most fun-loving as he rocked on his rocker and had himself a ball watching the traffic tie itself into knots on the morning of the hearing.

> "Ain't seed such a hoop-de-doo," he beat his gums at the people hurrying by, "since the Indians snatched old chink Ah Tai outten a courtroom and sliced 'im up into chop suey—right there on the street the year I was born, cackled odd skin full of bones. Slippery then, too. But 'twarn't snow—just blood," he snickered.

> Ear-piercing police whistles shattered the falling snowflakes. Looking more like Batman in storm

capes, highway patrolmen and deputy sheriffs waved, shouted, and tootled the snow-covered cars to skidding stops to let bundled-up Monoites slip and slush across 395 to the Courthouse.

Immediately the stopped drivers banged on their horns, and kept banging—the more musical beat out rhythms, the more wrathful long steady wails. Police ears can only take so much—so they'd toot the pedestrians to stop and waved the honking cars through. Muttering, the teed-off drivers spun their wheels on the getaway, splattering rooster tails of mud and slush all over the hated pedestrians. Women screamed, men cursed, police angrily blew staccato sixteenth notes.

Half the cars, of course, were filled with Mono natives in town for the hearing. They jammed things up good by stopping in the middle of 395 to yell: "Officers! Where can I park?" "Any place!" the steamed-up officers shouted back. "Move on! Move on!"

But what really knocked old toothless off his rocker was to see groups of rugged individuals— poo-pooing all this law-and-order stuff—make a dash for it on foot across the moving traffic. That would trigger such a pandemonium of dodging, splattering, tootling, honking, and shouting that it sent old bone-bag into a hysteria of cackling and knee-slapping.

For weeks now the dreary overcast sky had dropped little hints of snow—white flakes fluttering down in scattered bunches like "surrender" leaflets dropped from planes. Early on the morning of the hearing, the hints proved real—the sky dropped the year's first barrage of steady snow.

But snow is a way of life for Mono natives. After putting on chains and snow tires, they peered through hardworking windshield wipers and took aim on Bridgeport. From the north and from the south; down from the peaks and up from the deserts, they zeroed in on the courthouse—their excitement whetted by the coming battle of the heavyweights (Boatcourt Gorski and Tony Caldwell) for the championship of the wilderness country. Schools were let out, stores closed, "Back sometime" signs were hung on doors. It was Fiesta Day in the Land of the Monos—and who knows? Maybe heads will fall and blood will run! Let's go!

Hours before, when every seat in the Board of Supervisors' room had been filled, people jammed themselves three-deep along the walls and windows. The adjacent rooms were filled to the flood stage by the river of humanity that poured into the main hall. And when the river was blocked by walls, it sent tributaries up stairways and into nooks and crannies. Outside the main doors the jammed-up river was backing up into an ever-widening humanlake of cold, shoving latecomers. The old courthouse steamed with human heat and rocked with native chatter. Fiesta Day! "Hi, Pete!... Hi, Elmer!... Look who's here! Maggie!..."

Deputy Sheriff Marty Strelnick told me early that morning that county officials realized they had been caught with their estimates down. Half a dozen deputies on patrol radioed headquarters that they could see lines of headlights snaking down from every side road. The dispatcher radioed Sheriff McMahon who was just getting out of bed. As usual, the diaphoretic sheriff blew his top and a quart of sweat, and phoned Supervisor Guy Hanford, getting him out of bed. Phone operators Betty and Olga Neilson (twins) giggled constantly when they recalled the conversation later.

"Guy!" bellowed the nightgowned sheriff into the phone, said Olga. "We're gonna have a riot on our hands... What?... Who's gonna riot? Don't you know that half of Mono County's on the way to the courthouse, now?... What's to riot about? What'll we do for water, food, heat, parking? And what about those two dinky two-holers you call washrooms over there?... More help?... Oh, sure...like I could call out the Marines... Hey, wait a minute! Marines... Goodbye, Guy."

The sheriff slammed down the phone, then picked it up and jiggled furiously on the little thingamajig, sweat oozing freely now.

"Hello? Olga?... Where's Olga?... Oh, you're Betty. Betty, this is the sheriff... Confidential call, understand? To Colonel Miller at the Pickle Meadows Winter Training quarters. Quick, will you..."

"Colonel Miller talking. Oh, yes. Good morning, Sheriff..."

Ninety minutes later, Colonel Miller said, the Marines landed on the courthouse grounds—a fast-rolling convoy headed by the colonel and a squad of MPs. In another thirty minutes they had the units in line facing the courthouse: A comfort station marked "Men"; a first-aid van with medics; a rolling kitchen stuffed with hot dogs, buns, and huge coffee kettles; a water tank with Dixie cups; and another comfort station for "Women"—the whole line covered and surrounded on three sides with canvas, leaving open the side facing the courthouse. Communications men rigged up two loudspeakers outside the courthouse, wiring them to microphones inside the hearing room. Thinking of everything, the Marines unloaded six oil-burning salamanders, placing them at intervals under the canvas. In a jiffy, they were glowing with welcome heat.

And when a band recording of the blood-stirring "The Halls of Montezuma" blared from loudspeakers, the patriotic fiesta atmosphere was complete. The three hundred or so spectators who had been standing and freezing outside rushed into the warm canvas haven, stomped their feet in march rhythm, gave each other exaggerated salutes, and began singing the Marine song with gusto, if not with harmony. Those sweating (and fainting) inside pried open a few ancient high windows and joined in the singing, the flashing light bulbs of Hoppy's two press photographers adding the final seal of status to the event.

Those were "da conditions dat pervails," as Jimmy Durante used to say when we heard a sharp knock on the door of our small room. We had been secretly led here after rapping on a small door at the rear of the courthouse, as we had been told to do. Our party consisted of my wife and me, Hoppy Hopkins and his wife, Boatcourt Steve Gorski (in a sedate dark suit, but with a flowing ascot tie—"so they won't mistake me for a fisherman"), Lefty Wakefield (in uniform minus badge and gun—face showing strain), Lefty's wife (a tiny woman, simple brown dress, strong face, no makeup, dark lines under her eyes, lips moving imperceptibly, and fingers thumbing invisible rosary beads), and Lefty's six children, from fourteen to four—and all girls!—wearing clean simple dresses of various colors; but all with long black stockings and all with straw hair in ponytails. Lefty had objected violently to his children being at the hearing, but Boatcourt (his public defender) insisted even more violently—proof, I thought, that he knew his Freud as well as his Blackstone.

Boatcourt opened the door in answer to the knock. A young uniformed deputy sheriff (the one who gave me the "okay" sign at the first hearing) stood there, hands braced on the doorjamb, braced against the pressure of the sardine-packed crowd in the hall.

"Ready for the hearing, folks," he announced. We all rose. Boatcourt waved us back while he had a few whispered words with the deputy. I caught only a word or two from the deputy: "Nailed them myself on the trees... No, I wrote... Lefty's in trouble...courthouse..." Boatcourt waved us to come on. My wife's hand trembled as she took my arm. I had been on many stages, talked before many mikes, but this show before an overflow audience, on a snowy morning, in the quaint courthouse of a backwoods county—this show was for real— with no script. Queasy with stage fright, I whispered an old joke in my wife's ear: "Honey, there's a flock of quail with broken wings in my stomach trying to get out..."

The poor thing has been tensed up for so long my silly remark unglued her. She sputtered into repressed giggles. I shushed her. She put a handkerchief in her mouth to stop the giggles. It increased them. Boatcourt gave her a wry look, then whispered to Lefty: "You're sure now, Lefty... Still want to take the witness chair? You'll be under oath, and he'll cross examine like a tiger..."

"I want to take the chair, Mister Gorski," Lefty answered quietly.

"He'll swear to God," broke in Lefty's wife with astonishing strength. "He's got nothing to be ashamed of, Mister Gorski."

"Fine. Good girl. All right. Here we go..."

I interrupted Boatcourt with a whispered question: "Those nailed-up notes were for Bear Bait and Dry Rot, weren't they? Why didn't you just subpoena them?"

"Stick to your movies, CB," he answered. He resumed lining us up. "All right. Here we go. Hoppy and Mrs. Hopkins first. Frank," he said in a whisper, "and no more giggles, please... Lefty...Missus Wakefield...and you children, youngest last. Let's go."

"Let us through, please," pleaded the deputy, opening a thin crack in the crowd. "Coming through, thank you, thank you..."

American crowds are usually good-natured, but any crowd tends to be against the individual; instinctively the herd dislikes the maverick. The people we pushed through craned necks to peer into our faces with wide-eyed anticipation. Prizefighters we are, I thought to myself, going down the aisle to the ring; haughty toreadors parading to Carmen music; horse thieves running the gantlet to the hanging tree.

Those nearest whispered our names to those behind them. The whispers spread and simplified into loud calls. "It's Hoppy the editor"... "There's the movie director"... "The old guy's Boatcourt." A half-stoned cowpoke, wearing brown high-heeled boots with ornamental intaglio flowers, swished, waved a red neckerchief, and cried, "Yoo-hoo! Boatcourt!" A raucous woman's voice, through megaphoned hands, yammered a Three Blind Mice parody; "Three Venal Man... See How They Run... We'll have all the fun..." That triggered my wife into another fit of giggling—which she stifled so hard the tears came as we reached the hearing room. Another deputy at the open doorway unhooked a rope and motioned us in.

The Marine record player cut off suddenly at the "Shores of Tripoli." Throughout the old building, even out under the canvas, the hubbub simmered down. Silence took over. The curtain was rising.

One end of the hearing room was roped for the contestants. Beyond the rope were "we, the people"—we, the eyes at the moment. Inside the rope we followed our deputy single—to our far "corner." As Lefty's six girls crossed the room in descending order of height, some hushed "oh's" and "ah's" rose from the crowd; photographers' light bulbs flashed. My wife, in front of me, managed to walk the room without a giggle—although with her head down and a hanky to her eyes and mouth, all she needed was a black veil to look like a widow leaving the grave.

In our corner, the women and children were asked to sit on chairs backed up against the converging walls. Lefty, Hoppy, Boatcourt, and I seated ourselves around a small table facing the spectators. I waved to many of our friends—the Wrights, the Kellys, the Pattersons, the Hewitts—but Boatcourt nudged me as he waved to his left. I looked, and saw what I had missed coming in—the five supervisors I seated in a row behind their large, raised official desk, flanked by flags, and kibitzed from above by the faces of GW and LBJ. The chairman—Guy Hanford (Mr. Weathervane)—smiled, raised his clasped hands—wishing us luck. In my hurry to return the compliment I nearly dislocated a vertebra, when he suddenly turned away from us—as did the spectators— his attention focused on the doorway through which we had entered.

The "other side" was coming in! Leading the contingent was Sheriff McMahon, resplendent, sad-jowled as ever, eyes darting this way and that—the underarm rings just beginning to show. Behind him came two deputies (aides), and a court stenographer (faceless as a Scotland Yard man), and with the magic of the faceless, sat at his stenograph—and vanished. Then three familiar faces (the civil service commission of the former hearing) walked in, smiling and trading "killing" cracks with friends that triggered overkilling roars, before taking their seats against the rear wall. Then in walked three more men (one a forest ranger), and three women.

"Witnesses they subpoenaed," whispered Boatcourt in my ear. "Know any of them?"

"Not a one," I whispered back. "Did you subpoena any witnesses?"

"None," said Boatcourt. "But if Lady Luck smiles on us…"

"You mean Bear—"

"Quiet! And get ready for Hail to the Chief," he said, turning toward the entrance door.

So far, with the possible exception of the three commissioners, the entrances of the "other side"—including the bouncy blonde secretary (Tony's) who had come in alone with papers and briefcase, sporting a yellow chrysanthemum and, as usual, tugging her short skirt after sitting—had been ritualistic and silent: an overture in pantomime. But now a hubbub began swelling offstage—presaging the entrance of the star. Suddenly the offstage crowd burst into loud applause and prolonged cheering.

"That's the planted claque of county employees whooping it up," whispered Boatcourt to Hoppy and me. "I got tipped off. That's why I made Lefty bring his six girls. The claque was supposed to boo us— but the little gals stopped 'em cold," said Steve with a sly wink. I was learning things—including how to make an entrance.

The prolonged cheering offstage reached its climax—and out of the climax, Tony and his stunning wife stepped into the room. Like a brushfire in a wind, the cheers leaped over them to start a spontaneous combustion in the hearing room itself. The applause was deafening. Those seated stood up—the women in a dither of adoration.

And no wonder. This had to be one of the handsomest couples I ever laid eyes on. She wore a lavenderish wool suit that I can't describe—except that on her it was a knockout. A simple string of jade-green crystals encircled her long swanlike neck. Small, pendulant jade earrings framed the Grecian perfection of her face and reflected the sparkle of her green eyes. Her platinum hair was slicked back and caught up in a perfect coil on the nape of her neck: a chignon, I think it's called in French. A small green handbag, through which flowed an autumn-hued scarf, gave her that final touch of beauty and charm so typified by Jacqueline Kennedy.

But the shocking surprise (to us) was Tony; Tony the Magnificent had come in as Tony the All-American Boy; in a plain gray jacket and slacks, white shirt, thin black tie, hair slightly ruffled and uncombed. Gone was the cold elegant arrogance of the prosecutor. In its place was the shy smile, the friendly eyes, the appealing embarrassment of the humble—a young, handsome man any mother could love.

"Does that remind you fellas of the White House?" whispered Hoppy.

"Good heavens, yes! Jack and Jackie," muttered Boatcourt in admiration. "If you're reaching—reach for the stars."

The photographers had wormed their way through the crowd to get close-ups. While they were focusing, Tony graciously turned his back to the cameras (and to the spectators) and clapped his hands in applause—for his wife. That wowed the people all over again. Blushing (which the audience ate up), Tony's wife took one of his applauding hands and, in a ladylike move to avoid the limelight, she pulled him to the back row of chairs—where he seated her prettily. Still holding her hand, he made a courtly bow and raised her hand to his lips. Well, this bit of old-world romantic gallantry shook up the natives. The women screamed their pleasure—especially when he walked up to his table wearing a sheepish, boyish grin that said ever so plainly: "Forgive me. I'm in love."

Boatcourt jumped to his feet, applauding madly, hinting to us to join him. Hoppy and I jumped up, clapping our hands into blisters. So loud was the noise from our "corner," the spectators stopped their applauding to look at us. Wondering whether we were trying to be rude or polite, they began sitting down, still looking at us. We redoubled our hand-clapping. Momentarily, at least, we had stolen the show. Tony had the ball. Would he fumble it or throw it back? He threw it back. Walking halfway toward us, he stopped, smiled, made a little bow, and said humorously, "My wife thanks you, gentlemen."

A titter ran through the room. That was a horse on us.

"Oh, we weren't paying tribute to her great beauty," spoke up Boatcourt with real old-world gallantry. "We were applauding the next First Lady of the Governor's Mansion."

That got the biggest applause of the day. It was a horse apiece now. Tony's lips still smiled, but not his eyes. He turned to the audience, shrugged, then strode back to his table. He put up his hands for quiet, got it, then courteously announced to the chair, "The people of the County of Mono are ready, Mister Chairman."

CHAPTER NINE

O LD "WEATHER VANE," SUPERVISOR Guy Hanford, banged his gavel. As the cacophony of an orchestra tuning up hushed to the tap of the conductor's baton, so did our Mono crowd mute its decibels. But not all the way. Suppressed murmurs of expectation rippled through the steamy hearing room, the halls and stairways, and the huddled foot-stompers in the Marine tents. Feet and torsos shifted and twisted into new positions.

At Lefty's table, Public Defender Steve Gorski's pallor was two sheets whiter, his mood three shades darker. He inhaled draughts of air and exhaled them through ballooned cheeks. Lu pinched her nose between thumb and forefinger to stifle her giggle spasms.

"Biggest crowd I've ever seen in Mono County," volunteered Hoppy.

"Hoppy," I whispered, "I've got that funny feeling in the old pizzazz. Like this crowd could be as wild and unpredictable as a film preview audience."

Through the tall open windows they saw the silent snowflakes fall. Focus on them long enough and they seemed to halt their fall to the ground so the room could rise to the sky...

Big Lefty sat as silent, arid, lumpy as ever, while his strong-willed tiny wife tolled her beads in sync with her silent lip movements. Behind them, their six ponytailed, black-stockinged daughters sat pretty all in a row, adding a bizarre bit of feminine charm to the proceedings. So theatric did they look that I half expected them to bounce up and do a saucy song and dance to the lyrics of "When we get our women's rights, all you men go fly your kites."

"Quiet! Quiet, please!" honey-dripped Chairman "Weather Vane," tapping his gavel and beaming like a lit-up Christmas tree. O happy politician! Heaven is a microphone and an audience. "Here we are, my dear friends," he purred. "All of us gathered together, voters and officials alike—as just...plain...people. Isn't it wonderful?"

He waited for the applause. None came. He pulled the mike closer. "Can all you good folks in the hallways hear me?" he asked.

"YES!" the hall crowd roared—squawking loudspeakers and rattling windows. Before the roar died, a raucous voice boomed out of the speakers, "We got a good-and-bad situation here in the halls, Guy. Good because we can't see you, and bad because we can hear you."

The crowd's exploding laugh was overkill.

Hoppy and Boatcourt exchanged uneasy looks. "The natives are restless, Boatcourt."

(Contents from Capra's original files are missing here.)

The chairman's weather vane spun and pointed at the district attorney. Tony Caldwell nodded "yes." The relieved supervisor banged his gavel and addressed the woman: "Madam, state your name, business, and whether your statement is germane to this hearing. Quiet, everybody!"

"Mister," answered the charged-up woman, "if germane means something I gotta get off my chest, then YES. I gotta helluva big germane. My name's Nancy Sparks, and me and my banged-up husband, we run a small café in Walker. And if we stay open day and night, we just break even. Especially since you big wheels just raised our taxes from two hundred fifteen dollars to four hundred fifteen dollars." Cheers and applause for Nancy.

"Now what I want to know is," shrieked Nancy, shushing the crowd. "What I wanna know is this: Did you raise our county taxes one hundred percent in one year so you could hold circuses like this?" She had to almost scream over the crowd noise. "I mean, these cameras, and microphones, and tents, and food, and extra cops, and petitions, and overtime for everybody's gotta cost thousands of dollars. And why? To listen to the bellyaching of a discharged employee? Or the gripes of dirty old beggars?" The unpredictable crowd was listening again.

"I tell you, Mr. Supervisor, that when news of this meeting gets out, every thief, beggar, and moocher that's run out of this county will want a public hearing, and every employee you fire will demand that half of Mono County be made to come to this courthouse and listen to his sob story. Oh, it's okay with me. Hold your stupid hearings. But I'm putting you all on notice. You're not going to do it with my money. Not with my money. Not one cent will I pay—"

The rest of her speech got lost in the bedlam. The old courthouse rocked with cheering, whistling, and applauding. And who do you think was up on his feet clapping the loudest? Paunchy Tom McMahon, the diaphoretic sheriff of Mono County. Yes, sir. Vox Populi made itself heard in Bridgeport that snowy November day. Made itself heard, and lost its head. Vox Populi became Vox Prison Break.

The five ashen faces of the supervisors huddled round their anxious whispers. What to do? What to do?

"Boatcourt, it's a mob now. They'll tear the joint down," said Hoppy.

"Only one man can stop them," said Boatcourt. "And he's getting up now."

Sure enough, Tony Caldwell was up on his feet adjusting the mike to his height. A Marine with a walkie-talkie on his back handed Tony a walkie-talkie phone. He talked into it, then handed it back and motioned the orderly to give the phone to his wife, Grace, who was sitting almost out of sight against the rear wall.

"Hoppy, Frank. Keep your eye on their act. I've seen them use it before," whispered Boatcourt.

Grace took the walkie-talkie phone, motioned the orderly to shield her from prying eyes, said a few words into the phone, then nodded to her husband. Tony nodded back, turned to the mike and spoke with the voice of authority: "Okay. Okay. It's my turn now."

That was the cue. Grace spoke one word into the walkie-talkie phone. And lo! It was the magic word. The shouting subsided immediately. As if Vox Populi had heard the voice of authority, and obeyed it as one—like a well-trained chorus.

"I've got it!" I whispered to Hoppy and Boatcourt. "When she gave the signal, the Marine in the control tent turned down all the mikes but Tony's."

"You're catching on," said Boatcourt. "And when their noise went silent, the crowd cowed themselves into silence. Like catching yourself talking too loud in church."

"Well, I'll be damned!" said Hoppy, in sheer admiration.

"He's one of a kind," added Boatcourt. "Watch. The best part of the act is coming up."

"Ladies and gentlemen," Tony's words came over the quiet loudspeakers in a soft, humorous tone—"this is Tony Caldwell, your district attorney speaking—"

His wife gave the cue into the walkie-talkie. A slight hum came out of the loudspeakers. The people's mikes were turned on again before anyone knew they'd been turned off. "And from all the cheering," continued Tony, smiling broadly, "I thought for a moment you had elected me by acclamation."

A burst of applause and laughter greeted him. Not cynical now, but pleasant, and as obedient as Toscanini's orchestra. One lift of Tony's hand hushed the hubbub. With polished sincerity, and in complete command, he went on, "I, too, applaud you, Nancy Sparks, for so vividly expressing your concern for skyrocketing taxes. It's the frightful penalty we pay for progress, and I sometimes wonder if it's worth it. But let me disabuse your mind, Nancy, about that big germane you got off your lovely chest. Not one single penny of your tax money, or anyone else's tax money, has been, or will be, spent on this hearing.

"All the microphones, speakers, heaters, tents, comfort stations were furnished, and gladly, by the Marine Corps as one of their numerous training exercises.

"The ad in the Minden paper was paid for personally by me, the sheriff, and our presiding chairman. And all the printing and secretarial overtime for counting the petition, which was plenty, was paid for by the foreman of our Grand Jury there, Mr. Kyle Sommes.

"And saving the best for the last, all the food—coffee, drinks— soft and hard—hot dogs, pies, doughnuts—was donated by the man who expects to beat me at the polls next Tuesday, Mr. Steve Gorski. Take a bow, Steve."

As he knew it would, the crowd good-humoredly booed and applauded.

"Now," he said, (a cue for his wife to decrease crowd noise). "Let's get serious. What we are about to discuss here today demands your most sincere, thoughtful attention. And it is not just a local problem, not one that just concerns neighbors you know well. It is a problem that is vexing the highest courts and chanceries in Washington, London, Paris, Moscow, Tokyo, Peking. And what is the problem? Well, at its very core there lies a question. And that question, simply stated, is this: 'Where does individual freedom end and social responsibility begin?'

"And that question, ladies and gentlemen, bears directly on your rather sardonic outburst at the outset of this hearing. An outburst that is symptomatic of a nationwide fear that we Americans, even we who live in a far off wilderness, are in the midst of a new kind of revolution. Not over labor and capital, or over race, political systems, or ideologies, but over values and personal attitudes; over fear for our civilization.

"For one thing, we don't believe anybody anymore. We don't believe our president, we don't believe our news media, and, as you've just shown us, you don't believe your locally elected officials. In fact, my Mono County friends, we have reached that sterile state in which we little believe, or put much trust, in any of our traditional institutions.

"For example, the reason we are here today is that a certain deputy sheriff declined to obey his chief's order because he didn't agree with it. Think of it! Didn't agree with the order so he said, 'No, thanks!'

"Furthermore, when relieved of his duties, he clamored for a public hearing so he could tell the world why he was right and the chief wrong about that order.

"Now tell me. If every soldier can pick and choose which of the general's orders he'll obey, and then demands, and gets, a public hearing to defend his views—well, my friends, we'll have the kind of chaos that certain highly motivated anti-Americans are working night and day to bring about.

"We go around saying: 'America is great, but—our faith is faltering. And when we lose faith in our country, friends, we lose faith in ourselves. And we hate ourselves for it. And when we hate, we fear!' And as Emerson warned:

'O, friend, never strike sail to a fear!
Come into port greatly, or sail with God the seas.'

"For fear is what makes us ripe to join mobs, and to riot and burn and demand mindless changes!

"Why? Because deep, deep down in all of us, we yearn to believe in something. Something certain, secure, incorruptible. And when we find that pearl of great price, that North Star that we can trust in a storm, that honest, trustworthy, incorruptible American to whom we can surrender our hearts and our souls, and to whom we can truthfully say, 'I believe in you,' then, my brothers and sisters, we will cease to fear, cease to hate. Then we will believe in ourselves again, and in our God, and in each other, and in the greening of our country."

His intense sincerity had completely captivated his audience. Not a cough, not a movement of the head. In the hearing room, in the halls, in the standing room tents, all was silence and rapt attention. So engrossed were the spectators that many in the hearing room, including Tony, overheard Hoppy's fed-up, irreverent whispered remark meant for only Boatcourt and me, "Why the cheeky son of a bitch! He's setting himself up as some kind of a messiah!"

A hot solar wind of dirty looks came wafting Hoppy's way from Tony Caldwell, a long, cold, contemptuous look. Then, signaling his wife with a nod—she turned down all mikes but his—and speaking with repressed anger, he said, "Ladies and gentlemen, you didn't come here to complain about taxes, or to hear Lefty Wakefield plead for understanding, or to hear us hash over the human rights of two worthless, inhuman wretches. No, indeed.

"You turned out in droves, this cold snowy day, on the outside chance that you might see blood flow, or some heads roll. Well, I can't promise you blood. But I can assure you that one head will roll. And that head will be mine or Mister Stephen Gorski's.

"And you, the citizens of Mono County—like the Soman citizens in the Coliseum—will decide whose head is forfeit.

"And if, in your good judgment, your verdict is 'thumbs-down' for me, I shall hand you my head on a platter, and will immediately retire from public life forever!

"But if you spare my head, I will commit myself completely—heart, brain, and my beautiful wife—to a lifetime of dedicated public service.

"You know," he said, pausing and smiling again. "Al Capp once said that 'the public is really a piano. You just have to learn what keys to poke.' Well, before we get on with the unpleasant stuff, I want to poke one key on the piano."

Quotations seemed to purl from his lips, gracing the pellucid flow of his English. Hearts aflutter, faces radiant, the enchanted women—be they old, young, white, or Indian—looked up at him with one common reverence: adoration. Had he stirred up visions long quiescent? Of gallantry, romance, passion, flame? Of Camelot knights and maidens fair?

And was this flair, I thought, this power to make banked urges glow, was this a partial explanation of the unexplainable riddle, "What makes a star?"

His voice cut into the writer's vaporings.

"You know," said Tony to a hypnotized audience, "I was born in Mono County—on a pig farm. And Mono's unmatchable beauty is very dear to me. But much, much more important—I love the incredible friendliness of Mono's people. You. And I can never, never forget the love and forbearance of my devoted teachers and professors who struggled mightily to prepare your little pig boy—that's me—to study under some of the world's most learned men: scientists, philosophers, and intellectual giants powerful enough to play world chess using ethnic groups and whole countries as pawns.

"But strangely enough I couldn't burn incense to these mighty pundits. They acted as though there was a great gulf between themselves and the rest of us, and that they were the born masters of the huddled masses—us.

"They rationalized that all that does not shrink into the few cubic centimeters within their heads is trivia. Egomania is the common disease of these great savants. Some leave pyramids, some leave tapes…and Clio, the Muse of History, symbolically offers them a choice between a fanfare of trumpets and the dripping clepsydra." He put up a hand. "Who knows what a clepsydra is?"

A young woman's voice shouted, "A water clock!"

"Correct! Nice going." He started applause. "That's the good news," he said soberly. "The not-so-good news is that in my argosy among the world's far-out intellectuals, I sensed an unspoken conspiracy that threatens the very existence of our way of life: an artistic and a scientific crusade against family and State. And that, wittingly or not, a world dictatorship of their own kind is their goal.

"There is a connection between crime and the extreme activists, not in the sense that the intellectual hires the criminal, but that he condones and encourages crime itself by advocating philosophies that state there is no sin or virtue; no good or evil; no assaulters or Samaritans.

"Laws are the Ten Commandments expanded into the working blueprints and specifications for the building of a community or of a nation. But some modern thinkers have lost faith in the whole structure of human society. They say there is no design from God because there is no God. And if there ever was a God, he is now dead.

"They say a rock foundation of absolutes is an archaic myth of the past; that a shifting foundation of swamp or quicksand is more fitting to modern thought.

"And for the solid, binding beams of social laws, they would substitute nonbinding, non-dimensional, 'anything goes' pillars of free thought.

"The intellectual doesn't just advocate promiscuous sex. He says sexual love is a romantic figment of the poets. That in reality it is just a biological pleasure of the flesh to be gratified at any time one feels the urge, with members of the opposite sex, or with his own sex, it doesn't matter which. He says it's no different from eating. And when you satisfy hunger with a steak, it doesn't really matter whether the steak came from a cow or an ox.

"The theme song of 'Police Brutality,' which intellectuals wrote, is not for justice against certain rare police actions. What they really mean is 'Police Abolishment.'

"Why shouldn't students riot and guerrillas hijack planes and assassinate innocents when their tutors teach the obsolescence of all laws and governments?

"Now I would like to point out to you that the end result of 'individual human rights,' unchecked by the 'rights of society,' must finally be a state of anarchy, in which everybody lives by his own rules.

"That is why the 'human rights' of Bear Bait and Dry Rot, who sought escape from society in the lonely woods and mountains of our county, have become so important for us to discuss and understand. For they touch upon the rights of all of us, as individuals or as nations. They represent the whole gamut of human relations, much as a single blade of grass has within it all the mysteries of biological life itself.

"There is a philosophical movement with its own priesthood which preaches that there is no evil and no good, no right or wrong, only the unassailable intellect. To them, punishment has created crime. There should be no punishment for anything.

"There are two main obstacles to their attainment of an earthly paradise where there is no sin and no virtue: Religion and the Law. The Religious and the Lawmen stand between them and the home, the family, and decency.

"So knock off the church people. A few intellectuals, a very few, were able to convince the Supreme Court that prayers in school were unconstitutional. Children can study socialism, communism, Buddhism; they can read about sexual abuses, they can experiment with hallucinating drugs; but they can't read the Bible.

"It is unconstitutional to study the Ten Commandments or the Sermon on the Mount, the twin lighthouses of justice and mercy, whose beacons pushed back the darkness of ignorance and fear. So knock off the church; snuff out the spiritual light, all in the name of free thought.

"And knock off that other big obstacle to anarchy: The Lawmen. Yell 'Police Brutality' if you're arrested for breaking any law. And so we have the frightening spectacle of policemen being the targets of rocks, bottles, and snipers' bullets. Of rioting mobs setting fire to whole city blocks, then shooting at the firemen who risk their lives to put out the fires; all in the name of Police Brutality.

"And if a lawman catches some slimy character selling pornographic smut to your twelve-year-old children, a whole battery of intellectual lawyers come to his aid; and without pay, they throw legal roadblocks, and appeal, appeal, appeal until they reach the Supreme Court, where likely as not they will get a decision in the smut-seller's favor. All in the name of 'human rights.'

"Laws under which we have protected society for over two hundred years are now suddenly being rewritten or declared unconstitutional, making the arrest and conviction of the killer, the robber, the rapist more and more difficult, if not downright impossible. And always, no matter how long the criminal's record, no matter how heinous his crime, always there springs up this battery of unpaid lawyers, posing as public defenders, working with unholy zeal to nullify just punishment with trickery and technicalities. And all in the name of 'human rights.'

"And are there smart lawyers who will defend, without pay, your home, your family, your community, your church? No. None. Why? Because these are the 'rights' of society...the society the extremists are out to destroy; to destroy by weakening and making ineffectual the two great bulwarks of society: Religion and the Law.

"And ladies and gentlemen, if you do me the honor of electing me, I shall change all this nonsense; I will reverse the breakdown of laws; I promise you peace of mind, and law and order; I promise you that the criminals will suffer and not their victims; I promise to forcibly break up and destroy this cabal of "free thinkers." That is my pledge. I want to give our country back to the decent, God-fearing people who do all the living, the paying, and the dying. And if we can't make our voices heard in the halls of government, we'll make them heard in the streets and in the meeting halls, whence all power comes.

"You may find it strange, or perhaps even wonderful, that in our insignificant, isolated, and little-known county of primitive wilderness, the great drama of our age is being played out in capsule form. Our stage may be tiny, but here we have the same plot and the same cast of characters that play on the world stage—down to the same bit actors.

"Here we have the reason for the play: two unfortunates, the 'downtrodden,' who of their own volition have cut off all ties with society. Two hermits, Bear Bait and Dry Rot, have been threatened with a harmless brush with the law. And I say 'threatened' because not one legal hand has been placed on them, nor has one official word been spoken to them, as yet.

"Here we have the powerful intellectuals springing up to the defense of their 'human rights' even before the law had taken any action whatsoever against Bear Bait and Dry Rot.

"We have the big-name attorney acting as the public defender at no pay. We have the biggest newspaper publisher, and the only newspaper publisher in the county, throwing in his enormous weight… and we even have star value: a Hollywood motion-picture writer joined in the holy crusade for the 'human rights' of the downtrodden.

"Oh, I know…this 'holy movement' is ostensibly to ensure justice and a public hearing for Deputy Sheriff Lefty Wakefield… But they know and I know and you know that Lefty is just a gimmick…a red herring…a legal trick to provide them an open forum in which to broadcast their intellectual philosophy of 'down with Police Brutality' and 'up with human rights,' 'up with the downtrodden: Bear Bait and Dry Rot.'

"And I'm quite certain that Bear Bait and Dry Rot haven't the slightest notion of all that's going on in their name and if they did, they'd probably say we're all nuts. And I'd agree with them.

"And now," said Tony into the mike, "I take pleasure in presenting a gentleman known to all of you as the Clarence Darrow of the Eastern Sierra. He is here today, playing what is certainly for him a most unusual and unfamiliar role—a public defender for a humble deputy sheriff. That's about as far out as lighting your pipe with an atomic bomb…"

"Mr. Chairman?" Boatcourt spoke into his mike. "If it pleases the chair, and"—pointedly to the district attorney—"if it pleases the pearl of great price, the North Star we can trust in a storm, I'd like permission to proceed with the sole and only purpose of this public hearing: to grant my client an opportunity to publicly explain why he, a humble deputy sheriff, refused to carry out a direct order from his superior, the sheriff of Mono County. I ask that my client testify under oath."

"Oh, he doesn't have to, Boatcourt."

"My client insists on it, Mr. Chairman."

"Very well. Bailiff! Let the oath be sworn to."

The swearing-in over, Boatcourt took the podium.

"Ladies and gentlemen, my name is Stephen Gorski. I have been assigned as public defender for ex-Deputy Sergeant Lefty Wakefield. Now, most of you know or have heard about two hermits who live in our midst.

"For twenty-five years these two men have accepted the descriptive names of Bear Bait and Dry Rot the community has pinned on them. And for twenty-five years the community has accepted them; yes, some even have learned to love them.

"Four different sheriffs...and seven different district attorneys have known them, tolerated them, investigated them.

"Now, after being with us a quarter of a century, they have suddenly become such undesirables that the present sheriff ordered their arrest on vagrancy charges, in order to manufacture a legal motive to run them out of the county.

"Why? Because a new Caesar has taken over, to whom we must all pay homage—not the intellectual, as Wonder Boy would have you believe, but the almighty Vacation Dollar. And Mono officials must now march to the drum of the new-money city lords; the real estaters, promoters, wheeler-dealers. And they want Dry Rot and Bear Bait and all their ilk run out of the county. Bad publicity. Blah, blah, blah.

"So cynical and unfair were these trumped-up charges that the best-loved deputy sheriff this county ever had, a man who had served the county faithfully under four different sheriffs without ever so much as a scratch on his record...this man, father of six children, couldn't stomach the brutal sham, and, laying his career and his future on the line, he refused to carry out the order to arrest Bear Bait and Dry Rot." Turning to Lefty, he started his direct examination:

Boatcourt: "Now, Mr. Wakefield, what was the order you refused to carry out?"

Lefty: "The order was to pick up those two bums, Dry Rot and Bear Bait, on a vag charge and bring them in...so we can roust them around and get them to leave the county."

Boatcourt: "Who gave you that order?"

Lefty: "My boss, the sheriff."

Boatcourt: "And what was your answer to that order?"

Lefty: "I pleaded with the sheriff against the order. 'Chief,' I said, 'that's not fair and you know it. I know the heat's on you to get rid of Dry Rot and Bear Bait because they don't fit in with the new Vacationland image. But if those hermits are vags, I'm Al Capone. No, Chief,' I pleaded with him, 'I can't pick them up. Even if it means my badge. I can't.'"

Boatcourt: "Well, Lefty was dismissed as expected. But what he didn't expect was the character-assassinating implications in the official county press release, which would forever blacken his career as a peace officer. Mr. Wakefield, will you read the press release to us?"

Lefty: (Lefty unfolded a clipping and read) "'As of today, Deputy Sheriff 'Lefty' Wakefield has been stripped of his badge and summarily dismissed from the Mono County Sheriff Department because of flagrant insubordination in refusing to carry out a direct order from his Chief, Sheriff Tom McMahon.'

"Well, I was so hurt by the press release I immediately asked the civil service for a hearing. They said, 'Forget it, and we'll get you a job on the highway department at an increase in salary.' And I said to them, 'Gentlemen, I didn't ask for this hearing *to* get my job back, or for any other job. All right. I disobeyed a direct order and got fired. Fine. The sheriff was right. But the press release wasn't the truth.'

"So your county officials have been kind enough to give me this opportunity to tell you all—my wife, my kids, my friends, and everybody else—the reason I disobeyed an order. I just couldn't make myself arrest two peaceful nobodies, falsely charge them with vagrancy, and run them out of the county. To arrest citizens without due cause would make me a criminal. That's all I want my friends to know. I want them to know that those two hermits were here long before the ski lifts and the shiny Las Vegas hotels...living alone, no more trouble'n a couple chipmunks. They ain't got money, they ain't even got names. But damn it all, they've got human rights! And I'm gonna fight, fight for 'em if I have to see the president..."

Boatcourt: (To audience) "Now, one might ask, why all this hullabaloo over two worthless derelicts? I'll tell you why...because to Lefty they weren't just two worthless derelicts...they were two human beings...children of God just as you and me...human beings seeking surcease in loneliness...trying to find something in nature they couldn't find in the society of men.

"Lefty knew they weren't dangerous. He had investigated them, taken their fingerprints. Not a mark against them.

"Well, friends, it happens to all of us. There comes a time in every man's life when he is faced with a make-or-break decision, a decision between his conscience and expediency. 'These are the times that try men's souls,' said Thomas Paine. George Washington faced such a time when he had to decide whether to remain on Mount Vernon as a rich gentleman farmer, or lead a ragtag Continental Army against Britain's famous Redcoats. Harry Truman faced such a time when he had to decide whether or not to drop the bomb on Hiroshima.

"Lefty's time to try his soul came in the shape of a decision between duty and conscience over the fate of two insignificant hermits, who probably wouldn't care two cents' worth whether they did their hermitting in Mono County or Podunk, Iowa.

"But within the conscience of each man it isn't the size of the decision that counts. It's the rightness or wrongness that tears you apart.

"So Lefty faced his moment of truth. Obey the order and keep everything he had. Disobey it and lose everything. His conscience won out. He refused to obey the order...and took the consequences.

"Most of us would probably say his decision was silly, imprudent. We might even call it stupid. And yet...a few of us could call it admirable. It is the kind of decision that gives a lift to our own puny souls.

"Think, ladies and gentlemen...these are the decisions that raise mankind above the jungle; that reveal to us a little better understanding of what Christ meant by the second of his two great Commands: Love they neighbor as thyself...even though your neighbor is an unlovable beggar...as unlovable as Bear Bait or Dry Rot.

"By this small insignificant decision, this one tiny deed of compassion...Lefty has affected me more than a hundred Sunday sermons. He has made me just a little bit prouder of the whole human race.

"Just as Emily Dickinson did with this bit of loveliness:

'If I could stop one heart from breaking,
I shall not live in vain;
If I can ease one life the aching,
Or cool one pain,
Or help one fainting robin
Unto his nest again,
I shall not live in vain.'

"One teenie incident between a gentle woman and a frightened robin. One teenie decision by a gentle deputy. And yet, be they ever so small, their common touch of compassion reaches the heart with more power than mountains of Vacation Dollars."

Handsome Tony suddenly threw up his arms, shook all over, and caricatured a man hitting the sawdust trail. "Oh, God, I hear you...I hear your call...I feel you all through me..." He kneeled and crawled forward toward Boatcourt. "I accept Jesus. Where is he? I accept him...I accept him...Here's my worldly goods..." He took out his wallet and threw it at Boatcourt's feet. "Give me Christ! I want to buy Christ!"

The crowd went into stitches. Tony rose and bowed like an actor.

"Sorry to interrupt your sermon, Mister Gorski. But I got carried away. Besides, I wasn't sure if you were talking about two worm-eating bums or about Hansel and Gretel."

Boatcourt's face was livid with anger. In a very even voice, each word cutting deep, Boatcourt said, "I blaspheme. But in your case, God should apologize. The Almighty seldom makes a mistake. But when He does, it's a beaut."

Then, lightning-fast as a cobra strikes, Boatcourt slapped Tony squarely and resoundingly across his face. Over the loudspeakers it sounded like a rifle shot. Five hundred people heard the words and the slap. Five hundred people held their breath.

Two men, one young (Apollo), the other old (and froglike), faced each other silently. The young one could destroy the old one with one blow. It never came. He had a crueler way in mind. Besides, the young man had a mission. The slightest loss of self-control could jeopardize it.

The young man yielded first—with a deferential bow to Boatcourt. Then he faced the audience, and using his controlled humorous cool, he rubbed his jaw and said, "You wouldn't think he carried such a wallop." He got his laugh and broke the audience's tension. "But I deserved it—and I accept it."

Then, his cool hardening to icy menace, Tony threw away all pretense. "But...if that old gentleman throws gauntlets around, I have to pick them up—with regret. Because I find dismantling fools distasteful—particularly old fools. Great lawyer of the Sierras," he said directly to Boatcourt. "You slapped my face, publicly. I will destroy you...publicly."

He arranged his microphone and glanced around at the hushed, tense faces of the Monoites. The silence both inside and outside the old courthouse was so intense you could almost hear the mellifluous whispering of snowflakes falling on the tents, the courtyard, and the sills of the tall opened windows. The pause intensified the drama as Tony planned it would. Good actor...fine timing, he thought to himself.

His first words were even more riveting. "'J'accuse!' said Emile Zola in denouncing the Dreyfus affair. And I accuse the Clarence Darrow of the Sierra, and his cabal of stooges, of plotting to do a snow job on us—no pun intended. Yes, friends, we are witnessing a cunning charade to make a Dreyfus 'affair' out of two worm-eating riffraff." Then turning to Boatcourt, "Mr. Gorski, you know that Bear Bait is a gibbering alcoholic. Where he gets his liquor, or where he passes out, what's the difference? He doesn't know—or care!

"Dry Rot...he's a walking ghost. Where he sleeps, no one knows not even he. He just doesn't want to see anybody. Fine. His privilege. But he can be alone in a million places. Why must he stay here and haunt people?

"Admittedly they are both recidivists devolving back to insect-eating. Of what are they being deprived if they are asked to move to a more primitive stretch of woods? Personally, I think it reflects the prudency of your officials. For who can be sure that these male malcontents are not prone to algolagnia, with—"

"I can be sure," interrupted Lefty, the fired deputy sheriff.

Tony was astonished. "You? You know what algolagnia means?"

"Of course. Doesn't everybody?"

"What does it mean?"

"It means," said Lefty, "getting your sexual kicks out of hurting people."

"Where did you learn that word?"

"Oh, old Boatcourt here gave me a list of about twenty-five long words he thought you might use to show off with."

A ripple of giggles ran through the crowd.

"Well, then, Professor Lefty, can you guarantee the good people of Mono that two lone scummy males will never have yens to rape women and children?"

"I can't guarantee anything. But I've known Bear Bait and Dry Rot for over eighteen years, and I swear to God they are as harmless as pet puppies."

"Yes, Tony," interrupted Boatcourt compassionately. "I can understand your confusion. Geniuses have often been puzzled by simple, unsophisticated truths." He turned to the audience. "But we, the ordinary people, 'the huddled masses' as your super-intellectuals call us, we understand. If your grandmother is endeared to the house she was born in, with all its beautiful memories, we can understand her unwillingness to be forcibly moved out.

"But what we also must understand is that our Constitution gives any American citizen the right to come, go, or stay anywhere in this country whether he's endeared to the place or not. And no authority can legally deprive Mr. or Mrs. Citizen of those sacred rights merely because he or she may not want them. Or is unaware of them.

"Should an idiot be deprived of his money because he doesn't understand the meaning of money? No. Is it less of a crime to steal from an innocent child than from a banker? NO.

"If a man is being beaten by a mugger, does he have to yell 'Help!' before a policeman goes to his rescue? NO.

"In short, do the rights of man become null and void if he chooses not to make use of them? No. Does he have to assert his rights every hour to make them valid? Absolutely NOT! He is endowed with those rights from birth. And whether he asserts them, is ignorant of them, or refuses them does not relieve society or the law from the obligation to respect his rights, providing he breaks no laws.

"Is getting drunk breaking a law? Yes, if you become a public nuisance. Bear Bait gets drunk, yes. But in peace. And alone. I can name you a dozen big taxpayers who get just as drunk, but not in peace, and not alone. Some become embarrassing nuisances not only to their families but also to the pilgrims who come to worship our wilderness and leave their dollars in our pockets. Why not arrest these big-shot nuisances and exile them from our county?

"Is Dry Rot breaking any law by seeking to live in complete privacy? We all seek privacy. We build homes on distant hilltops, surround them with high fences, or plant trees around them to ensure privacy.

"Does Dry Rot, as shy of humanity as a golden eagle, become a public nuisance because his tortured soul seeks mercies in nature rather than in men? He has many illustrious predecessors. The Nazarene spent forty days alone in the wilderness conditioning himself for his mission of redemption. Saint Paul communed alone for fourteen years before he set forth to bring Christianity to the gentiles.

"History is filled with famous ascetics: John the Baptist, Saint Anthony of Egypt, Franciscan Monks, Trappist Monks. The pen name of the great poet Shelley was 'The Hermit of Marlow.' Thomas A. Kempis wrote *Imitation of Christ* when he was recluse. Daniel Boone kept moving west to get away from people. Henry Thoreau built a hut on the shores of Walden Pond to live alone and write his immortal thoughts on the simple natural life. 'A man is rich,' he wrote, 'in proportion to the number of things he can afford to let alone.'

"According to Thoreau's definition, Dry Rot is the richest in this county. And then we have our own great hermit of the Sierra... John Muir."

"Sure, sure," Tony interrupted, "and Thoreau was thrown in jail as an antisocial malcontent stirring up trouble. Shelley was a revolutionary agitator who was forced to flee his native England.

"But forget the venalities and the motives for the moment. I don't want any person in this room or in this county to get the idea that I'm against the rights of man...whether he's a hermit or a king.

No, sir. I'll stand on my two feet and defend the rights of man against all comers. But 'the rights of man' is a two-faced coin...the other side being responsibility.

"What social rights can any person claim who withdraws from human society? Who refuses to identify himself, even by name? Society has the right to know the identity of anyone claiming the rights of man. What man? Is he a murderer? A robber? A thief in hiding? If not, why refuse to identify himself?

"No court of law, of equity, or of morality would give a hearing to the plea of anyone who refuses to identify himself. It is an axiom of our social order, that if you wish to count you must stand up and be counted."

And at that precise time—magnificent actor that he was—Tony increased the pitch and tempo of his resonant voice, and the intensity of his outrage. The crowd stilled. Hands raising glasses stopped in midair.

"Think with me for a moment, ladies and gentlemen. Let your reason uncover the motive that has maneuvered you into the rigors of this cold, dreary day. Was it to hear good Deputy Lefty tell us he has a conscience? No. Everyone in Mono knows Lefty is honest and incorruptible. He has even been offered high posts in other county departments at an increase in salary.

"Was it to keep two hermits from being pushed out by newcomers? Nonsense. True hermits seek seclusion. They themselves flee any encroachment upon their solitude.

"Then why the big guns, here? The big Berthas? The biggest lawyer? The biggest newspaper publisher? They are here to make a young independent district attorney, who aspires to be your assemblyman, look like a heartless brute who despises the little man. They are out to beat me at next Tuesday's election so they can maintain their present political control on Mono County. They like the status quo. I don't. I want change! Change for a better shake for us, 'the huddled masses,' as they sneeringly call us. I am young, smart. I'll match my brain against any intellectual in the world! I want to go to Sacramento to represent you. Because I'm modern, progressive— Boatcourt's old. He is yesterday. I am tomorrow."

He looks scathingly at Boatcourt. "And oddly enough Boatcourt has been my protector, my campaign manager—my... But let me digress for a moment, so that you will understand.

"My bizarre affair with this—uh—face-slapper..." he waited for the laugh to die down, "goes back to my graduation from Bishop High School, where I gave the valedictorian address on the subject, 'The Evils of Compromise,' and Boatcourt's commencement speech was on 'The Values of Compromise.' As he handed me my diploma, I said to him, 'You see, sir, we don't agree!' And to this day we never have.

"Yes, I detested this man. Still do. He repels me. But, oddly enough, he adored me. Like a son. Still does. Only recently I found out that he paid my way through grammar school, high school, college, Harvard Law School, and a Rhodes Scholarship at Oxford. How? By setting up blind scholarships for the best Mono student each year, knowing I would win them all. Did I thank him? No! He took away my self-respect. I thought I was making it on my own. I hate him for it!

"Yes, ladies and gentlemen, all that I have and am today I owe to this queer-looking man with whom I had nothing in common. He took me into his law office. Then he talked me into politics; ran me for county tax assessor, then for district attorney, and begged to run me for state assemblyman. I didn't want, nor did I need anyone to pay for my schooling. And I don't want, nor do I need, any James Farley to run my campaigns; to do my thinking for me. And I told him so.

"And he answered: 'Wonder Boy, from the moment I saw you, and read your incredible grades, I knew you were something super special. I fell in love with you, and began to dream "The Impossible Dream," as the song goes. I envisioned you as a young, audacious Lochinvar. First—in the governor's seat in Sacramento; and then—so help me, I saw you in the White House. Another Jack Kennedy, graced with the wisdom of a Lincoln, and the drive of a Patton. I saw you calming our fears, healing our wounds, and bringing fresh, vigorous hope to a war-sick world...'

"Then he gave me his pitch:

"'But you need me to advise you, to tell you it has all happened before. To warn you that without the mellowing graces of moral principles, men gifted with your superior capacities have become monsters!

"'Listen to history, my boy,' he said. 'All rulers who have lacked compassion, pity, or moral principles have had to rule by terror, decree, and mass executions of the opposition. They became monstrous failures, dying ignominiously by murder or suicide. And it can happen again. To YOU! As it did to Genghis Kahn, to Nero, to Caesar, to Hitler...'

"I couldn't take any more. All my revulsions against him poured out of me: 'Monster!? Moral principles?' I shouted. 'Why you mealy mouthed old fart, it's a sin, a reversal of God's and nature's law for the weak to lead the strong; for the parasites to govern the hand that feeds them. Nor will I play your cliché games of 'being nice to Big Business,' or of 'groveling to Big Labor,' or 'kissing the combined asses of that rabble of Cretans we call minorities.

"'No, indeed, my ugly friend,' I said, 'I intend to reverse that trend, and put nature's law back on the right track, I intend to emancipate our citizens from the phony chains of compassion, pity, and humility. And our people will listen—as they are listening here now. And I fully intend to become president before I'm forty-five! And on my own platform!

"'So, rich man, fairy godfather, boy lover, or what the hell ever you are—thanks for the favors, and GOODBYE! AND STAY THE HELL OUT OF MY LIFE!'"

"Out of our lives, darling." Tony's beauteous wife had slipped up alongside him and put her arm around his waist. Tony turned to her and pounded his head with mocking fists.

"Oh, how stupid of me. Come here." They embraced; he covered her face with kisses. Then to the crowd, with mock horror: "This could cost me the women's vote... Ladies and gentlemen of Mono County, allow me to introduce you to Grace Caldwell, my new campaign manager." That brought down the house.

From his corner, Boatcourt broke the gloom. "Well, she's prettier than I am."

Grace advanced to the mike, smiling, bowing. "Thank you, thank you... It's time women get smart enough to manage a few simple things—like their husbands!"

Cheers and applause from the women. They were with her now.

"And I'd like you to know that I don't think my husband got the worst of the deal when he traded Boatcourt for me. Mr. Gorski may have a great talent for law—but I've got talents he's never heard of."

"Oh, man! Has she!" added Tony with exaggerated leering looks. "Like dishwashing," she quickly added. The laughs got bigger. "And don't you guys in pants howl too loud, because this gorgeous 'monster,' here, is more gung ho on women's rights than I am. You elect him to the assembly and he'll use all his talents, wit, and charisma (and who has more?) in seeing that women get treated as the equals of men—in wages, promotions, politics, and sex."

She threw up both arms and shouted, "ARRIBA THE WOMEN!"

En masse they rose.

The gloom in Boatcourt's corner thickened. It was a route, a walkway, a piece of cake.

I leaned over to whisper into Boatcourt's ear. "Do you still think your Wonder Boy has terminal cancer?"

His eyes closed, his head drooped sadly into his hands. "Yes, Frank. I'm sure of it now."

I shivered. Tony had beaten him to a frazzle, but Boatcourt still believed his Wonder Boy had terminal cancer; that he was "pure diamond."

Lu had been intensely following the now—to me—nonsensical proceedings.

"Lu, my head's spinning. If Tony's got terminal cancer, what difference does it make if he wins the election? Win or lose he'll soon be dead. And they all know it. So why doesn't someone get up and say it?"

"Because both sides are running scared," said Lu.

"Scared of what?"

"Scared of mentioning the word 'cancer' to that hooch-filled audience."

"Boy, is this an ad lib script. I haven't the faintest notion of what's going to happen next, or why? Do you?"

"Don't worry about it, Frank. Maybe that's the way they write scripts up here. You know. The Chinese way. Make 'em guess."

An unusually big crowd reaction brought him back to earth. Beauteous Grace was still pouring it on.

"Now, ladies, just listen to this for kookiness. Know what old Boatcourt did when Tony told him to 'get lost'? He waddled breathlessly to the courthouse and filed to run against Tony for assemblyman. To 'SAVE AMERICA FROM A MONSTER!' he shouted. (Aside to Tony, 'Oh, you beautiful monster!') So the Clarence Darrow of the Sierra, and his dear friend, Publisher Hopkins, and a crackpot film guy, together with a deputy sheriff who had received 'the call direct from God,' conspired to blow up a routine occurrence into the 'Second Coming.'

"And what was the routine occurrence? Well, new families moving into Mono County got panicky when they heard that two slimy, drunken hermits were running loose. Just the kind that rape and kill little girls. So they complained to the sheriff. A softheaded deputy refused to bother the drunken bums because he said they were angels with wings. He got fired.

"Well, of all the bleeding heart caterwauling! Boatcourt had found an issue to beat Tony with; *police brutality*. And get this. Not brutality against the possible victims or even against the two bums. No. It was brutality against the kind-hearted deputy!

"The cry went out. Save the deputy's job. Sign petitions. Hold a public hearing. What stupidity. They lost, of course. But my 'monster' husband here felt sorry for the dumb deputy. So here we are—joined together to hear the crybaby complaints of a 'born-again' lawman, and, God help us (indicating Boatcourt) the heartrending wails of a jilted queer."

The applause was deafening. And there was much stomping and whistling. The day was darkening, and the snow was coming down thicker than ever, but the Monoites were drunker than ever. This was their day to howl in the sacred sanctums of their leaders. But they howled and yowled at the oddest times. But who cared? They booed, bellowed, and applauded as the spirits moved them.

But two men and a wife cared. For them it was all or nothing. They aimed each thrust for the other's jugular.

The first one in our group to lose his cool was the publisher, Hopkins. He ran to the nearest mike. It was dead. To another. It was dead.

"Give me a mike, somebody!" he roared. "You, there, beautiful. Give me that walkie-talkie."

Grace tried to hold it back but he jerked it from her hand.

"Who do you two bunco artists think you're playing with?" he yelled into the walkie-talkie. "Hey, you Marine punks. You open up all the mikes in this room or I'll expose your whole crappy deal in my next issue. You got it? Or should I go to the colonel?" A Marine officer rose in the back and ran out.

Hoppy roared back to our table mike. It was alive. Hoppy sizzled. "The DA's wife," he shouted, "and some scurvy Marine have been screwing around with the chips. Up and down with the volume when it suited them. Pretty cheap trick for a Rhodes scholar. But I'm not here to make a speech. Only to correct an error of fact. Despite the innuendos, Stephen Gorski, here, is not a queer. Not a homosexual.

"What is he? First of all, he's royalty, not scum. His father descended from Polish kings. And his mother, adored by Picasso, was a niece of the murdered Romanov Czar.

"And when the commies took over Saint Petersburg, and began shooting and hanging anyone who could read or write, Steve's mother took her two children—Stephen, ten, and Ludmilla, twelve, and their governess, and tried to escape to Finland at night, during snowstorms. They almost made it, when a commie ski patrol spotted them and opened fire. The mother was killed, the daughter was killed, the governess was wounded, and little Steve got an exploding bullet in his rectum that blew out all his sex organs. The wounded governess dragged him as she would a wheelbarrow. Ugly loops of torn intestines began slipping out of his crotch, leaving a trail of blood and stench. But Anitchka, pulling her heart out, dragged our boy across the border—and fainted.

"Miraculously he lived. They came to America. He went to USC Law School, graduated, and became one of the most brilliant lawyers in California, a feat that matches anything Ulysses had to do.

"That's all I've got to say. Just wanted to correct a factual error. Boatcourt is no queer. He is a eunuch, he has no sex.

"But he has courage. And he has a heart. Big enough to make him the most charitable man I know. Big enough to send many Mono kids through college. Big enough to create a Mr. Wonderful—like the DA here. Thank you." He sat down.

The commanding authoritative voice of Hoppy Hopkins had cowed the slaphappy crowd. The word "eunuch" disarranged their already befogged brains. During the momentary silence, Stephen (Boatcourt) Gorski, head held high, walked majestically to the center of the podium, stood erect for all to see, and slowly scanned the crowd. He was the aristocrat facing down the hoi polloi. Not with the contemptuous snarl of a Coriolanus, but with the gentle, good-natured smile of an Einstein.

Necks in the hallways craned to get a better look. Unbelief was the prevailing expression. But on Tony—eyes wide, startled, and riveted on Boatcourt—a strange mixture of disbelief, awe, and wonder played across his handsome face. And underneath them all, one could sense the bitter pig boy's horror—looking at another boy lying in a pool of warm living blood smoking on the cold, white snow—his writhing innards, shredded and ripped, oozing out of a ghastly hole in the little boy's body. And here he was…a great man, a great, good man.

But the compressed silence needed but a spark to explode. And who sparked it? Tony's wife. She had been intently watching her husband's face. And when she saw a tiny glimmer of wetness in one eye, she grabbed the mike and shouted: "All right, I'll bite. What the hell is a eunuch?"

Yahoo! Course howls and bawdy jokes rattled the old courthouse. Amazing the volume of corny gags a word like eunuch can spawn in seconds. Grace kept the laughs going. "Anyone want to buy a slightly used eunuch?" she shouted over the mike. "Guaranteed to be a perfect partner on a honeymoon!"

The head supervisor (Weather Vane) banged and banged his gavel. In between bangs, he leaned over to a fellow supervisor and asked out of the corner of his mouth, "What the devil is a eunuch?"

"Don't know. Think it's like when they castrate a bull."

"Oh, poor fellow."

He got a signal from Boatcourt. Weather Vane banged and shouted over the mike, "Mr. Eunuch has the floor." The crowd howled. Weather Vane could bite his tongue. He made many "forgive me" gestures to Boatcourt. But Boatcourt laughed hardest of all at the gaffe.

The audience laughed with him, now. Tony and his wife exchanged worried glances.

"I don't blame you for laughing," said Boatcourt. "Eunuchs are funny. They used to be the watchdogs of the harems, you know.

"Can you imagine men walking through roomfuls of naked beauties without giving them a second look? But really, being a eunuch is not all bad.

"No, I've never experienced the carnal exaltation of sex. And since I don't know it, I don't miss it. But I have experienced the spiritual exaltation of love—in good measure, pressed down, and running over. And as when one arm is cut off, the other arm doubles in strength, so has my love of friends increased. You see, my love is the love of brother for brother, of father for son; the love that Jonathan had for David; the love that Christ had for his Apostles— 'greater love hath no man than this, that a man lay down his life for his friends.'

"So you see, it comes natural for me to love things and people. It is one way we are recompensed for our loss of sexual love. Of course, just as Christ had his favorite Apostle, I, too, had found my favorite—a young orphan boy who rose to prominence like a shooting star. To me, he was my son, my dearest love. But he was also my cross. He detested me as a boy. Hated me as a man.

"And here we are today, running against each other for the state assembly job. We stand at opposite poles. With him it's all black and white—no compromise. Yet black is but the compromise of blue, green, and orange; and white is a compromise of all colors.

"My love for him cries out, 'Elect my Wonder Boy...the marvel of our times...young...unafraid...knowledgeable about atoms and galaxies.... He is the hope of tomorrow...'

"But my love for my adopted country warns me to cry out, 'No! Don't vote for him. He's for one-man rule... No compromise... He makes sport of the importance and freedom of each individual. He's all brain and no heart; doesn't believe in compassion, pity, or mercy. He believes in power! Personal power. Now. Tomorrow.

The survival of the fittest. His genius can and will fool enough people who will give him enough time to remold our democracy to his liking.

"I know these are big words. But I must plead, implore, and shout to you that this tiny election, in the smallest assembly district of our state, can shape the future of our America. If Tony Caldwell goes to Sacramento with a huge majority, he has the brains, the savvy, the guts, and the backing to take him to the White House without a hitch.

"This election gives you, the people of Mono County, a clear choice: Tony Caldwell...genius...superman...power-seeking, hard-nosed hell-raiser with a healthy slice of Fort Knox behind him. Or you can vote for a soft-nosed eunuch—but a helluva good lawyer. Yes, you can vote for an elitist who thinks of himself as a God-sent messiah—sent down to rule us, the huddled masses. Or you can vote for one of us huddled masses who thinks of Tony as a treasonable jackass who has already been conned into spearheading a hate-oriented secret political party, a party of the super rich who privately call themselves 'The Takeovers.'

"And get this; Tony's father-in-law is their leader. Their führer. Can I make it any plainer to you why it would be catastrophic to vote for Tony Caldwell? Oh, yes. Tony will hobnob with tycoons who light their cigars with ten-dollar bills, but I'll have to sit in the last seat of the last row. So much for the political importance of this election.

"Now for the emotional importance that will affect your gut decision: I am old, a eunuch. But I believe in the self-evolution of our democracy—giving all Americans of all colors, or climes, or creeds equal opportunities to dream, create, achieve, and to enjoy all the personal liberties guaranteed by our Bill of Rights. I stand with Walt Whitman's statement to every man, woman, and child: 'The sum of all known reverences I add up in you whoever you are.'

"I believe my precocious opponent would prefer George Orwell's famous statement: 'All animals are equal, but some animals are more equal than others.'

"And so, my friends of Mono County, with all the passion I can conjure up, I ask for your vote in the name of the America we all love and revere; the America our forefathers built with hard work and free, independent minds. The America I love—and would die for.

My opponent does not love this America. He loves himself. I thank you, ladies and gentlemen, for the opportunity to stress to you the national, yes, the world importance of your vote.

"Well, so much for politics. And so little for the reason we called this public meeting." He walked over to where Lefty had been sitting in the witness chair all this time. "There is a rather large man here, larger than Job, but just as patient, who, with his tiny but very precious wife, and his six darling daughters all in a row, has been waiting to tell us his hard choice between conscience and comfort."

Boatcourt: "Now, Lefty. Remember, you are under oath. How long have you known Bear Bait and Dry Rot?"

Lefty: "Eighteen years. I met them during my first year as a deputy."

Boatcourt: "Did you investigate them thoroughly?"

Lefty: "I saw them almost daily for a while. Not a mark against them, except one against Bear Bait. And that was... Well, a call came in from a very frightened woman that a terrible-looking man had seized her six-year-old daughter and ran with her. But she screamed so loud he dropped the little girl and disappeared.

"I was assigned to the call. I knew right away it had to be Bear Bait. So I went to his hideout to question him. He said, 'Oh, no, no, Mr. Lefty. The little girl was walking right into... Come, I'll show you.' And he took me where he had picked up the little girl. She was heading right for a nest of rattlesnakes. I saw them myself. So he picked her up, took her away from the rattlesnakes, and dropped her, then ran away from the screaming mother."

Boatcourt: "Would you recognize the mother if you saw her?"

Lefty: "Oh, yes. She's sitting right over there. Her name is Mrs. Boyle."

Boatcourt: "Mrs. Boyle, would you mind standing up?"

A middle aged, good-looking lady stood up.

Boatcourt: "Mrs. Boyle, is Mr. Wakefield telling the truth?"

Mrs. Boyle: "Exactly. I'm sorry I never saw Mr. Bear Bait again to thank him personally."

Boatcourt: "Thank you, Mrs. Boyle. Is your presence here in answer to a subpoena that was served you?"

Mrs. Boyle: "Yes, sir."

Boatcourt: "Who subpoenaed you?"

Mrs. Boyle: "The district attorney."

A loud guffaw swept the crowd. Tony gave his busty secretary a withering look. She broke into tears.

Most speakers who address large gatherings know and fear the unpredictable mood-changing of their audiences. Like a chameleon's hues, a gathering can capriciously fluctuate up and down from an assemblage to a crowd to a mob to a vulgar herd almost instantaneously. Many famous names have tabbed crowds with pithy monikers; Horace Greeley said a crowd is "one immense ass." Max Grlnik said they were "monkeys outside the cage." And Machiavelli called them "a wild beast." Mark Twain said a mob "is merely a multiplied me."

Anyway, the Mono County cold, whiskey-smelling, yahoo mob yoyoed their cheers and boos between Wonder Boy and a smart, fun-loving, wide-track eunuch. There was much betting, of course. Reporter Jake Ziffren was my runner and tout. The odds started at thirty to one against Boatcourt. They shot up to fifty to one when Tony and his wife wowed them with their old-world curtsying and hand-kissing. You couldn't give away a hundred to one after the crowd heard Boatcourt was a eunuch. But strangely enough, the odds shot back down to twenty to one after Boatcourt made his humorous remarks about eunuchs. Jake said, "move in now." I gave him two tens—one for him—and said, "Lay it on Boatcourt."

"Your witness, Mr. Caldwell," Boatcourt said to Tony.

The crowd shifted around and murmured. The pints of hooch were upended. They all expected—and wanted—excitement. Wonder Boy would murder Lefty.

Tony approached Lefty, taking his time, knowing his prey was on edge. Then, suddenly—

Caldwell: "What did you say your name was?"

Lefty: "I didn't say."

Caldwell: "Better cooperate, Lefty. You're under oath. One lie can mean five years in the pen. Understand?"

Lefty: "Yes, I understand you're full of shit. Is that a lie?"

A boffo from the audience. More drinks and hoopla.

Tony turned to the audience and feigned surprise. Then he bowed low to Lefty. He had the great trick of turning away points against him with laughs.

Caldwell: "He must be a Don Rickles fan. Now, Mr. Comic, will you tell me why you chose to testify under oath?"

Lefty: "That's none of your goddamn business."

Caldwell: "Ah! But my next question is my business. Because your answer will be a lie. A felony, remember?"

A uniformed deputy handed him a long rectangular piece of bark with writing scribbled on it. Tony showed the writing to the audience. It read: "Lefty in trouble—Courthouse." The words were clumsily scratched with blackened burnt wood. Then he showed the sign to Lefty and asked, "How many of these signs did you nail on trees along Highway 395? Think before you answer. I want the exact number."

Lefty: "The exact number is zero. I never saw that sign before."

Caldwell: "Do you know who made and nailed them to trees?"

Lefty: "No. Of course not."

Caldwell: (Bearing down hard) "You're lying. Aren't you? AREN'T YOU? These are signals for Dry Rot and Bear Bait to come to your help. Aren't they? AREN'T THEY?"

Boatcourt: "WHOA! WHOA! WHOA!"

Lefty: "You're out of your mind…"

Caldwell: (Without a break) "Who scribbled these signs? Who nailed them up? Boatcourt? Hoppy? Your wife? Your kids?"

Lefty rose with clenched fists. "One more word about my kids and I'll break your neck!"

Caldwell: "That'll just add assault to perjury. You're lying, aren't you? You're LYING… Admit you're lying."

Sheriff: "Lay off, Tony. Lefty isn't lying. He doesn't know how to lie."

Caldwell: "Well, if he isn't lying, who nailed these signs to the trees?"

Sheriff: "You know damned well who did. It was me! You demanded that I produce Dry Rot and Bear Bait as witnesses, so I had the signs set up as bait to trap them. And we did. And if

I'm not mistaken, that siren outside means my deputies are bringing in Bear Bait and Dry Rot right now."

Heads turned and necks craned toward the siren's whine, which seemed to die at the courthouse entrance. Someone shouted, "It's Bear Bait and Dry Rot!" The stampede started. An entrance by Gable and Lombard wouldn't have caused such a rush. "Bear Bait and Dry Rot! They're here! They're here!"

In the communications truck, Marine Colonel Miller sensed a possible riot. Moving fast, he pressed the red button, which activated the alert horn. "Captain Fields, here," crackled over the intercom. "Bernie, I don't like it," said the colonel. "Assemble your platoon on the double and protect that sheriff car. No bayonets without my approval."

"Aye, sir."

Captain Fields's "assembly" whistle materialized twenty marines. "A double-line wedge. Guns only. Play it cool. MARCH!"

I pushed my way to an open window, just in time to see a deputy sheriff unlock his car and pull out two of the most ragged, dirty, emaciated, blue-cold, clownish-looking human beings he ever saw. Their feet were wound with clumps of muddy, snow-wet rags. Round the short one there hung a snow-heavy, torn, shapeless, oversized thing that once may have been an overcoat. The taller one was covered with a soggy toga of sewed-together cement sacks. To my surprise, the two shivering, pitiful, bareheaded derelicts were handcuffed together.

I hadn't seen Bear Bait for years. The grime on his face seemed thicker. But his features, wrinkled as a raisin, had scrunched together into a perpetual pleading grin, which, accompanied by perpetual body jerks and pitiful little whines, meant the thousand little devils gnawing his insides for alcohol had also become perpetual.

Dry Rot, the taller, frailer, but still bright of brain, held up one of the pieces of bark with the scrawled words, "Lefty in trouble— Courthouse," as the reason for their being there. "Where's Mr. Lefty?" Dry Rot kept shouting.

During all this, the drunks and non-drunks had pushed and climbed over each other for a glimpse of Mono County's two legends, whom very few had seen. At first sight, they laughed, then cheered and applauded. "Bear Bait and Dry Rot! Yahoo!"

The stiff-necked deputy who had picked up Dry Rot and Bear Bait had had a bellyful of this improper procedure. "All right, stand back. We're coming up," he barked, pushing the handcuffed misfits ahead of him.

Little did he know of the mountain of fury that was coming down to meet him. With the suddenness of a desert flash flood, the Monoites sardined on the first floor came hurtling through the open courthouse doors, piling up over the marines and each other. Through the squealing mess strode Lefty, tossing people right and left.

The two hermits threw themselves into his huge arms. "Oh, Mr. Lefty. Thank God, thank God…"

"It's okay, now. I'm here, I'm here." Then he saw the handcuffs. He looked at the unhappy deputy. "Gabe, you son of a bitch! Handcuffs on two pitiful…" He grabbed the handcuffs and, without unlocking them, he easily pulled out two weakened, shriveled hands. Lefty threw the handcuffs at the white-faced deputy. Then followed by picking him up and throwing him over the marines and into the crowd. Carrying Bear Bait in one arm and holding up Dry Rot with his other, Lefty yelled, "Gangway!" And, man, did those Monoites gang.

Up in the hearing room there was utter confusion. The apoplectic supervisor (Weather Vane) had broken the handles of three gavels, and was now banging for order with a beautifully carved coat hanger.

Lefty entered the hearing room with Bear Bait and Dry Rot. He was met at the door by the sheriff. "They're freezing, Chief," said Lefty. He saw a coatrack with some fur coats and hats on it. "A couple of those coats, Chief. Quick."

Weather Vane and the four other supervisors threw a fit.

"Here! Here! That's my best coat. Sheriff, marines. Order! Order! I'm in charge of this meeting. Put those coats back, I say…."

But Lefty put a coat around Bear Bait and another around Dry Rot, and led them to chairs on the podium. Bear Bait's body jerked constantly now. He pled with his hands; he cried; he knelt down and grabbed Lefty's knees. "A drink for him," pleaded Dry Rot. "He needs a drink, now, now. He may not make it—"

Lefty asked the crowd, "Anybody got a flask? Any kind of booze—Chuck, you've got a flas—"

"Use mine," said the sheriff, pulling a flask out of his back pocket.

While Dry Rot held up Bear Bait by his armpits, Lefty poured bourbon into Bear Bait's mouth. He let him drink half the flask. The eyes of the pressing crowd bugged out.

They sat Bear Bait in a chair again. He quieted down and for the first time saw the people, most of whom were standing and gawking curiously at the two derelicts. When Bear Bait grinned at them, they grinned back. And, for reasons not understood, they applauded him. He applauded with them, but his hands didn't hit each other. Like a child who wants to please, he took another long drink and grinned idiotically. Again they grinned back and applauded.

Boatcourt had not left his seat at their table, nor uttered a word during all these goings-on. And neither had Hoppy. "Aw, the poor fellow," managed to escape Lu before she broke into stifled sobs.

Tony and his wife smugly sat in two chairs behind the distraught supervisors. From there, smiling cynically, they watched the sansculotte, the lunatic rabble called the human race, make asses of themselves. Some laughed at the two hermits, then turned away holding their noses. Others applauded and mimicked their idiot smiles. Others held up their flasks and made scurvy toasts: "To Bear Bait and Dry Rot. They're beautiful but stink a lot."

And the more Tony and Grace saw, the more they smiled. Grace cracked, "People! Scum. Dumb."

"There they are," added Tony. "'The glory, jest, and riddle of the world,' Pope called them. 'Brainless suckers' would fit them better."

Dry Rot sat shivering in his chair, yet he put his borrowed coat over Bear Bait's feet. Between his legs, Dry Rot's hands tolled invisible beads. He closed his eyes and said to himself, "Father, not my words, but thy Son's: 'Forgive them, for they know not what they do.'"

Lefty gently took the bottle away from the grinning Bear Bait. He was bursting with rage. Addressing himself to Weather Vane, he leaned over the bench, grabbed the supervisor's tie, and asked, "I want to know from you, you... What inhuman bastard ordered these two innocent souls to be arrested and brought here to be humiliated by these laughing hyenas? Who did it? TELL me!"

"I did it," said a well-trained voice. Lefty turned to face Wonder Boy Tony. "It was my idea—and a spectacularly good one, evidently," said Tony. Then, addressing the crowd, "I brought them here, not for you to humiliate them, God forbid. I wanted you to see for yourself the two human derelicts our opponents were trying to use to smear the integrity of your elected officials. And their motives were not humanitarian, not idealistic, not a crusade for the 'rights of man.' No! Ladies and gentlemen. Their motives were venal and self-serving. A cruel, satanic trick it was, to use these human caricatures as a cause célèbre against me. I want you to know that these two unfortunates chose their own lives. My motive in asking them to move farther into the woods was to save them the humiliation from a growing population. Our opponents fought to enhance their humiliation. But what matters inhumanity if it serves their political PURPOSE?

"Mr. Gorski spoke eloquently about this: 'That a drop of madness is needed to spark life; that all martyrs, saints, and poets have it, and surely hermits have it. Mavericks they are, born to seek, to strive, to reach for the stars; rebels, fighting against being herded into the bovine chutes of conformity. Oh, yes, hermits have it.'"

Then, turning to the idiotic Bear Bait, he said, "Now there's a man for you. A seeker; a reacher for the stars, or, as Mister Gorski would have us believe...'a hermit with a touch of madness fighting against conformity.' What this poor idiot wretch is really seeking is a pint of liquor. Why? Because he fought against conformity, against society, against the traffic lights of red and green. He said, 'I want to be free of all laws, of all conventions.' And he succeeded.

"Look at him...." Bear Bait grinned broadly. "Tears your heart out. But, ladies and gentlemen, he's the end result of free thought, of anything-goes-but-law-and-order. And there are millions like him—pitiful derelicts with no anchor, no compass, no destination...drifters on the waves of chance. Now think, think with reason on this... Free thought leads to NO thought. And permissiveness leads to regression. Mark this. Permit all our pet dogs, all the purebreds, man's best friends and companions—permit them to roam uncontrolled...and they will revert back to their common species...the wolf.

"The evolution and advancement for both Fido and man comes out of conformity to the leash. The nonconformists, given complete license, reverse evolution. The mavericks devolve into Bear Baits. It is the irreversible Law of the God of Nature."

Elbows on the table, head in his hands, Boatcourt still sat statue-like—bewildered, hurt, reeling, praying.

Dry Rot rose and in a cultured voice addressed Tony. "Sir. It is most presumptuous of me, and I ask your forgiveness... But will you be kind enough to grant me the privilege of speaking a few words?"

There was a hush. Despite the dirt, the wetness, and the cement-sack toga, Dry Rot had a dignity that no rags could hide. His long white hair and white beard practically met at his waist. His face was very thin, his skin like dirty parchment. But his eyes were startlingly blue—a hypnotic blue that riveted attention.

"I speak not for myself, but for my friend and companion of twenty-five years. Yes, he is now an idiot, an alcoholic idiot. He has not talked for three years, and he hardly hears and barely sees. But he is now a happy idiot. He remembers nothing—a blessing which God saw fit to grant him a few years ago. For this half-man was once a very great man, carrying a very great sorrow which he sought to forget and expiate in loneliness.

"He did not believe in God. So he sought forgetfulness by depriving himself of creature comforts, and living like a lone animal in the woods. Time and again he was but a breath away from starving or freezing to death. But he could not forget; nor could he die.

"A stray fisherman left a bottle of whiskey in his shack. He drank it down. His sorrow became easier to bear. Now he needed alcohol. At night I'd get a drop here and a drop there from empty whiskey bottles in garbage boxes in the back of stores. I learned to make alcohol by fermenting rotten fruits and vegetables. I scrounged from garbage cans. Raccoons objected. I carry scars of their fangs and claws.

"Three years ago, during a blizzard, he went a week without alcohol or food. So intense was his suffering that, glory be, his mind snapped. He couldn't talk or remember anything, not even my name.

And for the first time he smiled and was happy. His past was erased. But he forgot one sorrow and picked up another one—liquor. He had to have it or die. And now he is an idiot for you to laugh at.

"But once he was a great man. He was Sir Andrew Parks, Canada's greatest surgeon, who joined the Canadian Army in World War I. He chose to be chief surgeon at a field hospital just behind the lines in Belgium, where he patched up so many torn bodies on a twenty-four-hour basis that he began to crack. He knew that for every young Canadian soldier he saw die in helpless agony, there were four British, six Americans, ten Germans, and fifteen Russian boys with faces shot away, legs and arms hanging in bloody shreds, guts hanging out...young men cheated of life...the monstrous violence...the mad insanity of tearing young lives apart...

"It was his third night without sleep. He could barely lift the saw he was using on an unconscious boy. And twenty more shattered youths moaned and waited for him—to die or be saved. He sawed off the boy's splintered leg. His nurse shook her head. The boy died. Like a zombie he glanced at the boy's face. So young. So young. He cracked. Went berserk.

"Grabbing the boy's cut-off leg, he ran screaming into the night. 'Stop this goddam war! Stop it!' He beat the nearest medics with the boy's leg. 'Stop the war! Everybody's mad! Mad! Stop it! Stop... Stop...'

"It took several shaken medics to catch him, down him, and give him a shot.

"Eventually they sent him to a psychoneurotic ward in Toronto, a broken, silent hulk. One day he walked away and disappeared. Months later he found some kind of peace for his tortured soul in the Jeffrey pines of Mono County; living alone, trying to find God—a God he never believed in. He didn't find Him.

"I came to the same woods for a far less noble reason. I was a young Catholic priest, Father Terence McInemy, from a small parish in New Jersey. There was a young girl. I lost my head and my soul. She became pregnant! In my shock and fright, I arranged for an illegal abortion. She died in horrible pain. I disappeared...I met Bear Bait in the woods. Gradually, we became friends.

"I tried to seek God's forgiveness in total abstinence and penance and prayer. God has not answered. My sin was too horrible for even God's great mercy. But I pray for forgiveness. I know nothing else. I have built a tiny chapel in the woods. No one will ever find it. I say Mass every day and pray constantly. Not for myself, for I am beyond mercy. I pray for all tortured souls who have lost faith in God and His infinite Love. Great souls such as Bear Bait; such as our dear friends and protectors—Deputy Lefty and his greathearted wife." Then kneeling, he continued, "And, dear God, bless the people of Mono County, bless their leaders, and please bless the gifted young man you will soon send to Sacramento. I ask this in the name of my friend..." He gasped.

Unnoticed, Bear Bait's head had slumped down on his chest, eyes open, a happy fixed grin on his face. He looked like a puppet with loosened strings.

Dry Rot crossed himself, closed Bear Bait's eyes, and whispered, "*Requiescat in Pace*." He rose and faced the crowd. "My friends, General Andrew Parks has found the peace he sought. God has called him to heaven to join the small group who thinks that war is the devil's cruelest masterpiece—invented to kill the young. *Pax vobiscum*."

Dr. Slingsby rushed up, examined Bear Bait's body, then announced into the mike, "I am Dr. Slingsby. Our friend Bear Bait is dead."

Lefty dropped his massive head on his little wife's lap and sobbed. A murmur went through the crowd, outside and inside. The snow was still falling, the day darkening. Streetlights went on, creating eerie halos around them.

A perceptible convulsion—as from a stifled sob—shook Boatcourt's seated body.

Colonel Miller punched a button.

"Aye, sir. Bernie here."

"Bernie, put Bear Bait's body on a stretcher, cover it, remove it from the hearing room to the private room, and wait for the ambulance I sent for."

"Aye, sir."

Four marines slipped quietly into the hearing room, laid the body on a stretcher, and covered it with Weather Vane's overcoat. "Here!

Here! You dullards. Not with Bay coat...." The marines did not look back. They were followed out by Dry Rot, and Lefty and his family; leaving Hoppy, his wife, and me and my wife standing around the slumped Boatcourt. Weather Vane, as usual, was feeling out for the right wind.

The wind came from an unhappy direction. Breaking the silence with his powerful voice, Hoppy the publisher stood up and demanded, "Mr. Chairman. I ask for the floor for five minutes, without interruptions."

"By all means," said the unsure supervisor.

Hoppy went to the podium and stood quietly before a microphone for a couple of seconds before he said, "Ladies and gentlemen of Mono County. I, for one, will long remember what we've seen here today. First of all, I want to apologize to General Andrew Parks and to Father Terry, hermits that we so jeeringly called Bear Bait and Dry Rot, for being one of the idiots who wanted them kicked out of our county. Oh, how wrong I was, and will say so in my papers.

"And, oh, how right Deputy Lefty was when he refused an order to arrest Bear Bait and Dry Rot as vags so we could roust them out of the county. And I admire Lefty for accepting dismissal rather than carrying out such an unfair order. And I further admire him for sticking to his demand for a public hearing to explain the battle between his conscience and his duty to his large family. Lefty's compassion and courage have been unequaled among us. And I will fight very hard for his reinstatement and promotion. Now, that finishes the only business for which we assembled here today: To hear Lefty's story.

"Normally, we would adjourn after finishing our agenda. But—but—there is a little unfinished business which I now bring up before you as a newsman." He took out a folded front page of his *Mono Herald*, unfolded it, and showed a double-track, huge headline.

He held it up to those who could read it, and read it into the mike for others. "This is the front-page headline of tomorrow's *Mono Herald*. It reads: 'A MONO TRAGEDY: OUR BELOVED TONY CALDWELL HAS INOPERABLE CANCER, SAID HIS DOCTOR.' For the first time in minutes, Boatcourt lifted his head.

"Where did I get this information?" asked Hoppy. "Right from the horse's mouth. A week ago, after the petition count had gone against us, Boatcourt, Lefty, the film man, and I got together in the backroom of the Sportsman's Lodge to lick our wounds. When in walked Tony, to tell us he had persuaded the supervisors to give Lefty a public hearing even though the petition count had gone against our side. He said, "Lefty is such a square, honest guy that he deserves a public hearing to let us all know why he refused to carry out a direct order from his superior.

"Then, in a businesslike way, Tony told us of the time, and details of the hearing, and asked me to publish the details in my paper. I said I would.

"Tony was on his way out when Boatcourt said, 'Lefty is no more honest today than he was yesterday. What's the other reason, Tony?'

"Tony looked back and said, 'Well, maybe I'm not the same guy today I was yesterday. This morning, Dr. Slingsby told me I have an inoperable cancer.' Then he walked out, leaving us shocked and speechless.

"I tried to check the story with Dr. Slingsby and was rewarded with a sharp lecture about his Hippocratic oath.

"So now, having disposed of all other business, I, as a newsman, must confirm this story Hoppy held up the paper. Mr. Caldwell, have you, or have you not inoperable cancer?"

Boatcourt suddenly raised his head and leaned forward with keen interest. Would the love of his twisted life prove to be a pure diamond? Of course—

Tony came up to Hoppy, looked him right in the eye, and said, "Well I'll be goddamed!" He turned to the audience. "Ladies and gentlemen, I've heard of slimy, putrid, sneaky, dishonest, inhuman election tricks, but this cancer bit...the devil himself couldn't think of that one. INOPERABLE CANCER? ME?" He looked for Dr. Slingsby in the audience.

"Hey, Doc, where are you? Stand up, please. Ladies and gentlemen, that is my regular doctor, Doctor Slingsby. Doctor Slingsby, when did you last examine me?"

"I gave you a complete physical examination yesterday."

"Did you find any cancer in me, inoperable or any other kind?"

"No, sir. As I told you after the examination, you are the healthiest guy I ever examined."

"But," insisted Hoppy, "if you haven't got cancer, why did you tell us four that Dr. Slingsby had told you that morning that you had inoperable cancer?"

"Why? Yes, why? Why do I stand here and talk to you penny-ante liars who'd sell your grandmothers to win an election? Friends, let me say this for the record, and then we're leaving. I have never uttered the word 'cancer' to this cabal of lying scum, or to anyone else in the world—for as long as I can remember!"

Face drained of blood, Boatcourt rose, trembling; his face contorted with pain and fury. Oh, how brutal was the raw truth! Tony lied! His pure diamond had lied!

Angrily dismissing it all, Tony dramatically threw up his hands and quit. "Oh, what in hell am I taking this beating from these cheap bums for? Go on. Send that scurvy Boatcourt to represent you in the assembly. And Grace and I will move to another county where politicians are not such lying shysters."

Shouts of "NO! NO!," were beginning to be heard.

"But if you want me to represent you, and fight for you in Sacramento, I'll have to know that you want me, that you're behind me. And I want to know it now! Not at election time. NOW! Or I take my name off the ticket, and leave the county.

"Okay, let's find out. There are enough of you here. All those who want to be represented by that toad, that fat eunuch toad—say 'Aye!'"

The courthouse exploded with No's and Boo's.

"Okay. Now all those who want to be represented by me, say 'Aye!'"

"AYE!"

"Louder."

"AYE!!!!!!!!!"

The courthouse shook with stompings and whistles and cheers. Every person in the room rushed to shake Tony's hand. The cry went up—"TONY...TONY...TONY..." Those outside stormed the doors to get inside. The ovation became hysterical. Tony stood on a chair and raised his arms in victory.

Waves of well-wishers jostled the benumbed Boatcourt. No one noticed him. Hoppy managed to come alongside him and say into his ear, "We weren't smart enough to stop the son of a bitch here. Damn! Damn! Damn!"

The two old gladiators slumped together in the jostling—beaten, defeated, vanquished. Tears came into their already watery eyes.

"God save America," whispered Boatcourt. Then he advanced toward Tony. The sheriff and several deputies and marines tried to keep the crowd from overwhelming the winner.

Tony caught sight of Boatcourt. Arrogantly, he pointed him out. "There he is, folks. My opponent! The Great Eunuch of the Sierra...."

The crowd around hissed and sneered their contempt.

Tony couldn't hold back his hate. "Told you, Boatcourt, that I was going to destroy you in public. Show him what you think of him. Everybody!"

The room shook with taunts and despicable words.

The sheriff came to Boatcourt's aid. With one quick movement, Boatcourt snatched the sheriff's gun from its holster, and fired three quick shots into Tony, then fired one quick shot into his own head.

Pandemonium broke loose. Marines and deputies charged here and there, keeping crowds, those who pushed to see the bodies and those who pushed to get away from the bodies, from crushing each other. Men panicked and jumped out of windows. Women fainted and were trampled. Stair banisters gave way under the human pressure. Men leaped and caught women who leaped after them.

Coolest of all was Tony's wife, Grace. When the shooting started she slithered silently behind and under the seats of the hysterical supervisors. A blob of Boatcourt's brains had splattered her dress. She was desperately trying to wipe off the filthy stuff when she saw Tony's secretary, the dress puller-downer, pushing herself away from Tony's bloody body, her face awash with tears. Grace pulled her into her hiding place. "Here, quick," she said. "Let me wear your coat and shawl. Nobody must see me leave. Understand? And, oh, a hundred dollars if you drive me to the Reno airport without anybody noticing me."

"There's a back way," said the tear-stained secretary. They scuttled to the secretary's little Volkswagen unnoticed. Grace slumped in the back seat while the secretary maneuvered her VW to Highway 395 through a jammed-up mass of honking cars. Distant siren wails added confusion to the bedlam.

Grace had made her escape unnoticed, a perfumed rat leaving the ship. From her back seat she harshly ranted, "Father warned me. 'Watch it, baby,' he'd say. 'Those who root with pigs grow a snout.' Can't you go any faster? Oh, hold it, hold it! I see a payphone." She leaped out of the car before it stopped and ran for the phone. Alone, the secretary gave way to sobbing—deeply, audibly.

"Wait a minute, Dad," she said hurriedly on the phone. "Let me repeat it back to you. One—I buy the car from her. Right? Two—I drive it full speed, not to Reno, but to the ammunition depot at Hawthorne, Nevada. Three—they will know to let me in. Four—the Lear Jet will be waiting for me. Five—give a soldier a couple of G's to burn the car. Okay. Got it. See you, Dad."

CHAPTER TEN

T HE MORNING HAD GROWN wackier and wackier; first sun, then snow, then a brutal blizzard. An extraordinarily large crowd of Monoites had gathered at first light at the small primitive county graveyard on the north shore of Mono Lake. But when the blizzard hit before the services started (the blinding winds burst on them from all sides like charging, screaming, mounted Indians), the deputy sheriffs quickly ordered all spectators to get into their cars and follow the snowplow single file because visibility was approaching zero, and the narrow road to the highway would quickly be obliterated.

These mountain people will turn tail for nothing on earth— except a blizzard. And the winds know it. In half an hour, the long procession of cars had disappeared in the blinding blasts.

Having disposed of the cars, the tormenting winds turned their fury on stuffy, haughty Mono Lake, provoking that caliginous loch into lashing back with angry waves that pounded and sprayed great blobs of salty foam on the white-encrusted towers and miniature castles that line its shores; and to snobbishly brag that unlike other dead sea waters, Mono Lake was teeming with life, because it had the secret of creating life. With the proper mixture of saltwater and fresh (from freshwater springs) and solar power, it created a profusion of microscopic life, which fed billions of shrimp and flies, which fed millions of birds, including, if you please, 95 percent of California's seagulls which fly over the Sierra to lay their eggs on Negit, Mono's little black island.

Yes, indeed! And the three-million-year-old lake has many more dark secrets yet untold to man, or even to witless winds.

But the wild winds couldn't care less. They had spied another sport. They whistled and swirled around something new: three plain pine coffins, lined up on staked-down green-carpeted sawhorses, alongside three graves carved out of frozen ground. Mounds of mixed snow and earth (dug-out material for filling the graves) were covered with heavy tarps weighted down with concrete blocks.

First, the zany winds zeroed in on the mounds of flowers, around and atop the two end coffins—the middle coffin (Tony Caldwell's) was bare. Off go the flowers flying in the wind—hothouse roses, gardenias, plastic wreaths, all took off like spooked birds; followed by the little stands and vases that went bouncing and toppling like men on crutches fleeing a fire.

Leaving only the bare coffins (with temporary three-foot black-lettered white signs staked into the ground in front of each coffin), the rampaging winds spied something new; the left coffin was covered with an unfamiliar flag—a Canadian flag was tied on the coffin. Well, they huffed and they puffed. But the strange flag held fast. Four Canadian military men—an honor guard standing stiffly at attention—knew their tie-downs. Foiled, the clownish winds went looking for easier prey.

In front of the Canadian coffin, the temporary sign read:

"**(two stars on top) SURGEON GENERAL ANDREW "BEAR BAIT" PARKS...CANADIAN INFANTRY...WORLD WAR II... BORN JUNE 7, 1897...DIED NOVEMBER 26, 1965."

The middle coffin was unadorned. The white sign read:

"TONY CALDWELL...WORLD CHAMPION "GO" PLAYER... BORN APRIL 10, 1939...DIED NOVEMBER 26, 1965."

At the third coffin, Anitchka and Hoppy Hopkins were unwrapping a beautiful, gold-rimmed Romanov coat of arms of inlaid wood. Her head trembling up and down and unable to speak, Anitchka laid the coat of arms gently on top of the coffin.

Then she kneeled, kissed the coffin, said a little prayer, rose, and asked to be taken away, her head continuing to shake up and down. She smiled at those about her and allowed herself to be taken to a car and driven away; remembering nothing of the past or of the immediate present, but living happily in her own small cocoon.

In front of the third coffin was the lettered sign:

"STEPHEN 'BOATCOURT' PIETAGORSRI...BORN, JANUARY 8, 1909...DIED NOVEMBER 26, 1965."

Among the spectators who had not left was the sheriff, standing stiff and hatless, about twenty feet in front of the coffins. Next to him stood Deputy Sheriff "Lefty" Wakefield, once again in possession of his badge and gun. Also hatless. Behind Lefty was a small bouquet of people, his wife and six girls all snuggled together, shielded by Lefty's wide bulk.

Another small group, huddled together against the icy blasts, comprised the five supervisors who shook and shivered and wished they were home. Right close to them were me and Lu and four of their neighbors. In front of them, of course, were the three coffins, the left one with its Canadian Honor Guard, and behind the coffins was the streaky, angry, convulsed surface of Mono Lake—its wild breaking waves yielding their spume and foam to the wings of the assaulting winds. We faced those spume-laden assaulting winds.

Hoppy Hopkins tried to adjust the height of the microphone he would have needed had the spectators not left. It was while Hoppy was testing the mike that Lu called my attention to a person at the rear end of Tony Caldwell's unadorned coffin. She looked like a woman all bundled up.

Yes. It was a woman—I recognized her as Tony Caldwell's secretary, the one who helped Tony's wife escape unseen. It was difficult to see her through the flying mist, but it looked as though she had put a heavy rock on Tony's coffin. Then she reached into her clothes and came up with a long pair of scissors, with which she cut off a large clump of her blonde hair that had been tied with a ribbon. Then she put the long braid under the heavy rock. The hair held and fluttered in the wind. Then she kissed the coffin and embraced it, her body racking with sobs. Oh, the power of true love. Lu began to weep. Tears rolled down my cheeks, and surely down many other cheeks.

Hoppy gave a signal to the Canadians. A trumpet appeared and blew Canadian taps under horrible handicaps of cold and wind.

At the end of taps, Hoppy went to the microphone. It worked fairly well. I had never seen tough Hoppy so moved. He began his eulogy.

"Friends, we are met this cold blizzardy morning, in this primitive cemetery which is proud to be the last resting place for some hardy pioneers; men and women with courage and vision who met the unknown at every level of hardship and danger. This morning we are here to perform a lamentable duty for three more extraordinary men; to return them to the dust whence they came. For 'dust to dust' is one of the very few biblical phrases that I can understand.

"I am not a priest, a minister, or anyone versed in God. So I speak to you as a fool.

"I did seek professional help from the various churches we are blessed with, but each denomination was loath to say 'yes' until I answered questions about the deceased: 'Were they Catholics, Protestants, Baptists, Mormons, Buddhists, or what?' For it seems that each sect has its own private arcane pipeline to God, which is geared to reach the very ear of God with prayers from their own kind only.

"However, they gave me to understand that 'any one of us could give you the short general service that offends nobody.'

"'It would offend me,' I said, 'and I think it would offend God, if there is one. Thank you.'

"As I said, I am not a priest, or a minister. I am only a newsman who seeks to report what he sees and hears, and tries to separate fact from fiction. Yes, I speak to you as a fool, for I know nothing about a soul, or why we should pray to God for special privileges for a soul. If God is who they say He is, He knows what's going on. And no amount of special prayers and jive is going to make Him believe that the souls of all who die will suddenly turn into souls of Good Samaritans.

"If death cleanses all sins, then the hangman is God.

"I speak to you as a fool, as a brother human being. For all humans are fools. Else why concoct wars to kill our young? Or send old pompous seniles to meet with other…pompous seniles to argue about boundaries, or races, or who should play with the biggest agate in a marble game?

"And so, speaking again as a fool with no hotline to God, I ask Him to accept the souls of our three friends—if they have any—just as they are. And if there is another life, I ask you, God, to give these three men a little better break than You gave them in this life. Thank you."

The winds suddenly quieted down. In the lull, Lu and I, conscious of heartbreaking sobs. They came from Tony's secretary, who still embraced Tony's coffin. With her face just behind the rock that held down the sacrificial offering of her hair, she covered the coffin with tears, and kisses, and prayers: "Oh, God, please be good to my Tony, I loved him, God…I loved him so much…so much…"

The harsh voice of the sheriff rent the air like a clap of thunder. "All right, everybody. Let's go. Let's go! The snowplow's back. Into your cars, everybody. Leave everything as it is. We'll finish the job when this goddam wind stops. Let's go! Let's go! You Canadian guards have to stay with your general? Okay, we'll send down some tents and some food. Okay, the rest of you. Let's *go*!"

I took Lu's arm and turned to leave. But she suddenly tore herself away and ran back toward the coffins. I made no attempt to stop her. I knew her. She almost fell into one of the graves, but she scrambled to safety on hands and knees. I watched as she reached the sobbing secretary—still embracing Tony's coffin. Lu put an arm around her and urged her to come with us. The weeping girl would not budge.

I saw a Canadian soldier approach, salute, and speak to Lu. He must have said, "It's okay, ma'am. We'll take good care of her." Lu hesitated. Then, taking off her favorite warm coat, she covered the freezing girl, kissed her, and came running back to snuggle under my overcoat. "I'm proud of you, honey." I kissed her head and hurried her toward the frantic sheriff. I unceremoniously squeezed us in with Lefty's family—in the paddy wagon Lefty was driving. "Hello?" said Lefty. "What's this?" He had found a folded note on his steering wheel. He read it out loud to us.

"'Dear Mr. Lefty, you good and great friend. With this note, I thank you for the kindness of your great big heart, and will say goodbye to you, perhaps forever if that be God's will.

"'For the past two days I have been in my little chapel asking our Merciful God to accept the souls of Bear Bait, Tony, and Boatcourt, to forgive them for their earthly sins, and to welcome them into the glories of His heaven. As for me, I am not needed here anymore, and though God has decided not to forgive my awful sin, I love Him with all my heart and soul, and the hell He will condemn me to cannot be much worse than to live unforgiven and unneeded on this earth.

"'But God's will be done, not mine. But I did ask Him for one last request: What a blessing it would be if He arranged for someone in hell to need me just a little bit.

"'I know you have looked for my chapel. It is a four-by-five, head-high cave I fashioned on the seldom-seen far side of the Obsidian Dome near Deadman's Summit. Its door, made of saplings and small pieces of obsidian, blends right into an obsidian slide. I roll away a large piece and pull open the camouflaged door. Three small Jeffrey pines both shade and hide my hideaway. The inside is a miniature chapel in which I have lived and said daily mass for twenty-five years.

"'This morning I said my last mass, closed the rock door, kissed it, and, surrendering myself completely to God, I walked away in the deep snow, facing the icy wind.

"'Some ten minutes later, I heard distant roaring sounds. I saw two specks in the distance coming in my direction. Two men in snowmobiles arrived and hurriedly introduced themselves as Father Savage, the priest of the local church, and Bishop Buddy, head of the diocese. Father Savage said that he had heard me tell my story in the courthouse, and that he had immediately notified his bishop, who in turn called my diocese in New Jersey to tell them about me and my belief that God would never forgive my sin. And that their answer was, 'Oh, for heaven's sake! Of course, God has forgiven him. Tell him to come right back to his parish, because we desperately need him here to replace many priests who have been martyred in Africa. Put him on a plane and get him here as fast as you can.'"

Smiling from ear to ear, Lefty turned to us and exclaimed, "How about that, huh!" We all cheered. "Wait," said Lefty. "There's a little more."

He read on. "'And so, Mr. Lefty, by the time you read this I'll be on a plane flying back to New Jersey, and I'm sure people will think I'm crazy because I'll be laughing and crying at the same time. How great and how merciful is our God! I keep saying, 'Here I am, Lord. I come to do Your will.' And, Mr. Lefty, you've never seen a happier man than I am at the moment. So goodbye, dear friend. And God's grace and blessings be with you and your wonderful family forever.

"'Yours in Christ,

"'Father "Dry Rot" Terence.'"

Well, there was whooping, cheering, and dancing in the paddy wagon. Lefty turned on his siren. Then, picking up a communicating mike and identifying himself, he shouted, "Chief, turn on your siren, Dry Rot's on his way back to New Jersey as a priest again. And the rest of you guys turn on your sirens, and let's give Dry Rot a great send-off!"

Sirens on all sheriff cars and highway equipment came on and deputies and working stiffs all shouted to each other, "Atta boy, Dry Rot!" And the word got back to June Lake, where the stores hung up "Closed" signs, and the bars ran out of liquor. "Atta way to go, Dry Rot."

END